PRAISE FOR JOHN D. NESBITT

"Nesbitt is a true artist…"

— *WESTERN AMERICAN LITERATURE*

"John Nesbitt knows working cowboys and ranch life well enough for you to chew the dirt with his characters as this tale unfolds."

— *TRUE WEST*

"Nesbitt has a nice turn of phrase and creates characters so real, you can hear them talk if you close your eyes."

— *ROUNDUP MAGAZINE*

"Nesbitt demonstrates himself a skilled wrangler of detail and character."

— *PUBLISHERS WEEKLY*

LOST CANYON

ALSO BY JOHN D. NESBITT

LOST CANYON

JESS DELAINE
BOOK 1

JOHN D. NESBITT

WOLFPACK
PUBLISHING

For Charles Pengilly and the friendship of younger days

LOST CANYON

1

THE TOWN LAY ALONG BOTH SIDES OF THE WIDE MAIN
street running west. Many of the buildings had false
fronts, and several had overhangs and board sidewalks.
Delaine saw the name of the town on one of the
smaller businesses, the Overton Shoe Repair, which sat
on his right between the Great Western Land Office,
also small, and the Prairie Star Bakery. Beyond the
main street, on his right, a woman was calling to a
child. On his left, between the main street and the railroad beyond, lay the shipping pens and the stockyard
office. Cattle were mooing. His horse moved on at a
steady pace, and Delaine read the names of more businesses on each side. He did not try to remember them.
If he stayed, he would learn them as he needed.

After two blocks, he crossed what looked like a
main cross street leading north out of town, and on the
right side of the next block, he found a modest-looking
business called the Sweet Auburn Café. Turning in, he
dismounted, tied his horse, and stepped up onto the
sidewalk.

Inside, as the bell tinkled behind him, he saw tables on both sides and a counter straight ahead. As he made his way to the counter, a woman with dark hair came out of the kitchen. She was about his age or a little younger, with a bronze complexion. She wore a dark-blue dress and a full-length white apron.

"Good afternoon," she said. Her voice was clear without much of an accent.

"Good afternoon. I wonder what you might have at this time of day."

"The cook is working on the supper menu right now. There's beef stew left over from lunch."

"That sounds fine to me." Delaine took a seat at a table near the counter as the woman walked away. She was familiar in a general sense, as she reminded him of the many agreeable people he had known in New Mexico, some of whom spoke only Spanish. He set his hat on a chair next to him and waited.

The woman brought a bowl of stew with two biscuits on a saucer by themselves. "Anything else? Coffee?"

"That would be good."

When she set down the coffee, she said, "I'm at the end of my shift, so I'll be going in a few minutes. I come in early."

"Shall I pay you now?"

"If you'd like. It's twenty-five cents."

He reached into his pocket, took out a quarter, and laid it on the table.

"Thank you."

"And the same to you."

He ate his meal in the empty café. Sounds came from the kitchen—an iron skillet clanging on a stovetop, a spoon being whacked on the lip of a pot, plates rattling. He thought there might be a cook and a dishwasher at work, but he did not hear any voices. A pair of quaint-looking illustrations hung on the far wall, not close enough for him to see details or read inscriptions. He finished his meal and left, with the doorbell ringing behind him.

He stepped into the street and stood by his horse, a brown animal with a mane and tail of a darker shade. Two doors down on his right, past the post office, he saw a business he had noticed earlier. The White Mule Saloon had a large square front, a wooden awning, and a board sidewalk. Delaine moved his horse to the hitching rail in front of the saloon and went in.

The bar ran along the left side, with a brass rail and a polished wooden top. In back of the bar, the woodwork included shelves for liquor bottles, two columns flanking a wide mirror, and a ledge above. A painting hung on the wall above the ledge.

It was not the typical painting of a nude woman draped in a sheet or of a man roping a steer but something more refined. A beautiful young dark-haired woman with a complexion that Delaine imagined to be Italian or Spanish, wearing a royal blue dress, sat sidesaddle on an animal that looked like a white donkey. Delaine assumed it was a white mule. The animal was walking in a terraced garden with fruit trees in the background.

"What'll it be?"

The bartender's voice brought Delaine back to the present, where a couple of patrons on his right gave him a casual glance. Delaine gave his attention to the man in the green brocade vest.

"Just a whiskey."

The bartender poured a generous ounce into a small glass. "Fifteen cents." He set the bottle upright on the bar and wiped his hand on the clean white apron he wore from the waist down.

Delaine set a quarter on the bar. "Nice day," he said.

"Looks like it. I haven't been out much."

"How's the work hereabouts?"

The bartender shrugged. "We're gettin' into the fall. You could ask Tom."

A man not far away on Delaine's right turned to him. He was a clean-looking fellow of about thirty-five with wavy brown hair, blue eyes, and a neat mustache. He wore a dark grey wool jacket, a light brown work shirt, a brown vest, and dark grey wool pants. He had brown boots with plain spurs.

"What kind of work are you lookin' for?"

"I do ranch work, but just about anything else."

The man's eyes passed over Delaine. "I can't speak for him, but the man I work for might could use another hand to bring some steers into town for shipping."

"That's something I could do."

The man reached into his coat pocket, lifting the flap, and drew out the makings for a cigarette. As he went about rolling a smoke, he said, "I'm goin' back out in a little while. You can ride along if you want."

"Thanks. I think I will."

The man lit his cigarette, blew away the smoke, and held his hand forward. "Tom Caswell."

"Jess Delaine."

"Pleased to meet you."

"And the same here."

Caswell turned to his drink on the bar, and Delaine did the same. He noticed his dime in change and took it. He did not know when his next money would come in.

A man farther down the bar said, "That's the way to do it. Work when you can find it. You never know what's next. Could be a long winter."

Barroom wisdom. But Delaine was glad he came in. A saloon was not a bad place to find out about work. The other chaff was just part of the scene. He couldn't expect the average customer to be as reserved as the lady on the mule.

———

CASWELL DID NOT SPEAK MUCH on the way to the ranch. The trail took them up onto rolling grassland and into taller hills that were dotted with dark evergreens. At about four miles from town, the trail forked, and Caswell led the way to the left. A couple of miles farther on, they rode through an archway with "Silver Pine Ranch" inset in dark letters in the plank spanning overhead. Dusk was falling when they rode into a ranch yard surrounded by pine trees. Delaine's glance went from a large, dark red barn with a gambrel roof to lower sheds, a bunkhouse, and a ranch house. The layout was neat and clean, and the buildings were well kept.

They stopped and tied up at the ranch house, and Caswell led the way. He knocked on the door frame. A voice inside called, "Come in," and Caswell opened the door and led Delaine to the doorway of an office on one side of the front room. The smell of tobacco smoke hung in the air.

A man of about forty-five stood up behind an oak desk. He wore a brown wool jacket, vest, and pants with a white shirt. He was clean-shaven except for a trimmed mustache, and he had neat hair. Behind him, a brown hat hung on a varnished board with brass hooks showing. To the right of the board and hooks hung a portrait of President Benjamin Harrison, and to the left hung a small and amateurish painting of a deer standing in front of a canyon in autumn colors with a snow-capped mountain rising in the background.

The man motioned with his hand and said, "Come on in."

Caswell took off his hat, and Delaine did likewise.

Caswell said, "Met this fella in town. He's lookin' for work, and I didn't know if you needed another hand."

The man looked Delaine over. "Can you help move a herd of steers?"

"I believe so."

The man held his hand forward and said, "I'm George Mace."

"Jess Delaine." They shook.

Mace said, "It's just for a few days. I can pay a dollar a day plus room and board, startin' tomorrow, but you can eat tonight, of course." He picked up a pipe from his desk, drew on it, and puffed out smoke. "Are you on your own horse?"

"Yes, sir."

"You can ride my horses while you're here. Tom can show you which ones. When we take the steers to town, you can ride your own horse, because that's where we'll finish."

"Sounds good enough."

"Tom will show you to the bunkhouse and tell Ambrose." Mace moved his eyes to Caswell. "Any mail?"

"None today."

Mace came back to Delaine. "Welcome to the Silver Pine Ranch. I think you'll find it a straight-up place." They shook again, and the meeting ended.

————

THE BUNKHOUSE and the eating area were together in one low building. Caswell introduced Delaine to Ambrose, a pale man with greying hair, rolled-up sleeves, and a stained white apron. He had a cigarette hanging from the corner of his mouth.

"Grub'll be ready in a little while. There's a few empty bunks. Take the one you want."

"Thanks."

Delaine took a bunk near Caswell's. He set his bag underneath and rolled out his blankets.

Caswell sat on his own bunk. "Don't you have a gun?"

"I keep it in my bag."

"Doesn't do you much good there."

"I'll wear it when we work, just like normal."

Caswell rolled a cigarette and lit it. "The others will be in before long, and then we'll eat. Ambrose feeds us pretty good."

————

CASWELL POINTED out a sorrel horse in a large corral with a dozen others. "You can ride that one this morning," he said. "We'll let the other fellas rope theirs first."

Chiddester and Bloom, the other two hands, roped out their two horses and led them away. The rest of the horses were not milling much when Delaine approached his. The sorrel seemed to know he was up, and he turned away, but he did not run. Delaine tossed his loop and caught the horse, then led it away so Caswell could catch one for himself.

Outside the corral, away from the others, Delaine tied the sorrel to a rail and put his hand on its upper shoulder. The animal did not flinch. Delaine took that as a good sign and began to brush it. The horse had saddle tracks as if it had been ridden in the recent past, and it did not pull back on the neck rope where it was tied. Delaine combed its mane and stood by its left hip as he combed the tail. He did not find many tangles in either place, and he took that as an indication also that the animal had not been out on its own for a long time.

He left the sorrel standing in the early morning sunlight as he went for his saddle and blanket. The horse stood still as he spread the folded blanket on its back and swung the saddle up and settled it into place. He reached under for the front cinch, drew it up by the ring, and ran the latigo through it twice. He moved to the back cinch and buckled it.

Delaine paused, put three fingers between the webbed front cinch and the horse's warm body, and pulled the strap another inch. He pushed the spoke into the hole in the leather and tucked the loose end.

The sorrel watched but not with a wide eye as Delaine took the bridle from the saddle horn and lifted it in front of the horse's head. He guided the bit into the animal's mouth and over its tongue, then slipped the headstall over the ears. The bit settled into the corner of the mouth, making a smile. No need to adjust the bridle. Delaine untied the neck rope and led the sorrel out into the open.

He had known horses to be calm all the way through the process and then start bucking before he could catch his right stirrup, so he took nothing for granted. He checked the cinch to see that it was still snug enough, then set the reins in place. After pulling the near rein enough to turn the horse's head an inch toward him, he grabbed both reins and a hank of mane with his left hand, grasped the saddle horn with his right, and poked his foot into the stirrup. In one motion, he swung up and into the saddle. When his right leg touched the other side and he felt the horse steady and relaxed beneath him, he knew he was all right. He found his right stirrup, clucked, and walked the sorrel out in a half-circle, its coat catching the sunlight.

DELAINE RODE with the other ranch hands to separate steers from a larger herd into a small holding pasture. Caswell and the two others did the sorting and cutting, while Delaine guarded the gateway to see that no unwanted cattle went through. The whole process was everyday life once again to Delaine. Cattle mooed, bellowed, pushed, and jostled. Some drooled, and some had green smears on their rumps. Flies hovered in the air, along with small clouds of gnats. The sorrel that Delaine rode was a good cow horse, and it responded whenever Delaine made the smallest motion to head off a cow or calf from going through the gateway.

At midday, the four ranch hands left their horses in the corral and walked to the bunkhouse to eat. Two horses were tied in front of the bunkhouse, and two men came out with George Mace.

One was a tall, broad man with a red beard. He wore a tobacco-colored suit, a cream-colored shirt, and knee-high brown boots with the pants tucked in. Closer, Delaine saw that he had blue eyes and a meaty face.

The other man was an inch below average height. He walked with his shoulders squared and his hands away from him, as if he was ready to grab the handle of his low-slung six-gun. He had blond hair, blue eyes, prominent ears and nose, and a frozen smile. A tooth-pick was tucked into one corner of his mouth. He wore an off-white hat, a buckskin vest, a dull white shirt, wheat-colored sackcloth pants, and dull brown boots with large-roweled, clinking spurs.

The two men nodded as they passed, but no one spoke. A few steps later, Caswell said to Delaine, "That's Cole Chamberlain in the red beard. He's going to drive his herd in at the same time we take ours. Between the two, we'll have a trainload."

"Is the other one his right-hand man?"

"He's got two of them. One on each side, you might say. They're brothers, and they look alike and dress alike. Their last name is Dodge. You can tell 'em apart because Earl has darker hair than Cal. The one we just saw is Cal."

"Will we be meeting up with them?"

"For a while. They'll bring their herd in from

farther east and north, and we're likely to meet them anywhere between the 'Y' and town."

"That all seems regular enough."

"Everyday work. Two outfits about the same size with about the same number of cattle to ship. Just don't let the Dodge boys get under your skin."

"In what way?"

"Oh, they strut around, cock-of-the-walk style. Don't step right in front of one of 'em or square off and bare your teeth."

"I don't tend to do those things."

"So much the better. Either of them will punch a man for stepping on his shadow."

———

After noon dinner, Delaine sat against the bunkhouse wall with the other three as they smoked. The sun was moving south at this time of year, and the rays were soft and comfortable.

Delaine saw, as before, that the ranch yard was surrounded by pine trees, a pale and brighter green than the evening before. But he did not see any silver pines. People called a land formation such as this one a pine ridge, although in reality it had quite a few dark cedars throughout. He knew the word "pine" became a general term for some people, taken to mean any evergreen tree with needles. He wondered if, at one time, there was a silver-colored fir or spruce tree that might have given the ranch its name.

Caswell said, "We need to ride out into the canyons and bring in some steers that slipped through the net earlier."

"Will we see any silver pines?"

"Ah, that," said Caswell. "I think it's just a name."

——————

ON THE WAY OUT, the men rode in pairs. Caswell let the other two hands go ahead, and he rode alongside Delaine. When the others were well ahead, Caswell spoke in a voice that was not loud but not low and confidential.

"It was good of the boss to say that this is a straight-up outfit."

Delaine laughed. "I've heard some pretty crooked fellows say the same thing, but I felt that he was saying it in earnest."

"He was." Caswell rode on for half a minute and spoke again. "Sometimes it seems as if he's insisting."

"Oh, yeah."

"Did you notice it?"

"Not so much, but I know what you mean."

"He says he trusts his men, but it seems as if he likes to sound 'em out."

"It may have gotten past me. And I'm not going to be here but a few days anyway."

"He knows that, of course."

Delaine frowned. "Do you think he was saying it for some other effect?"

"I don't know. I wondered what you thought."

Delaine tipped his head to one side. "Hard to say. I don't know him. but he seems to be like a lot of 'em, always on the lookout to see if someone from the inside or on the outside is makin' off with something of his."

"That might be what I mean."

Delaine said, "Not to make any assumptions, but I

think just about every puncher, at some time or another, has a chance to do something. If I ever did, it would be a long ways away and, I hope, well in the past."

"Oh, yeah. Anyone with a head on his shoulders will figure out, sooner or later, that he needs to go straight. It's just that it's not always easy. Sometimes a fellow is in too deep, and someone else doesn't want to let him go."

Delaine had a faint glow of recognition, a sense of where Caswell had been going with the conversation. He felt himself resisting. He did not want to be drawn into a confidence or even to seem receptive or sympathetic. He said, "I know what you mean. It's hard to change, even when you know it's time."

Caswell must have understood, for he did not bring the topic back to the angle he had been taking. He motioned with his head toward the other two riders. "We have a good idea where the steers are, and the country's not that rough. We go up into the head of each little canyon and push out anything that's in the trees or brush. You know how to do that."

"Sure I do."

"We should be able to find more than a dozen steers among the rest of the cattle. The boss would like to have fifteen to round out the number we've got, so if we get that many, we can take 'em on in." Caswell reached into his coat pocket as if he was going to take out his tobacco and papers, but he drew his hand out empty, as if he had changed his mind.

Delaine recalled the moment the day before in the saloon. Caswell seemed as if he had a little liberty when he went to town to pick up the mail and, Delaine imagined, to send messages to people like Chamberlain, the man in the red beard. Delaine wondered what else Caswell did when he was on his own, and he told himself he would be better off not to think about it. It was better to think about small things, such as why men shouldn't smoke on the open range when the grass was dry.

2

———

Delaine was riding his brown horse when he and the other riders pushed the sixty steers out of the holding pasture in the morning. When they had the cattle onto the trail, Caswell rode on the left flank, Delaine rode on the right, and Chiddester and Bloom took up the drag. The drive did not shape up to be a difficult task, as there were no cows and calves to be separated in the mass and go looking for one another, and there were no lame or slow animals. Delaine knew they did not want to move the steers fast and run the weight off of them, so it was just a matter of keeping the bunch together and headed in the right direction.

They reached the fork in the road that Caswell called the "Y" at midmorning. From there, the country opened up with fewer trees and lower hills. While the outfit rested, the steers began to graze in the better grass. After a few minutes, Caswell gave a loud whoop and set the bunch in motion again.

About halfway from the "Y" to town, Delaine saw another herd moving from the northeast. As Caswell, had said, the herd was about the same size as the Silver Pine's, and from what Delaine could see, it had four riders as well. The Dodge boys were on the flanks, and two other men were visible in the dust at the rear. Mace had set out ahead that morning, and Delaine assumed that Chamberlain had done the same. The steers moved at an easy pace as the country sloped downhill toward town and the river. The shipping pens lay on the east end of town, so Caswell had the herd pointed in that direction. The day was calm, and nothing was hurried. The sun moved across the sky, and it was past the high point when they brought the steers down the last slope, across the road, and in through the arched gateway of the first corral. A stock-yard man stood back on each side, one with a long, thick cane and the other with a stick large enough to be a cudgel.

The steers slowed as they went into the large pen and were funneled into an alleyway. Caswell called out in a friendly tone to the man on his side. The steers lowed, and hooves thumped on corral planks. Bits of dust and dried manure rose on the air.

When all the steers were in, the four riders moved off to the side to wait for the second herd and to be ready to help if any animals broke loose.

Caswell said, "Chamberlain's men had to start quite a bit earlier to bring 'em in all in one day. They're goin' to be hungry, so we'll let them get in the grubline first."

The men in his own crew chatted on, and Delaine listened. He understood that two men, Bloom and a hired hand of Chamberlain's named Fitts, were going to go with the train to Chicago. They would ride in the caboose, and at every stop, they would have to get out and prod through the slats of the cattle cars with poles to make sure that none of the steers stayed down. It could be a dirty job with all the manure, and if it rained or snowed, there would be muck on the ground as well as in the cars.

"But you get to see the city," said Caswell.

"The ass end of it," said Bloom. "Nothin' special about that. Even if I had the time and the money and a new set of clothes, I wouldn't feel that I fit in downtown. So we stay over one night and come back. Sleep in the caboose the whole time."

Caswell rode over to talk with one of the men on the ground. Some men, like Chiddester, kept to themselves, while others had it in their nature to want to get along well with others. After a short while, Caswell came back to join the Silver Pine group.

Chamberlain's herd came in. The Dodge boy on the near side had darker hair than the other, so Delaine assumed he was Earl. The man gave what looked like a self-satisfied smile to Caswell and the others, then gigged his horse and slapped his thigh as he hollered at the steers.

"Hep! Hep! Hep!"

The herd slowed as it moved into the corral. One of the riders in back, a light-haired fellow in a dust-colored, wide-brimmed hat and a sheepskin coat, waved to the Silver Pine riders.

Bloom said, "That's the one who's goin' to ride in the caboose with me. Hiram Fitts. He's all right. He's not afraid to get in the cattle car if he has to and get manure up to his knees."

When all the steers had been driven in, pushed down the alleys, and put into smaller pens, Caswell said, "We can put our horses in one of these pens and go eat."

Delaine followed the others past the train station and telegraph office to an eating house, still on the same side of the street. A sign with red letters proclaimed it to be The Knight's Table.

Inside, the aroma of grease and cooked meat hung in the air, and men's voices made a hubbub. Mace and Chamberlain were already seated at one of the tables. Chamberlain's men were in the front of the line, followed by a couple of men who looked like towns-folk. A couple of railroad workers in denim overalls came next, then and the two stockyard men who had stood at the gate. Caswell and the others took up the end of the line.

Before long, Delaine saw the layout of food being served. A large, oblong basket of sliced bread was followed by steaming pans of boiled carrots and boiled potatoes. After that came the centerpiece, a roasted pig with an apple in its mouth and all the meat on the far side carved away. Beyond that, Delaine saw a large basin of what looked like applesauce.

The men in line served themselves. An attendant moved back and forth behind the food while another was scraping away pork fat from the cutting board and keeping sliced meat in the pans. A man with a cloudy, overbearing expression, who had the air of being the proprietor, gave orders to the two attendants. He had wavy brown hair, blue eyes, ruddy cheeks on a full face, and a heavy upper body covered in part by a full-length white apron. Delaine guessed him to be close to his own age of thirty-eight but worse from the wear of whatever life he lived.

"That's Goodwin," said Caswell. "He owns the place."

Delaine nodded. The eating house was more common-looking than the sign outside suggested, as it was more like a mess hall with tables and benches and no adornments except a three-foot-by-three-foot poster with the name of the establishment in red letters above an illustration of a helmet and a halberd. It looked like a good place for drovers, freighters, railroad workers, and the like, not the kind where men took off their hats to eat.

The men sat in their groups, and the atmosphere relaxed. Once everyone was seated, individuals got up as they chose and served themselves more food. The Dodge boys made their way together, spurs clinking, and returned to sit on opposite sides of their table. Hiram Fitts, the light-haired fellow in the sheepskin coat, sat at the same table but not close to them.

"Good grub," said Caswell. "I like pork when it's been seared on the outside like this. Say what you will about Goodwin, but he puts on a good feed. Of course, the bosses are paying for this, and others come to the trough."

Delaine thought he was referring to the two townsmen, as all the rest were part of the work crew in one way or another. One of the attendants arrived with a coffeepot and four cups, and no one spoke.

As the man set the cups down and filled them, Goodwin appeared at his elbow and said, "Griggs, get over there and help Andrews turn the cutting board around." The proprietor moved on without speaking to any of the men at the table.

Little by little, the clacking of utensils diminished. Griggs and Andrews began to distribute saucers with dessert, which Delaine identified as bread pudding with raisins.

By now, one of the townsmen had gotten up and was going from one table to another in the manner of an ambassador of goodwill. He was a man of average height in a loose-fitting, dull brown suit and a hat with a small crown and a short brim. As he came near, Delaine saw that he had straight hair the color of old straw, a fleshy face, dull blue eyes, a fixed smile, a nose that almost met his chin, and a protruding stomach.

He passed the table where Delaine and his fellow riders sat. He smiled and nodded, not looking straight at anyone with his vacuous eyes.

When he had gone on to the next table, Caswell said, "His name's Herbert. Ed Herbert. He has the land office on the other side of the street."

Delaine nodded. He remembered seeing the sign.

Herbert passed a couple of more tables and stopped at the table where Mace and Chamberlain sat. He shook hands with each of them and said something, which, from the smile and the nod, Delaine imagined might be thanking them for the meal. Herbert then walked past his own table, gave a small wave to the man who seemed to be his associate, and walked out.

The other man remained seated. He had kept to himself all along and had not gotten up to serve himself more food. Delaine thought he had seen him cast an expression of recognition at the Dodge boys and a less certain flicker at Caswell, but he did not watch the man because he did not want to be caught looking at him. Instead, he took him in with brief glances.

The man was about forty or a little older, lean,

and dressed in a grey wool jacket and pants and a dull black hat. He had dark hair with streaks of grey, and he was clean-shaven with a sallow complexion and close-set beady eyes. A line that looked like a thin scar ran straight down the left side of his face between his eye and his ear and faded at the jaw. He had a prominent Adam's apple and an overall dry look.

Griggs came by with more coffee.

Bloom said, "The bread pudding was good. So was everything else."

"Glad you liked it," said Griggs.

The conversation at the tables began to pick up. Delaine saw that the slender man in the grey suit had left. He thought it might be time for him to leave as well, but he did not know what the others were going to do.

Someone touched his elbow, and he looked up to see George Mace.

"I think your work is done," said the boss, "and I thank you for it. I have your pay." He held his hand downward with large coins between his thumb and his first three fingers.

Delaine held his hand forward and received two silver dollars and a fifty-cent piece. "Thank you," he said.

"Two dollars didn't seem like much, so I added a little bonus."

"I appreciate it. And this has been a fine meal."

"Glad you liked it. Roast pig is good, once in a while." Mace took in the other three men. "I guess I'll see you boys whenever you get back to the ranch. Don't drink the town dry."

"We won't," said Caswell. "Just a little nip."

The boss raised his eyebrows and lowered them as he turned to walk away.

Caswell motioned with his hand toward Delaine. "Why don't you join us for a drink at the White Mule? Don't worry. We won't drink up all your wages."

"I guess I could. I need to stop at the stable on the way, to leave my horse. I'll meet you there, at the saloon."

———

THE MAN who ran the stable emerged from the shadows carrying a pitchfork upright. He had a blocky build and wore a short-brimmed hat, khaki work clothes, suspenders, and crusted work shoes. As he came to a stop in better light, Delaine saw his mouse-colored hair, rough complexion, and sparse stubble. His frown may have been a permanent fixture. He stood with the tip of the pitchfork handle on the floor, turned his head, and spit out a small quantity of tobacco juice. He wiped his lower lip with his free hand and said, "What do you need?"

"I'd like to put my horse up."

"For how long?"

"I'm not sure. I just finished a little job bringing some steers into the pens, and I plan to stay long enough to see if there's any other work."

"There isn't much." The man's pale-brown eyes went to Delaine's horse and came back. "What's your name?"

"Delaine."

"Delaney?"

"No, Delaine. It's a kind of wool."

"You lack a syllable to be Delaney, then."

Delaine waited a couple of seconds to answer. "I'd like to roll out my bed somewhere in the straw, as well."

The man tilted the pitchfork to move the head. "Over there. It'll be another twenty cents. No smokin' inside. Don't want no fires."

"I don't smoke."

"No candles, either."

The man held out his hand as if to take the reins.

"I'll unsaddle him myself. I'm used to it. And I'll leave my bag and bedroll there where you said."

"Suit yourself."

"I plan to be gone for a while and come in later."

"That's why I said what I did. Men come in drunk."

Delaine waited another couple of seconds. "The fellow who runs the eatin' house put on a good feed. Roasted a whole pig. Small one, but good."

"What I hear."

———

DELAINE STAYED on the south side of the main street. He walked past the blacksmith shop, crossed the inter-section, and noted the other businesses still on the south side—a farm and implement outlet, a rooming house, a place that looked like a beer and ale house called The Three Hermits, a freight yard, and a coal yard. He crossed another street, passed an empty building, and reached the end of town.

He turned north and walked across the main street, facing a saddle and harness shop. To the left of it sat a butcher shop, with what looked like a slaughter-house in back. To the right of it, on the corner, sat a laundry that advertised alterations in small letters and had a painted image of an iron with a goose-necked handle. The phrase *the tailor's goose* ran through his mind. He turned east and headed toward the main part of town again, passing the businesses he just saw, then the mercantile on the next corner and arriving at the entrance of the White Mule. Music and voices and laughter sounded normal to him as he walked in, and the decor was familiar.

At the far end of the bar, in good lamplight, red-bearded Cole Chamberlain stood with his two hired men, the Dodge brothers, all in colors of tobacco, buckskin, and wheat. Delaine took a place at the bar where, when he looked up, he saw the painting of the lady in the blue dress riding the white mule.

The bartender was the same as before, with his dark-green vest and white apron. He addressed Delaine in a familiar tune. "Whiskey?"

"Good for me." Delaine saw himself in the mirror as the bartender turned away. He also saw the dry, slender man in the grey jacket who had been sitting with Ed Herbert in The Knight's Table. He was walking farther into the saloon.

The bartender set a glass on the bar and poured whiskey. Delaine put his half-dollar, Mace's bonus, next to the glass.

Delaine took a sip and appreciated the taste. The music was coming from a piano against the opposite wall. One man was seated, playing, and two men were standing by, singing, with drinks in their hands. Delaine recognized the song as a sentimental tune about a man who had gone to prison and would never see his sweetheart again.

A figure appeared in the mirror, and Delaine recognized Caswell. Delaine turned to greet him and saw that he had a companion with him. Delaine nodded and shook as Caswell made introductions.

Delaine caught the man's name as Hensley. He was about Caswell's age and looked like a plausible acquaintance. He wore a dusty hat that seemed to have discolored from black to a dark brown, plus a blanket-lined denim jacket that went down past his waist. He had a light-blue shirt, a brown cloth vest, denim pants, and scuffed, dull-black boots with no spurs. Returning to the man's face, Delaine observed his straight, dark-brown hair, dark eyebrows, brown eyes, and dark stubble.

"Buy you a drink?" said Delaine.

"Wouldn't turn it down," said Caswell. "How about you, Paul?"

Hensley said, "Sure."

Delaine caught the bartender's attention, pointed at his change, and made a circular motion to indicate Caswell and Hensley.

The bartender poured the drinks, and Delaine handed them to the other two men. As he did, the man in the grey jacket passed by again on his way to the door. Caswell's eyes followed him even as he smiled and thanked Delaine for the drink. Hensley thanked him as well. The man in the grey jacket went out through the front door. Delaine reflected that he had not stayed long enough for a drink.

Another song was playing. As Hensley sang along, Delaine recognized a version of the song about a high-lopin' cowboy and wild buckaroo.

> I've been in Montana and in Idaho
> I've been down in Texas and old
> > Mexico.

"Where are the other two?" Delaine asked.

"Chiddester and Bloom? They'll be along." Caswell looked to one side and another. "You don't find women in here."

"But I imagine they're somewhere."

"They always are," said Hensley. "Waitin' to separate a man from his wages."

Delaine wondered where Hensley earned his wages, but as with other things, he figured that if it mattered, he would learn it in its own good time. He said, "I wonder where I might look for work next. I don't like to go down Main Street, knockin' door to door."

"That's in a song, too," said Hensley.

"I guess I've heard it."

"Walkin' down Canal Street, knockin' door to door. Dum-dum son of a bitch, tryin' to find a whore."

"Well," said Caswell, "I think I heard Al at the shippin' pens say somethin' about wantin' to do some repairs, put in new posts and such, before the ground freezes."

"I could try that."

"Sure. He might even remember you. He was there today."

"Thanks for the suggestion."

Caswell glanced each way again. "I don't like to stay in these places all night. There's somethin' I wouldn't mind mentionin' to you if we were in a place where we wouldn't be eavesdropped on or interrupted."

Delaine raised his eyebrows. "Well, I've arranged to stay in the livery stable. I could meet you there later on if you'd like. Say in about an hour."

"That sounds fine. I'll be by myself. But don't worry about Paul. He's all right." Caswell pushed his fist against Hensley's shoulder.

Hensley put on a silly expression and said, "Sing polly-wolly-doodle all day."

Delaine smiled.

Caswell and Hensley finished off their drink, thanked Delaine, and left.

Delaine sipped on his whiskey. The men at the piano were having a good time. So were the men at the end of the bar, from appearances. The Dodge boys were standing in their self-assured poses with their hats tipped back and their thumbs in their gun belts. Both of them had broad smiles, while Cole Chamberlain, taller, held his right index finger in the air and was speaking with the air of a man being witty.

"Another?" said the bartender.

"No, thanks. One's enough for me tonight. I have to look for work in the morning." He left the nickel on the bar for a tip, and he had the familiar experience of wondering if sometime in the next couple of weeks he would wish he still had it.

———

A LANTERN HUNG from a rafter near the harness room, and a dull light reached the area in the straw where Delaine rolled out his blankets. He wondered how long he would have to wait for Caswell.

He sat on his blankets for a while, then pushed himself to his feet and walked to the door. The night was not cold. He left the door open and stood outside where he thought a person could see him.

After about ten minutes, a voice at his right said, "Is that you?"

"It's either me or the wild buckaroo." Delaine realized he had the tune of the song running through his head.

Caswell said something that sounded like "That's a bet." His boots sounded on the hard ground, but he must have taken his spurs off, for no sound came from them. *Quiet*, thought Delaine.

Caswell drew near, and in a low voice, he said, "I don't mean to be so top secret, but you never know who's around."

"I think we're pretty much on our own here."

"I do, too." Caswell took out the makings, rolled a cigarette, and lit it. "Good weather we're still havin'."

"Not bad at all."

Caswell sniffed. "Don't mind Hensley."

"Oh, he didn't bother me."

"That's good." Caswell took a drag. "You may recall somethin' I said the other day, about how hard it is to go straight."

"I guess I do, but if it seemed like the thing to do, I might not remember it at all."

"Could be that, too. I don't know how long you plan to stay around."

Delaine felt the same resistance he had felt on the earlier occasion. He did not want to seem too open or sympathetic or confidential. At the same time, Caswell had made what seemed like a sincere gesture of friendship. "I don't know how long either," he said. "Depends on whether I find work. I'll talk to the fellow at the stockyards tomorrow."

"Sure." Caswell took another drag. "You never know if any of it amounts to anything. But I'll say this. You want to be careful."

"I always try to be."

"Just a word to the wise." Caswell took a long breath. "You know, we all have to look out for ourselves."

"Uh-huh."

"And I'm still tryin' to get loose from bein' tied up with bad company. Sometimes I have a feelin' that it might be somethin' harder than I can do."

Delaine thought Caswell was talking around something he might like to say in clearer terms, but Delaine did not want to be brought into it. He wondered why Caswell was telling him to be careful—whether it was for being friends with Caswell or if it was a more general warning about some of the other men with whom he had crossed paths.

"I don't know what I can do," he said, "other than, as you say, be careful."

"Neither do I. I just wanted to say that."

"Well, I appreciate it."

"Don't mention it." Caswell took a long drag on the cigarette, dropped the stub, and rubbed it out with the sole of his boot. He held out his hand. "It was good to work with you. maybe we'll do it again."

"It was," said Delaine.

As Caswell walked away in the darkness, Delaine had the sense that the man wanted to say more but held his tongue. Delaine felt a shadowy guilt for having cut him short. Maybe there would be more in a later conversation.

Delaine looked down at the snuffed-out cigarette butt. He knew a man once who did not like to smoke while walking down the street because it did not look dignified. He could imagine another man not wanting to make a target of himself in the dark.

3

———

GREY LIGHT APPEARED IN THE STABLE, AND THE shifting of horses' feet in the stalls was accompanied by a low human voice that sounded like the stable man's. Delaine rolled out of bed, rubbed his face, and put on his hat and boots. He found his blanket-lined canvas jacket and put it on. After rolling his blankets and checking around to see that he had not left anything in the straw, he tied his bedroll onto the back of his saddle where he had left it on a rack. After another look around, he stepped outside in the first light of dawn.

He crossed the street and was not surprised to see the haberdashery, the drugstore, and the newsstand all closed and dark. A light shone in the general store, but the door was not open yet, and no articles had been set out onto the sidewalk. He continued walking east, crossed the street, and noted a mercery, millinery, and women's wear business, also dark. Light was shining in the Prairie Star Bakery, so he went in.

A slender man below average height, with white

hair and a clipped mustache, was setting a rectangular wicker basket of bread rolls on the counter.

"Are those fresh?" Delaine asked.

"These are yesterday's. A penny each."

"Then I'll take three of them."

The man had a humorless air about him as he set the three rolls on the counter and took the three pennies without comment.

"Thanks," said Delaine.

"Same to you."

Delaine walked back west and took a seat on a bench outside the newsstand. As he ate his bread, he heard the sounds of morning—a rooster crowing, a dog barking, a voice calling. Movement on his left caught his eye as a man in a green apron came out of the general store and set an armful of brooms on display. The town of Overton seemed like many others Delaine had seen, tending to business and getting through from one day to the next.

He stood up and brushed the crumbs from his lap. He could see the shipping pens, but nothing seemed to be stirring. Not wishing to pass the stony gaze of the baker, he angled across the street toward the train station and went east from there.

A dull light showed in the stockyards office. He walked past it and saw that the pens were empty. He assumed that all the steers had been loaded and that Bloom and Fitts were in a caboose chugging across the sandhills of Nebraska.

He walked out to the end of the pens, which was also the end of town, and lingered. It seemed early to be interrupting anyone's work or routine, and if he didn't have luck in this first place, he was going to have to wait for other businesses to open.

He watched the morning light grow by the minute. As long as the weather was good, a fellow could enjoy the feeling of freedom, of not being tied down to drudgery and payments; but when the cold weather hit and the icy storms came over the land, he would be glad for a job and a bunk inside.

A clank of metal came from the blacksmith shop two blocks away. He did not care for the smudge and the smoke and the smell of melted flux, but a forge was a good place in winter, if only for a few minutes.

Some people said they couldn't remember the cold when the weather was hot. On any day of the year, he could remember riding into the icy streets of Ratón after midnight, chilled to the core of his body, and feeling himself lucky to find a room even though it had a door to the street and a one-inch gap at the bottom.

A bell sounded, like a church bell. Now that he thought of it, he had not heard that sound as much on the northern plains as he did in any little town in New Mexico.

For a moment, he saw himself in this new place as others might—as a loiterer at the edge of town. He hunched his shoulders. After standing in one place for a few minutes, he felt the chill of morning. He put his hands in his coat pockets and began walking.

He stopped and turned in at the stockyards office and knocked on the door. A voice inside called, "Come in," so he did.

One of the men Delaine had seen the day before sat at a small wooden desk, looking at papers by the light of a kerosene lamp. He was wearing a creased hat and a canvas jacket, and he had a weathered face with a trimmed mustache. He looked up and said, "What can I do for you?"

Delaine took off his hat. "How do you do? My name's Jess Delaine. I helped bring in the steers for George Mace yesterday. My work with him is finished, and I was wondering if there was anything you need to have done here."

The man took in Delaine at a glance. "Word travels. I just said yesterday that I was thinkin' of doin' some repairs before the ground freezes. I've got posts to be dug out and replaced, which means takin' planks down and puttin' them back up. How are you with a diggin' bar and a shovel?"

"I can hold my own."

"You'll use a crowbar and a sledgehammer, too, as well as a hammer. I've got another boy lined up to start tomorrow. You take turns on everything, so one fella doesn't have to do all the hard work."

"Of course."

"He's Mexican. But he speaks English as good as you or me, and I don't want someone to think he can put anything over on him."

"I get along fine with Mexican people. I even speak a little Spanish myself."

"You won't have to."

Delaine decided not to make things better.

"What did you say your name is?"

"Delaine."

"Are you staying here in town?"

"Yes, sir."

The man let out a breath. "Then I guess I'll put you on. You can show up at this time tomorrow."

"At seven?"

"It's a little past that right now, but, yes." The man glanced at his paper and raised his eyes again. "By the way, my name's Al Portman."

"It's a pleasure to meet you. I'll see you tomorrow."

"I'll be here."

On the street again, Delaine did not have a good idea of what to do with his time for the rest of the day. If he was in a bigger town, he might go to a warehouse or a materials yard and ask if anyone needed a day laborer, but he had not seen any such places, and he did not want to seem as if he was begging for work. On the other hand, he did not want to sit on a bench all day and look like a vagrant.

He went back to the stable and found the proprietor brushing a sleek bay horse.

"Good morning, sir."

"My name's Kent."

"Very good."

"What's on your mind?"

"I've got a job starting tomorrow with Al Portman at the shipping pens, and I was wondering if you had any work that I might keep busy at today."

Kent frowned. "I don't make much as it is. I have one hired man already. When he goes, I've got another lined up. I try to keep money going in my direction, small amounts that they are. But if you want to put in a day's work cleanin' stalls, I can put it against your bill for keepin' your horse here. And I won't charge you for sleepin' here another night. If you have a regular job, I'd just as soon you stay at the roomin' house or the hotel after that."

"That sounds fair to me. Something to keep me busy."

Kent gave him a critical glance. "Keep you out of the barroom, if nothing else."

Delaine worked through the morning and into the early afternoon. Because he wasn't making any money, he put off buying something to eat. His hunger got the best of him, though, and he told Kent he was going to find a meal. Kent shrugged and said that everything would be there when he came back.

Delaine made his way to the Sweet Auburn Café, hoping he did not have too much of the odor of the stable on him. The same woman waited on him as on the day he came to town.

"It looks like I missed the main mealtime again," he said. "What do we have?"

"Beans with bacon rind, biscuits on the side."

"Couldn't turn it down."

On this visit, he sat on the other side of the center aisle, close enough to see the lithograph illustrations he had noticed before. One picture showed an old-fashioned village street with a legend below it in a flowing script, *Sweet Auburn, loveliest village of the plain*, followed by an attribution to *The Deserted Village*, by Oliver Goldsmith. In the other illustration, he saw a rose growing in a spare landscape with an excerpt below, in the same lettering as in the first illustration, that read, *Full many a flow'r is born to blush unseen, And waste its sweetness on the desert air.*

Below it was an attribution to *Elegy Written in a Country Churchyard*, by Thomas Gray. The reference to the second work seemed familiar to Delaine.

The woman returned with a bowl of beans and two biscuits. "We have plenty in the pot," she said, "So if you want more, don't be shy. No extra charge."

"Thanks. I might take you up on it. Are you at the end of your shift again?"

"Not till you're done, and it's not quite time yet." She did not seem to be in a hurry to leave him. "I get up at four, and I come in to have the oven going by five. I do the baking in the morning, and then I wait on customers."

"I see. Well, it's nice to meet people in this town."

"Have you found work?"

"I helped bring in some cattle for George Mace, and I'm going to work tomorrow for Al Portman at the shipping pens. Today I'm doing a little work at the livery stable, to stay out of mischief."

She nodded.

He said, "Would it be too forward to ask your name?"

She took a couple of seconds to answer. "My name is Rachel." After another short pause, she added, "No one's name is a secret in a small town like this, anyway."

"I don't imagine. My name is Jess Delaine, though I don't suppose it matters much."

"Why do you say that?"

"Well, I'm new in town, and no one knows how long I'll stay."

She shrugged. "Every person matters."

"Thanks."

She gave a faint smile. "Let me know if you want another serving."

———

DELAINE AWOKE AGAIN in the first light of morning. He stared at the rafters above and remembered where he was. After his one full meal in the afternoon, followed by a couple of more hours of work, he had gone to bed early and had slept right through. He tensed his body and relaxed. Time to roll out. He had a day's work ahead of him. As he turned the blankets aside and sat up, he saw a human form in the straw not far away.

Focusing his eyes, Delaine saw that the person was Tom Caswell, huddled on his side in his grey wool jacket with his knees drawn up to his midsection. He was still, and Delaine wondered if something had happened to him. Then Caswell brushed his nose and let out a short, heavy breath.

Delaine imagined that Caswell must have stayed up or stayed out late, so he made as little noise as possible as he put on his boots, hat, and jacket, stored his bedroll, and walked out of the stable.

The morning felt colder than the day before. He buttoned his jacket and took out a pair of gloves from the left pocket. He felt hungry enough to eat a full breakfast, but mindful of his money, he crossed the street and walked east to the bakery again.

The impassive baker sold him three day-old bread rolls and gave him change for a nickel. Outside, Delaine sat on the sidewalk in front of the dark and empty land office and ate his bread. He kept an eye on the stockyards, telling himself that if someone else showed up, he would make haste to get over there. As it turned out, he had time to finish his modest meal, brush off the crumbs, and walk across the street.

Al Portman met him at the door. His light-brown hair and brown eyes were more visible than the day before, and he was smoking a cigarette. He was wearing his hat and jacket, a vest, a shirt, and pants, all in sand-colored tones. He took the cigarette from his mouth and said, "You're a few minutes early. I'll take you out and show you where you'll work. Benny should be here any time."

Portman stepped outside and led the way around

to a shed in back. He opened the door and took out a digging bar and two shovels. "Hold these."

He reached inside again and came out with a sledgehammer, a crowbar, and a clawhammer. He tipped his head and looked past Delaine.

Footsteps sounded on the hard ground, and Delaine turned to see a young man in tan work clothes and a grey wool cap with a short beak.

"This is Benny," said the boss.

Delaine had the digging bar in one hand and the two shovels in the other, so he nodded. "How do you do?"

The young man had wavy dark hair and a medium complexion, and his teeth showed as he smiled. "Just fine. And yourself?"

"Doin' well."

"You take these," said Portman. He handed the sledge, crowbar, and hammer to Benny.

The boss led the way to a gate on the west side of the corrals, opened it, and went through a pen to another gate. "Might as well start here," he said. "This post is about to break off at ground level. You need to take the planks off, dig out the post, and put in a new one. For the planks, don't just beat 'em on the other side. You splinter 'em that way. Tap 'em out a little ways, or pry 'em, and tap 'em back, so the nail heads show, and then pull the nails with a crowbar. Don't leave any nails on the ground for a cow to pick up with its hoof." His cigarette was down to a stub, so he held his thumb and forefinger close to the damp tip, and he squinted as he took a last drag. "Benny knows all this, includin' which end is which on the diggin' bar."

The young man smiled.

Delaine had noticed that one end of the five-foot

bar was flared for digging, and the other end had a metal disk, two inches wide and three-quarters of an inch thick, welded onto it for tamping.

"If you need anything, you know where I am." The boss walked past them and left them to their work.

Delaine set the shovels and bar against a plank they were not going to work on. He held out his hand and said, "My name's Jess Delaine." He had worked with Mexican men in the past, and he knew that they often shook hands at the beginning of each day and had other courtesies as well, such as offering a cigarette. He also knew that some white men did not like to shake hands with Mexicans, Chinese, or Negroes, and he did not want to seem like one of those, even though his hands had been full when the introduction was first made.

Benny shook and said, "Benny Escalon."

Delaine noticed that he gave his last name an English pronunciation. In New Mexico, Delaine had heard the name pronounced with an accentuated long *o*. "I suppose we might as well get started by takin' off the planks."

They separated the planks as the boss told them, prying the boards and then pulling the twenty-penny nails with the crowbar. When they had the post standing by itself, they began to dig.

Benny was cheerful and conversational. He said his family had lived in town for about ten years. He knew most of the people. He had worked in town and in the country, on ranches and farms.

Delaine told of his recent work with the Silver Pine, and Benny said he knew the boss and the men who rode for him.

The only sounds for a few minutes came from the

chipping of the bar against the hard-packed earth and the scraping of the shovel as they lifted out the loose dirt.

Delaine said, "This seems like a quiet, peaceful town. Except when the train comes through."

"Oh, yeah, it's quiet," Benny said. "Calm. You know, as far as what everybody sees."

"On the surface."

"Yeah. But it's not like…nothing ever happens."

"Oh." It was Delaine's turn with the bar, and he was careful not to scrape his knuckles on the post. He moved around to continue digging and to let Benny take out the loose dirt they had chipped.

Benny said, "Some things people don't talk very much about."

Delaine drove hard with the bar.

"Couple of years ago, a little more, there was a girl who worked here in town, and she disappeared."

"Little girl? Older?"

"She was about nineteen. A year younger than me."

"You knew her, then?"

"Yes, I knew her. And I liked her. But it was never going to work out for us, I could see that, and then she disappeared."

"What kind of girl was she?"

"She was white. But there were other things that don't matter much now, but they made it impossible then. Other men. But that's all in the past."

"That's too bad. Sometimes things happen, and then it's too late to make things better."

"That's what happened here."

Delaine drove another dozen times with the bar,

loosening flakes and chunks. He rested as Benny dug out the loose stuff.

Benny held his hand out to take his turn with the steel bar. Silence seemed to fall for a moment as he said, "Her name was Nora."

———

AN OLDER WOMAN in a dark shawl, sweater, and dress arrived with a small bundle wrapped in a towel. Benny introduced her as his aunt, and he said she had brought him lunch. He asked Delaine if he would like some.

Delaine was sure the woman had brought food for only one person, so he said no, thanks. He left Benny to his meal and made his way to the general store, where he bought soda crackers, cheese, and a few dried apples. When he returned to the corrals, the older woman was folding the towel. She smiled and took leave in Spanish.

Delaine sat down and ate his lunch. Benny handed him the water jug that Portman had left with them at midmorning, a one-gallon wine jug wrapped in sewed-up burlap. Both of them had drunk from it, and now Delaine drank again, taking care to brush the crumbs from his mouth first.

They had replaced the first post and had nailed the planks on again, and they had dug out the next post Portman showed them. Like the first one, it was a corner post, almost a foot thick, but it was deteriorated at ground level and cracked from livestock crowding against it. The old post lay on the ground near the open hole with fresh dirt in mounds.

Delaine set the jug in the shade and said, "Let's see

if we can get the new post into the hole without knocking in a bunch of dirt."

The two of them held the heavy post upright and dropped it clean into the hole. They were tamping in the first portion of dirt, Delaine with the bar and Benny with the tip of a shovel handle, when the sound of a man clearing his throat caused them to stop and turn.

Delaine recognized the straw-colored hair, fleshy face, and fixed smile of the man named Ed Herbert. Delaine recalled that Herbert had the land office across the main street. The man was wearing his hat with a small crown and short brim to go along with his loose-fitting brown suit. As before, he seemed to lead with his stomach. He had his hands in his pants pockets. He tucked his chin and said, "Looks like you're doin' a good job there, boys." The nearness of his nose to his chin was noticeable.

"Thanks," said Benny.

Herbert jingled the change in his pocket. "Good weather for it. Not too hot, not too cold."

Delaine and Benny continued tamping.

"Good thing about Al. Likes to keep things fixed."

Delaine drove the bar downward with both hands, thumping on the fill dirt.

"Well, I'd better move along. Let you boys do your work."

When he was gone, Benny said, "That's Mr. Herbert. He has the land office over there. He buys and sells other things, too."

From the man's appearance, Delaine imagined him buying and selling used furniture. He said, "I saw him the other day when we were all eating, and one of Mace's men told me who he was. I suppose he takes it up on himself to see what anyone else is doing."

"Oh, yeah. He's nosy. He knows everyone and goes everywhere."

"Maybe he knows who I am, then. He's seen me twice."

Benny laughed. "Maybe he thinks he'll sell you something."

———

DELAINE ASKED about a room at the rooming house he had seen a couple of times. The clerk told him it was forty cents a night or two-fifty a week. He could have food in the room, but he could not cook. Many of the railroad workers stayed there as the trains came and went, so he would hear men coming and going at all hours, but no one wanted to hear loud men coming in drunk. This was a place for men who got up early and needed to sleep. Delaine said he would take a room for a week.

When he had moved his bag, bedroll, and rifle from the stable, he went downstairs. He paused at the door and turned as another man came down the stairs. As a habit, he liked to know who was behind him. He felt no reason for concern as he saw a young man about thirty, a little taller than average, with sandy-colored hair. He was clean-shaven, not slender but not filling out yet, and he was wearing a plain, very light-brown suit.

"Going out?" said the man.

"Yes, I am."

"So am I."

Delaine held the door open and followed him out.

The other man said, "I'm on my way to the café across the street."

"That's what I was thinking of doing."

"If you don't mind, we can go together." The man did not have a hat, and he raised his head to face the light breeze. He smiled and said, "Not to make a formal occasion of it, I'm Bernard Gresham. I'm the local schoolteacher."

"I'm Jess Delaine. I've been here a few days. I helped bring a herd of steers into town, and now I'm working at the shipping pens." As they shook hands, he was glad to be able to say that he was employed.

They crossed the street and went into the café, with Gresham handling the door this time. The bell quieted as they made their way inside.

A waiter met them and said, "Good evening, Mr. Gresham."

"Good evening, Phil. I think my fellow lodger and I will take a table together."

The evening meal was roast beef, mashed potatoes, and gravy. The waiter made himself inconspicuous, and the schoolteacher was sociable. He said that he came from Kansas and was in his second year in town. The first year, he boarded around with families, which was uneven because many of his pupils came in from the country, and the school was in town, so the families he stayed with had to settle with the others. Now he had a room of his own, which was much better, modest though it was.

Delaine said, "I grew up on the northern plains and worked in New Mexico for several years. I decided to come back, but I feel as if I'm like many of the people you meet here, who are from somewhere else."

"It does seem that way."

The conversation lulled as they ate their plate dinners. When Delaine finished, he said, "I'm sure you've noticed those two illustrations."

"Oh, of course. Many times. The one about the deserted village refers to a poem with that title, by Oliver Goldsmith, written in 1770 or so. Sweet Auburn is the name of the village itself. The other illustration, with the rose, comes from a poem called 'Elegy Written in a Country Churchyard,' written by Thomas Gray in about 1750."

"I saw the inscriptions, and I think I've heard the lines about the desert rose."

"It's a well-known poem, and those lines are often quoted along with 'The paths of glory lead but to the grave.' Good sentimental stuff, not all that morbid. The poem opens with the tolling of a bell and is nice and melancholy all the way through. And it's a good companion to the later poem, both of them in a sentimental period when there was a growing readership of common citizens—but you don't need to hear a summary of what I heard in lectures in college."

"It's all interesting."

The schoolteacher laughed. "As one of my professors used to say, 'This is interesting. At least to me.'"

On the way back to the rooming house, Gresham said, "There's The Three Hermits. As a general practice, I don't go there or to the saloon, because of my public image, but I don't mind having a growler in the room."

"A bucket of beer?"

"Yes. And I don't mind drinking in company. Maybe sometime later in the week."

"I don't mind it myself."

"I could quote you long passages from *Paradise Lost*."

Delaine gave him an uncertain look.

"Just a joke. It's a long poem from the century before, about falling from grace—man's first disobedience—but I had better not get started on that."

"Good enough. I'll look forward to a growler."

"Oh, yes, and The Three Hermits is handy. Right next door."

———

Delaine and Benny were taking the tools out of the shed in the cold air of morning when shouting voices carried from somewhere closer to the middle of town. Delaine listened but could not pick out any words.

He and Benny walked out to the front, where Al Portman stood on the doorstep of the office. He lowered his cigarette and said, "I wonder what the hell is going on."

The commotion rose again, as if men were shouting back and forth across the main street.

Portman said, "Why don't one of you run down there and see if someone needs help. Both of you go. If it's something serious, do what you can. If no one's hurt or dying, come on back to work."

Delaine and Benny jogged in the street. Voices continued to rise, and a man holding a hat on his head ran across the street on a diagonal from the general store to the livery stable. The door of the stable was open.

A couple of other men had gathered inside as well, so there were four, including Kent, blocking the view.

A lantern hung on a rafter above the area where Delaine had slept for two nights.

The soles of Delaine's boots slapped on the ground as he and Benny came to a stop. The four men turned. Delaine went through the doorway with Benny behind him.

Delaine tried to catch his breath as he said, "Al Portman sent us down to see if anyone needs help."

Kent rubbed his lower lip with the back of his hand. "I think he's beyond help."

As Delaine and Benny walked forward, the men separated two on each side. A man in a grey wool jacket lay face-down in the straw.

"Don't touch him," said Kent. "I already did, to see if he was alive. But he's cold."

The storekeeper, who had arrived just ahead of Delaine and Benny, asked, "Do you know who it is?"

"Sure, I do," said Kent. "He comes in here from time to time when it's too long of a ride back to the ranch." He looked at Delaine. "I think you know him, too. His name is Tom Caswell."

The storekeeper said, "I know him. He's kind of young to drink himself to death, isn't he?"

Kent spit to the side. "I'll leave it to the coroner to say, but I don't think that's what did it. He's got some purple marks on his throat. Quiet way to do things."

4

Delaine stood in line in the general store, waiting to order groceries to take back to his room. All day long at work, he had been visited by the after-effects of seeing the deceased Tom Caswell in the stable. In one moment, he would feel guilt at not having been able to do anything for the man, if only in a small way such as listening to what he wanted to say. In another moment, he would feel the familiar resistance of not wanting to be associated with or sympathetic to a man who was guilty of something and had enemies. Delaine was trying to keep his own life on a better track, and he did not need contact with any of those earlier ways.

The woman in line ahead of him said, "I hope someone can do something. This is not the kind of thing we can have. We're keeping our door locked at all times, and my husband took a pistol to work in his coat pocket after he came home at noon."

"It's terrible," said the storekeeper. "I saw the body myself."

The woman took her groceries away in her cloth bag, and the line of vision was cleared for the storekeeper, who gave Delaine a look of recognition. "Good afternoon, or evening, almost. What would you like?"

"Some food items to take to my room and to carry to work." He had the list rehearsed. "Some bread, cheese, dried apples, raisins, canned tomatoes, canned peaches, canned sardines, and canned meat."

"Beef or pork?"

"I prefer beef."

"One can of each thing?"

"Yes."

"How much cheese?"

"About a pound."

The grocer gathered canned goods and stacked them on the counter. "Do you have a bag?"

"I think I can take off my jacket and use it to carry the things. It's just across the street."

"Have you heard anything?"

"About—?"

"Well, yes, about the body."

"No, I haven't."

"Neither have I. This is not good at all. It's not like one man shooting another out in the open, in an argument, although that's not good, either. But this is a crime, and we have to wait for the sheriff's office to send someone. People have to live in fear."

Delaine frowned. He imagined it was natural for people to think of something like this in terms of what was happening to them. Even he had taken it that way with his feelings of guilt and resistance. But the person who deserved the most consideration couldn't feel anything anymore.

Delaine awoke to early morning light in his room. After a cold breakfast of bread and canned peaches, he wrapped bread, cheese, and dried apples in a clean handkerchief for lunch, put the bundle in his coat pocket, and made his way downstairs and into the street. He was glad to leave his narrow room behind him and to breathe the fresh air. The sun had not yet risen, and nothing was stirring on the street, so he decided he had time for a cup of coffee before he went to work.

The café was empty when he went in, but the aroma of fresh-baked bread was agreeable. The woman named Rachel came out of the kitchen as he took a seat at a table near the counter.

"Good morning," she said.,

"And good morning to you. I'll just have coffee, if it's not too much trouble."

"Not at all." She turned and left. She came back with a black enamel coffeepot and a tan crockery mug. As she poured the coffee, she said, "Did you know the man they found in the stable yesterday?"

"Yes, I did. I worked with him when we gathered the steers and brought them into town."

"I thought you did."

"I didn't know him very well, though."

She nodded. "Didn't you say you were going to go to work at the corrals?"

"Yes. I've been there a couple of days now. I work with a young fellow named Benny."

"Oh, yes. He's a good worker."

"He seems to know everybody."

"He's very likable. I think it made him sad when the girl disappeared. Did he tell you about that?"

Delaine thought the mention of the girl was abrupt, but he answered the question. "He's mentioned it both days. Said it happened a couple of years ago."

"Yes, it was before I came here. I know her sister, not very well. She works in a store here in town." Rachel paused. "It's like what happened yesterday, except no one is sure whether she is still alive. But in another way it is similar. It might seem like a small thing to people who live in big cities. Unimportant. But it is important to the people who know the person, and it is important in a bigger way. Every person has a life and deserves a chance."

Delaine had the impression that the recent event had reminded the woman of the earlier one and had brought out her larger concern. "I agree," he said. "And if something happens, they deserve someone finding out why." Delaine picked his words, not wanting to repeat the familiar phrase that somebody should do something.

"Not everyone is a brother or a sister," said Rachel. "Everybody is a daughter or a son, but even at that, some people don't have anyone. They still deserve, like you say, the truth."

Delaine was thinking of how to phrase his words. Again, he did not want to respond with a common phrase. At that moment, the door opened, ringing the bell.

A man in a long traveling coat and a homburg hat came in with a newspaper under his arm. "Good morning," he said. "Are you serving breakfast?"

"Yes, we are," said Rachel.

"Good. I'd like some bacon and eggs while my driver has my horse fed." The man took a seat on the other side of the café.

"Right away." Rachel turned to Delaine and lowered her voice. "No charge for the coffee. I'm sorry I talked so much."

"Not at all. It was good to hear you."

"Thanks. But please don't leave anything." She turned and walked to the kitchen.

As Delaine drank his coffee, the traveler opened his newspaper and gave it his attention. Delaine was sure the newsstand was not open yet. The man must have carried the paper with him and found it useful at times like this.

———

THE WORK at the corrals proceeded in its regular way. Delaine and Benny did not talk much when they were prying off planks or nailing them on or when one of them was breathing hard with the digging bar. In the interludes of tamping, which called for more even exertion, they returned to conversation, sometimes picking up a topic suspended earlier.

At one point, Benny said, "I wonder how long it will take for the deputy to come to town."

"People in town seem anxious."

"That doesn't mean they will do much. Unless it's someone important."

"Important in the sense of being a prominent citizen. I didn't invent this idea, but I think you would agree that everyone is important. Just making conversation."

"Oh, of course. Everyone is important. It's just that some of them are not treated that way."

Delaine waited. He could sense that Benny had something he wanted to say.

"Like Nora. They said she prob'ly ran off with someone. Just because she went with men in the evenings."

"Oh. I hadn't heard that part. Not that it makes her less important."

"It shouldn't."

"No, but it helps someone understand the story. You said the other day that you could see that things were never going to work between you and her, and it's none of my business, but it seems to make more sense now, or be clearer. Again, not wantin' to be personal. It all seems rather sad."

"That's what it was. She was going with them in the evenings, and I wasn't going to pay her money just like them. It was two different things. Crazy, in a way. Just a big thing that came between us, and I had to see it, that she was not looking for someone like me. Not then."

"That's too bad. And you're pretty sure she didn't run off with someone?"

"I'm sure. She didn't go with anyone like that."

"Like that—do you mean with that kind of interest, of eloping, or someone with that kind of money?"

"Either one."

Delaine tried to think of a more pleasant aspect. "What did she look like?"

"She was pretty. Brown hair and blue eyes, like her sister. The one who works in the tobacco and candy store."

"I don't know what store that is."

"The one where they sell newspapers." Benny pointed toward the middle of town.

"Oh, I know the place. I haven't been in there, though."

———

THEIR WORK TOOK them to the front of the pens, closer to the street. Again, they were working on a gatepost. When noontime came, they sat inside the corral with their backs to the planks and the sun shining down. A young boy had brought Benny's lunch and left it, so the two of them sat by themselves with their backs to the street.

A man came trudging through the open gate. He was of average height and build, with dark blond hair and plain features, about forty years old. He was wearing drab, dusty clothes and a cloth cap, and he had a knapsack over his shoulder. He turned to stand in front of the two workers and said, "How-do?"

Delaine shaded his eyes and said, "Good afternoon. Can we help you find something?"

"Happiness," said the man. "Ha-ha-ha. What does it look like I need?"

Delaine said, "I could make a better guess if you didn't stand with the sun in back of you."

"Oh, I'm sorry." The man stepped around and stood on Delaine's right, perpendicular to him.

"I don't know," said Delaine. "It looks like you've been walking. Do you need to find the stage line?"

"Not yet. Do you mind if I sit down?"

"Go ahead. We need to go back to work in a little while. I hope you don't mind if we eat our lunch."

"Please do. And don't mind about me. I plan to eat in a little while."

"It makes me feel guilty to eat in front of someone who doesn't have food."

"I'll have something in a little while, I assure you. I know you've got to eat if you're goin' to work, so don't let me bother you." The stranger looked at Benny and said, "I know the Mexican people are superstitious about eating in front of a pregnant woman. If they don't offer her food, the child'll grow up with its mouth open, always lookin' for somethin' to eat. But don't worry about me. I'm not in that condition. Ha-ha-ha."

Delaine and Benny exchanged a glance.

"You look like a couple of honest working men, toiling along the side of life's highway."

"Are you traveling on foot?" Benny asked.

"For the present. You don't mind if I sit down, then?"

Benny said, "Dirt's free."

The man set his knapsack on the ground and settled next to it, facing the two workmen. He sat with his hands around his knees. "I'm a little bit like you fellas," he said.

Delaine looked at him and waited.

In a lower voice and a less artificial tone, he said, "I do a little digging myself. I'm what they call an investigator. I don't tell everyone, and the ones I do tell, I don't tell right away. I like to have the feeling that I can trust someone."

Delaine nodded. He wondered if the man took them for bumpkins or did feel that they were thinking people who could be trusted. Benny was showing no response.

The man went on, still in a low voice. "I know it

doesn't do any good to ask someone not to say anything, but the more other people talk, the harder it is for me. Still, I have to start somewhere, and I'm startin' with you two fellas because you look like honest men who wouldn't be opposed to helpin' me find a missing girl."

Benny's face was rigid.

Delaine said, "Where is she from?"

"Eastern Colorado. Seventeen years old. Blonde hair and blue eyes."

Benny shook his head. "I haven't seen anyone like that."

"Neither have I," said Delaine. "I've been in town just a few days. How long has she been missing?"

"Well over a month," said the man, all serious now.

Delaine said, "I hope you find her. We just had a death of a different nature here. A ranch hand, found dead in the livery stable, and from the looks of it, at someone else's hands. If you talk to people in town, it's liable to come up right away."

"I try to let people talk." The man waited a few seconds, and after looking around, he continued. "My information has taken me to here. I believe you two when you say you haven't seen her, but you might yet." He reached inside his shirt and took out an envelope. From it, he drew out a photograph and handed it to Delaine. "This is the girl," he said.

The image was not of very good quality, as if it had been cut out of a larger photograph and duplicated in some way, but it showed an identifiable image of a blonde girl with her eyes open and her mouth closed in a serious attitude such as people assumed for a family portrait. Her hair was tied back, and she wore a high-collared blouse and a jacket.

"Her name is Evelina Ralston," the man said, keeping his voice low but clear. "She has parents who are worried sick about her." He paused. "Whenever I tell anyone anything, I know it's a risk."

Delaine handed the photograph to Benny, who looked at it and handed it to the stranger.

"What's your name?" Benny asked.

"My name is Jerome Richards. I plan to be in town for a couple of days at least, maybe more, and I'll be staying at the hotel. If you happen to learn anything, you can look for me there or leave word." He put the photograph in the envelope and tucked the envelope inside his shirt. He stood up, reached down to shake hands with the other two, and said, "Thanks, men." Putting on his simple smile from earlier, he picked up his knapsack and walked out of the corral.

Benny turned to see that he was gone. "That's something."

"It sure is. He seems to be on the square about looking for the girl, though."

"He does. I think it's good that someone is looking for her. I wish someone would have done that for Nora."

"So do I," said Delaine. He recalled Tom Caswell as he had seen him last, and he wished someone would do something for him, too.

———

DELAINE DID NOT SEE any signs or illustrations in The Three Hermits. It was a plain, narrow establishment, not very deep, with the bar across the back. Four spittoons sat along the bottom of the bar, which had no rail, and two kerosene lamps hung overhead. Midway beneath the two lamps stood a tall man with greying brown hair covering his ears, a beard of matching color, and a pullover collarless grey shirt that fell straight down from the circumference of his tun-like girth. Delaine did not think he was one of the original hermits, as his hair and beard and shirt were all clean, and his hands, which he rested on the bar, looked pale and soft.

"Evenin'," he said. "What would you like?"

"I'm staying at the rooming house next door, and I'd like to take a growler with me."

The tall man raised his eyebrows. "Were you friends with Tom Caswell?"

Delaine kept himself from frowning. "I worked with him for a short while."

"I was sorry to hear about what happened to him. When it's someone you know, it seems like something that could happen to any of us."

"I haven't been in town very long."

"Do you know Mr. Gresham?"

"Yes, I do. He's the one who suggested a growler."

"Thought that might be. I seen the two of you together the other evening." The man slid his hands from the bar, backed up, and turned his head as he stooped. He came up with a grey enamel bucket with a lid and a bail handle, about a half-gallon in capacity. He turned his broad back to Delaine as he filled the container from a tap and watched in the mirror. Drawing himself straight up with a breath, he swung the pail around and set it on the bar. "Twenty-five cents." He put the lid in place.

Delaine set a quarter on the bar. "Thanks."

The man slid the coin toward him with all four fingers. "Thanks to you, friend. What's your name?"

"Delaine."

The man nodded. "My name is Butch."

"Pleased to meet you. I may be back for another one."

"I'll be here. Give my best to Mr. Gresham."

———

THE SCHOOLTEACHER HAD two water glasses and was adept at pouring from the pail. "Thanks for fetching it," he said. "It's not forbidden for me to go into those places. I just don't hang around."

"I met Butch. He sends his greetings."

"Nice enough fellow. Somewhere between curious and inquisitive, but nothing out of the ordinary for a small town like this. I think he has the smallest amount of jealousy, but more about that later. Here's to your health." Gresham raised a glass.

Delaine raised the other, and they drank.

The schoolteacher had two cane-bottomed chairs, which took up a considerable amount of space, as the small room also held the iron bedstead, a washstand, a dresser with a mirror, and an unpainted wooden wardrobe with its doors open. He must have been conscious of his place as Delaine glanced around, for he said, "Welcome to my modest dwelling. Let's sit down."

They sat facing each other, less than three feet apart. Beyond the schoolteacher, in the open closet, Delaine observed three plain suits in tones of grey to tan, one of which the man would have been wearing when Delaine met him.

"Everyone seems concerned about the man who

was found dead, and with good reason," said Gresham. "I didn't know him."

"I worked with him for a couple of days, and I happened to look in when they first found him, so it was real to me."

"It's a bad thing to happen. Something like this is unsettling for a little while, and then the townsfolk go back to their personal concerns, and life rolls along on the surface."

"That seems to be the way. You've been here a couple of years, have you?"

"A little less. As I mentioned, I came from Kansas. Small towns there, too. I came from a difficult family situation, and I saw other families where there was drinking and fighting as well, so I'm used to seeing something other than the 'smiling aspects' of life. But I got past it, thanks to encouragement from a couple of teachers, and I went on to become one myself."

"Education is to be appreciated."

"I'm glad I had what I did. I took the teachers' curriculum and a little more. You know, some of these country schoolteachers, on the frontier, went straight from high school to teaching, when they were only seventeen or eighteen years old themselves. I'm sure they did some good, and a great deal of the material is very basic—numbers and letters on a slate—but I think a teacher needs to know ten times more than the level at which he is going to teach his pupils. I've heard of people, even at the teacher's college, who got the book just before the beginning of the term and had to keep ahead of the students. I guess I could if I had to, but I'm glad I don't, or I haven't so far."

"And you've been here less than two years."

"Yes. Is there—?"

"Just a matter of conversation. I work at the ship-ping pens, fixing corrals, with a young fellow named Benny Escalon. He's mentioned more than once a story about a girl who went missing. Talk of this recent death seems to have brought up more mention of her."

"Nora."

"Then you've heard of her, too."

"Oh, yes. I've heard of her through her sister, Marian. Their last name is Peele, like the orange peel, with an *e*. Like the English playwright."

"Don't know him."

"Most people don't. He lived in the time of Shake speare. At any rate, I know Marian, rather well, I might say, or I hope to. Well, you know what I mean. I hope I'm not getting ahead of my story, but I think that's why Butch has a little bit of jealousy. I think he likes her, too."

"Not enough to poison your growler, I hope."

"Ha-ha. I hope not. There are stories about that, too, in the old plays and poems. The poisoner ends up drinking his own potion, or two men kill their partner, who brought poisoned wine from town, and then they drink the wine and they die, too. And then in other stories, the wrong person gets the poison."

"That's what I would worry about."

"Well, I don't think Butch would kill us both. Did you tell him this was for me?"

"Yes, I did."

"I think if he was going to poison me, he would have done it by now. It would make a good story—turn his back to me as he poured in the poison, and then smile in my face as he handed me the pail."

Delaine made a dry swallow.

"That's all story, though. I should be more serious.

You asked me about Nora, and there's nothing light about that." Gresham took a drink. "The two girls came from a difficult background themselves, in the grimy parts of Pittsburgh, and they were adopted by a farm family that came out here. The girls worked on the farm and in the household until they were of age, first Nora and then Marian. They came to town here, or rather, Nora came, and Marian joined her, and they rented a room together. Marian still lives there. She works at the newsstand, where they sell tobacco and other smoking materials as well as candy, newspapers, and magazines."

"I've seen the place."

"It's honest enough work. The lost sister, if I may call her that, worked at the laundry."

Delaine recalled the sign with the goose-necked iron. "I've seen it, too."

"It was honest work, too, but she did not make much money, and even before her sister came to town, she fell into other ways of making money. It wasn't all that lucrative itself, sort of a plain business, I guess, with cowpunchers, teamsters, railroad workers, and the like, and she didn't get the full fee because some of it went to the place where she did the business, of which I know very little. But in the end, when she turned up missing, the townspeople did not have much sympathy because she was something of a soiled dove, and it was easy for them to say she might have run off with someone."

"Benny says he is sure she didn't."

"And so is Marian. The two of them stayed together in a rented room, and Nora disappeared without a word and without taking anything with her."

"But that didn't seem to make much difference."

"Nah. Public opinion is hard to change. And if you scratch below the surface, I think you'll find a general lack of sympathy for this fellow named Caswell. He's said to have been carrying on with someone, though I haven't heard any names, just that it was a married woman."

"Oh."

"Mind you, this is just what I heard, and please don't repeat it. Or at least don't say I aid it, because I don't know if it's true, and I don't like to spread gossip. I was just relaying it as a way of saying why I think some people might be—well, if not indifferent, unsympathetic."

Delaine raised his eyebrows and took a drink from his beer.

Gresham drank as well. "Not knowing anything for sure, I don't have an opinion to express. And even if I did know more, I've seen enough of the unpleasant side of life to believe in the saying about not casting the first stone."

"It must be hard for the families. I'm sure Caswell has relations somewhere, just as this girl did, even if it was only her sister."

"Oh, yes. It has been very difficult for Marian. She has carried the sadness with her. She tries not to let it show, but it grieves her to know that people care so little about her sister disappearing." Gresham raised his glass. "But enough about these mournful things. Tell me a little about yourself."

"Well," said Delaine. "I think I told you the main story the other evening. I grew up in this part of the country, worked in New Mexico, and decided to come back."

"Have you been a cowpuncher all your life?"

"As the old joke goes, not yet."

Gresham laughed. "I'll remember that one."

"To answer the question, yes, I've been a hired man on horseback for most of my working life. I have done other work, like I'm doing now."

"Of course. I've done my share of manual work, just to get where I am, and I never assume that I won't go back to it."

"Good way to be. When I was young, I had to skin animals that had died, just for the wool or the hide. I remember the smell, and I never know when I might have to do work like that again."

"Do you have a horse of your own?"

"Yes, I do. I keep him in the stable right now."

"That seems to me like a valuable thing, though many people take it for granted."

"It's good to have your own horse and saddle."

"I'd like to. I'll have to work a while longer before I can have a place to keep one, but it's an ambition of mine. In the meanwhile, I'd like to go out riding some day before the weather turns bad. It wouldn't be that great a hardship for me to rent a horse from the stable for an afternoon."

Delaine guessed that the schoolteacher would rather not undertake the whole process by himself. He said, "I should take my horse out to give him some exercise. I'd be glad to bear you company."

"Thanks," said Gresham. "And I'll buy the beer afterwards. Meanwhile, let me pour us another glass. This doesn't seem to have poisoned either of us yet."

5

———

THE DIM SKY TOLD DELAINE HE HAD TIME FOR COFFEE before work again, so he crossed the street to the café. A customer sat at a table by the left wall, looking down, as Delaine closed the door behind him. As he made his way to a table on the other side of the café, he saw that the person was Ed Herbert. He was wearing glasses as he read in a ledger or notebook, about six inches by nine, and made notations with a pencil. He looked up, gave Delaine a bland smile, and returned to his work.

Delaine sat down as Rachel came out of the kitchen. "Good morning," she said. "Coffee?"

"Yes, please. Just coffee, if it's not too much trouble."

"Not at all." She turned and walked to the kitchen.

Delaine was conscious of watching her, but Herbert did not pay him or the waitress any attention. He made small noises in his throat, then coughed, took a drink of coffee, and gave an audible sigh.

Rachel returned with the dark coffeepot and a tan mug. She poured coffee for Delaine and moved across to Herbert's table.

The man spoke in a loud voice. "No more for me, my dear. Thanks. I'm about ready to go." He cleared his throat for the equivalent of three syllables, took off his glasses, closed his notebook, stood up, and pulled his small hat forward. "Here's this." He pressed a small coin into her hand and made his way toward the door, shuffling in his flat shoes.

Rachel cleared his table of a cup and saucer. A couple of minutes later, she came out to Delaine's table.

"That was Ed Herbert, wasn't it?" he asked.

"Yes. He has the land office. He helps people buy and sell land, and he helps people locate land that they have bought or claimed."

"I've seen him a couple of times."

"He is kind of a dealer, also. He buys and sells other things, like horses and wagons. I heard that he bought and sold beans, also, in some quantity."

Delaine said, "An entrepreneur."

"Yes," she said. She made a small motion as if she was ready to go to the kitchen.

Delaine took his opportunity. "I know I shouldn't take up your time at work, and I need to go to work myself. I wonder if you have time—well, at some other time—for what some people would call a social visit."

She brushed at the hair on the side of her head. "I don't stay up late, because I have to go to work early, but I do have time in the evening."

His spirits picked up. "That would be very nice. Is there a place—?"

"You could visit me where I live. I rent a room with an older woman, a widow. It is a modest place, but it is decent, and I can have visitors there, in the front room."

"In the evening. Would this evening be all right?"

"It should be. Sometime between six and eight." She pointed as she spoke. "I live on Green Street. If you turn right going out the door, you come to Sterling Street. Turn right, go two blocks, and turn left and it's the second house on the right. There is a little statue of a Dutch boy with a white cap, yellow hair, a blue jacket and pants, and yellow shoes. They're supposed to look like wooden shoes."

"I should be able to find it."

She held her hand above waist level. "It's more than three feet tall, made of plaster of Paris, so it doesn't blow over."

"Very good. I'll look forward to it."

She smiled and left him to finish his coffee.

———

DELAINE CHECKED on his horse at the stable after work, and he paused on the street when he came out. Across the street and a little to his right, light showed in the window of the newsstand. A thought occurred to him, so he crossed over.

The name of the business, Lone Trail News Stand, was painted in white letters on the window. The door was open. He walked in and saw the display of newspapers, magazines, story papers, and dime novels on a set of painted shelves on his left. Packages and dishes of candy were arranged on the counter, while a variety of tobacco products, some in a glass case, sat under lamplight behind the counter.

Soft footsteps sounded, and a young woman came into the light, which shone on her light brown hair and blue eyes. She wore a striped grey apron that did not conceal her figure, and she had clean, straight teeth that showed when she smiled.

"Good evening. Something I can help you with?"

"I thought I might buy some candy."

"Very good." She waved with her hand at the top of the counter. "What kind do you like?"

"It's for someone else, and to tell you the truth, I don't know what she likes."

"It's hard to go wrong with chocolate. We have some gift boxes—"

"Nothing that elaborate. Something small."

"Oh, I see. This might go well." The young woman touched a package wrapped in illustrated paper.

"I'll trust your judgment," he said. "How much is it?"

"Five cents for that one. There's another for three, and of course there's hard candy for a penny."

"I'll take this one," he said. He put a nickel on the counter.

"Anything else? Tobacco? Papers?"

"This will be fine." He observed her face again, noting the clear, open features. He recalled Benny saying that she looked like her lost sister, and he recalled the schoolteacher's comment that she carried the sadness with her and tried not to let it show.

She smiled as she handed him the package. "Thank you for coming in."

"Thank you, and good evening."

———

DELAINE FOUND the house with the little Dutch boy in front as the light faded in the evening. He knocked on the door, and he waited as footsteps approached and a key turned in the lock. The door opened, and an old woman in a yellowed head scarf faced him.

"I came to visit with Miss Rachel."

The woman stepped aside and looked him over as he walked in. He was glad he was not wearing his six-gun. He heard the door lock behind him as he took off his hat and waited.

Rachel came into the room, neat and trim in a dark-blue dress with white lace at the throat. "Good evening," she said. She gave him her hand to touch, then took it back. "This is Mrs. Vanderhoven. And this is Mr. Delaine."

"How do you do," said the woman. "I'm sorry I don't have anything to offer you to drink."

"That's quite all right," said Delaine, smiling with his hat in his hand.

The woman's head had a slight swaying motion as she stood there. "Well, I'll leave you to your visit." She walked through an open doorway to a lit area that appeared to be the kitchen.

Rachel showed Delaine to a cushioned chair and took a seat near it on the end of a couch. Before he sat down, he took the small package from his coat pocket and handed it to her.

"Oh, you shouldn't have," she said.

"A small thing. I hope you like chocolate."

"Of course I do. I'll share it with Mrs. Vanderhoven." She lowered her voice and said, "She doesn't mind a drink of brandy once in a while, but she seems to be out of it."

Delaine smiled. "I'll remember that for a future occasion."

Rachel set the candy aside and said, "Well, tell me about yourself."

Delaine took a couple of seconds to answer. "It always seems like such a dull subject, and I think I've told you a little already. But to give it to you in one piece, I grew up here on the northern plains and ended up working in New Mexico. To begin with, I stayed there for the mild winters, but as time went on, I found myself working in the mountain ranches, where cattle were harder to keep track of and the winters were hard, and the fellas who wanted it easy were winnowed out."

Rachel nodded and smiled. "Go on. It's interesting."

He felt at ease. "Well, I was a seasonal cowhand, so work in the winter was sometimes separate. There's a way of making money at that time of year, and it's called mavericking. A fella can make about five dollars a head by putting an outfit's brand on an animal, most often a younger one, that hasn't been branded yet. It's not illegal, but it's what you might call relaxed or informal. I decided I wanted to get away from that casual kind of practice, so I moved on to Colorado, working in the high country of parks and mesas. But it seemed in that area that it was easy to fall in with the same kind of work and the same kind of companions, so I came farther north."

"To your home."

"Somewhat, though it wasn't the same as when I

left. More people from different places. As for myself, I felt that I might be ready to change from being a seasonal hand to having a place of my own with more than a cot among others in a bunkhouse. But for the time being, I'm just hoping to find honest work and keep at it."

"Is that what you want, then?"

"I don't have a detailed picture of it, but in more general terms, I want to make my own way and do what is right, not just what is most convenient or beneficial to me." He was surprised she had gotten him to say as much as he had. He said, "Now it's me who's talking too much."

"Not at all. Everyone's story is important."

"Well, then, I should like to hear some of yours."

She kept her hands folded in her lap and sat with good posture. After a moment, she spoke in a steady voice. "My story is one of sadness, but I do not want to tell it as if it were of sadness only. I have had some happiness, though it was short." She took a breath. "I have been married, and like many other women, I am a widow. And I know what it is like to lose a child."

"I'm sorry to hear that. I would not have known."

She made a small wave of the hand. "It is in the past, in the sense that we have to do the best with our lives, but it also stays with us. I had a lovely girl, Emilia, but she died of the whooping cough. There was nothing that could be done."

"They say that losing a child is the greatest sadness."

"It may be. I may not have seen them all." She paused, settled her hands, and went on. "My husband died when he went to help some men move a herd of horses. I never had a satisfactory explanation of how he died. I was told that he fell from his horse when it 'took a tumble' at high speed, but the foreman did not tell the story in much detail. So I did not know how convinced I was. I wonder if he, too, was caught up in some kind of work that was, as they say, not on the up and up."

"It's not always clear."

"This was in southern Colorado, near Durango. I came here to help some relatives with their houseful of kids, but they wanted me to work for my room and board and nothing more, so I went to work at the café and I rent a room here." She turned her palm upward.

"It sounds as if you have had more than your share of hardship and you've managed it well."

"I do not know how much is one's share or how well I've managed." She smiled. "There was a saying we learned in school in Spanish. It said that we are the architect of our own destiny. Of course, the church tells us that it is all in God's hands, but I also believe we have to make our own decisions and be responsible for our own lives."

"It sure seems that way to me."

"These are things to talk about. When one person gets to know another."

Delaine wondered if he was in the middle of a process or a set of forms that people went through. He was familiar with patterns of conduct in which a man first asked the father if he could visit the daughter, then asked for each succeeding step, such as going for a walk or going to a dance. Asking questions seemed to be patterned as well. In the times that he had gotten to know Mexican people, they often asked similar questions, not very intrusive, such as where his family lived, how many brothers and sisters he had, and so forth.

He wondered if his small gift had been seen as some part of a process. He did not think so. Still, he felt that Rachel was giving the visit some significance, as an occasion to learn about one another and to ask each other questions. He was glad he had cleaned up in his room and had changed into clean clothes.

He said, "Is there anything else you'd like to ask about me?"

"No," she said. "I'm not very—I don't ask many questions that are personal or, as we say, indiscreet." She smiled again. "And you?"

"I don't know your last name."

"Oh." Her head went from side to side in a calm motion. "As you may know, Mexican women often use their original last name even after they are married. They call it *apellido de soltera*, what you call a maiden name. Mine is Valera. My husband's last name was Juárez, the same as the famous president, Benito Juárez, but no relation."

"I've heard of him. Benito."

"It's Benny's name in Spanish, too."

"Oh. I hadn't thought of that."

"Anyway, to be clear about your question. The last name I go by is Valera."

"That's good to know."

Silence hung in the air until Rachel spoke. "I would like to say that I am sorry for what happened to your friend and that nobody seems to be doing very much about it."

Delaine thought he was recognizing another form of courtesy, giving condolence, combined with introducing a new topic of conversation.

"Thank you," he said. "We were friends only in a

passing way, as people are when they work together." Delaine paused, and her attention encouraged him to say more. "I didn't know him well, but he seemed to have things that weighed on him—things that related to something that he might have done. Questionable work."

Rachel did not speak in a loud voice as she said, "I have had the impression that he had something to do with a man that some people would call a rough customer. But I don't know in what way, and I would prefer not to mention names."

Delaine envisioned a rough customer on the basis of some he had known—a burly fellow with thick arms, big fists, and a .45 on his hip. He assumed that Caswell's most likely association with such a person would have been for something like rustling or changing brands. As before, he felt a need to keep a distance. "Sometimes it's better not to know," he said. "On the other hand, thanks for telling me that much. It helps me know what to avoid."

"That's good."

He recognized the phrase as a common one that had its equivalent in Spanish.

After another short silence, she said, "It was very nice of you to bring the chocolate."

"I had already forgotten. I hope you like it." He had lost track of time, but he remembered she turned in early. "I should let you go," he said. "And I need to work in the morning as well."

"Don't be in a hurry." Her voice did not seem to be pleading for him to stay.

"I think it's time to go." He stood up.

"Very well. I'll see you to the door." She rose from her seat, walked to the door, and unlocked it. Before she opened it, she gave him her hand. "Thank you for coming."

"Thank you for having me. And give my best to Mrs.—"

"Vanderhoven."

"Yes. I was afraid of saying it wrong."

She smiled. "You didn't."

"Thanks to you." He heard the door close and lock as he walked into the night. He repeated Rachel's last name to himself. *Valera.*

———

AL PORTMAN WAS WAITING in the doorway of the office when Delaine arrived at work the next morning.

"Half a dozen steers got out of a pen last night, and the fellas who brought 'em have gone back to their ranch for more. As soon as Benny gets here, I need the two of you to go bring 'em in if you can. I think they're out northeast of town, up in the grass. At least that's what I heard. We want to try to get 'em before they get into the trees. I've talked to Kent at the stable, and he'll have a horse for Benny. If you want to use your own, I'll pay you what I pay Kent for Benny's."

"That's all right with me. What's the brand on these steers?"

"Bar BW on the left hip."

"We'll do what we can."

———

SUNLIGHT WAS MELTING frost on the dry grass when Delaine and Benny rode up the sloping land out of town. Benny rode a bay with dull colors, and Delaine was on his brown horse.

"It's good to get away from the corrals for a day," Benny said.

"It is. I don't know how easy it'll be to find these steers. There's been quite a few animals through here, horses and cattle, goin' one way and another. Lots of tracks. It's not been that long since we brought those two herds this way, and I imagine Chamberlain and his men, and others I don't know, go through here as well."

The rolling country had dips and rises, with pine and cedar trees in the low spots. A few miles ahead, the trees became thicker, and the land rose up into a ridge.

Some of the creases in the land were deep and long enough to be called draws, and the two riders separated and rode out each way for half a mile or so before coming up on to higher ground and heading back toward one another, covering the area in a broad zig-zag pattern.

Delaine was glad to find the six steers in a grassy swale, not spread out very far from one another. The brands were easy to read. He rode to a high spot and waited, and when Benny appeared, Delaine waved his hat.

The sun was warming the slopes when they brought the six steers together and headed them toward town. Not many flies hovered, and Delaine figured that a few nights of frost had done some good.

Their route toward town took them up and down hills until they came to a trail that looked like it threaded through the swells and would not require so much wear on the cattle. No matter whose they were,

Delaine did not want to run weight off of them if he didn't have to.

They had not been on the trail very long when they met another rider coming up a smaller trail in a wide draw. For all Delaine knew, it might be one of the Bar BW riders. Delaine called to Benny to wait up.

The rider was on a dark horse, not quite black except in the mane and tail. The man wore a dark hat and a denim jacket. He did not seem to be in a hurry to meet anyone else. Delaine had the sense that the man was like some he had known, who came forward so they would not seem suspicious.

When he was about fifty yards away, the man raised his hand to chest level in an expression of greeting. Something seemed familiar about him, and as he came closer, Delaine recognized the dark features of Tom Caswell's friend, Paul Hensley.

"Mornin'," said Delaine.

"How do you do."

"I think we've met. One night in the saloon. You were with Tom Caswell."

Hensley nodded as he drew his horse to a stop. "I remember you."

"I was sorry about what happened to him. I didn't know him well, just worked with him for a couple of days, but to that extent, he was a friend."

"I was sorry, too." Hensley cast a short glance at Benny. "It was a rotten deal. What have you got here?"

"These steers got out of the shipping pens, and Al Portman sent us out to find 'em."

Hensley looked over the animals, which had stopped to graze. "I know the brand." He sniffed. "I thought 'most everyone had shipped."

"So did I. We've been fixin' corrals."

"Uh-huh." Hensley did not glance at Benny. "Good to see you again," he said. "Maybe I'll see you in town one of these times. Have a drink."

"Sure." Delaine noticed a more somber quality about Hensley than in their earlier meeting in the saloon.

"Good luck." Hensley reined his horse aside.

"Same to you."

Delaine and Benny put the small herd into motion. The animals strung out and followed the trail and did not need much flanking at the moment.

Benny rode next to Delaine and said, "I don't know that man."

"I don't know him very well. His name is Paul Hensley. He was a friend of Tom Caswell's, so I can understand why he wasn't very cheerful. I don't know where he works or if he does." As he said it, Delaine had the thought that Hensley might have been interested in stray cattle. He looked ahead. "I'm glad we found these without much trouble. Al should be happy to see 'em back in the pen."

"Oh, yeah. And another one for us to fix."

———

DELAINE STOPPED at the Prairie Star Bakery on his way home from work. He did not have to check on his horse, as he had ridden it earlier in the day, and he thought he would buy a couple of sweet rolls to go along with the basic fare that he ate in his room.

The man ahead of him at the counter ordered doughnuts. Delaine thought the voice was familiar, but he did not place it. When the man turned to leave, Delaine recognized the dark blond hair and plain features of

Richards, the investigator. The man had changed out of his drab traveling clothes and was wearing a light-blue suit and a white shirt with no tie, plus a white straw hat. He must have bought the hat and perhaps the suit here in town. He smiled and said good evening to Delaine, with a glance of recognition but no indication that they had spoken on a serious subject. Rather, he had the air of a man on vacation, saying hello to local residents as if he had bought an ice cream on the beach.

———

DELAINE WAS on his way up the stairs when he met Gresham on his way down. The schoolteacher was still wearing a tan suit from his day's work, and he was not wearing a hat.

"What-ho," he said. "I was just on my way out, on the way to the newsstand. Care to go along?"

"Why not? Let me put this in my room, and I'll be right with you."

Delaine met Gresham on the street, and they crossed on a diagonal. The schoolteacher walked with his head up, and the breeze ruffled his sandy-colored hair.

"Have a good day?" he asked.

"It was all right. We went out to chase steers for a little variety."

"Not a bad day for it, I would guess. I spent a minute now and then looking out the window, wondering how long the good weather would last."

"What they say is true. It can change any time."

A buckboard drawn by two horses raised a low cloud of dust as it passed.

"Never fails," said the schoolteacher. "That's what I get for being in the street for so long."

When they came up on the other side, he wiped his forehead with his handkerchief and looked at the cloth.

Past the bank, the haberdashery, and the druggist, they slowed at the newsstand. Delaine stopped by the bench and insisted that Gresham go in first.

The young woman in the striped grey apron was standing behind the counter. Her face brightened as she smiled at the schoolteacher, and her glance went to Delaine. She came back to the fair-haired man and said, "Good evening, Mr. Gresham."

"Good evening. I brought along a friend, a fellow lodger. This is Mr. Delaine." He paused. "And this is Miss Marian Peele."

Delaine took off his hat. "Pleased to meet you, Miss. I was in here once before, for a minute. Just yesterday, though it seems longer."

She smiled. "I remember you."

Delaine observed her calm features and recalled again that Benny had said her sister looked like her. Not wanting to stare at her, he shifted his gaze, and his attention fell on what looked like a stack of student papers.

"Are you looking at the school paper?" she asked. "They're from Mr. Gresham's students. When he has marked their papers and returned them, some of the children bring their papers here and trade them for candy. We use the paper, then, to wrap things like candy and tobacco."

"So some lone sheepherder can review his multiplication tables."

Marian smiled. "If he wants to. Or he can use it to light his fire in his little sheepherder's stove."

"No worry about student names falling into… undesirable hands?"

"They write in pencil, so they can erase their names. Or smudge them out. And most of them put only their first name to begin with."

Gresham said, "If I was a parent, I would want to see the child's work, and some of them do."

"Oh, yes." Marian smiled at both of them. "Is there anything I can help you with today?"

Delaine said, "I don't care for anything at the moment, thank you. I just came along for the exercise."

"I'll have the *Cheyenne Daily Leader*," said Gresham. "See if there's anything other than political propaganda."

"Help yourself," said Marian. She made a mark in a small notebook.

Gresham took a newspaper from the shelf and folded it. "Thanks. I guess that's all." He hesitated and said, "I'll see you again."

"Very well," she said, and turning to Delaine, "it was a pleasure to meet you."

"A great pleasure for me," he said. He thought it discreet that the two young people did not show that they knew each other any better.

Out on the street, Gresham said, "Sometimes I buy the Chicago paper. Read about people's misfortunes far away. But I feel that I should stay informed on what's going on here."

"This was just a territory when I lived here before. I suppose it's even more political now. Not that I had much to do with political things."

"Nor do I. But it's good to know what rumblings are going on." Gresham glanced at the street. "By the way, I'm still interested in going horseback riding, if you haven't changed your mind."

"Not at all. I rode my horse today, but I'm always ready to take him out again. What do you think of this Sunday?"

"I think it sounds good. I'll get my mind ready."

"By reading the newspaper?"

"No, to the contrary. By trying to forget about it."

6

———————

Music was playing in the White Mule Saloon as voices mixed in a sea of conversation. A haze of tobacco smoke hung above, and light shone from the lamps overhead. Delaine took his place at the bar and signaled to the bartender. He set a quarter on the bar, the quarter that Al Portman had paid him for the use of his horse, along with six days' wages. His whiskey came, and he took a sip.

A man at the piano was playing a tune but not singing. A short man on Delaine's left with a muddy complexion and a gravelly voice was talking to another man about buying cheap horses at this time of year.

Delaine turned to watch the man at the piano, who leaned from one side to the other as he came down on the keys. Movement on Delaine's right caught his attention, and his pulse jumped. Recognition settled in as Cole Chamberlain, tall and red-bearded, strolled along with a Dodge boy on each side. Delaine practiced differentiating them. Earl was the one with darker hair. Cal was the lighter one. They were both dressed as usual, in light-colored hats, buckskin vests, dull white shirts, wheat-colored pants, and dull brown boots with large-roweled, clinking spurs. Each wore a brown holster with a six-gun as well.

Chamberlain, with his pants tucked into knee-high boots, accentuated his height with a high-crowned hat that was a tone off from his tobacco-colored suit. He, too, wore a holster and gun. His blue eyes, set in his meaty face, looked straight ahead, while his two attendants, with their spreading smiles, gave small glances to either side. The men standing at the bar went on talking, and the man at the piano continued working on a simple tune that sounded like "The Little Mohea."

The trio paid no attention to Delaine. He wondered if they recognized him, and he did not think it mattered much.

The tune at the piano changed, or seemed to, as it became stronger. Delaine thought it was "The Railroad Hotel." He turned to the bar and took another sip of his drink. He tried to ignore the man with the rough voice on his left who was now talking about some task being the easiest thing in the world. Just drag it out and drag it back.

In the mirror, Delaine saw a man in range rider clothes pass in back of him. He did not place the man, but something was familiar. Delaine liked to know who walked behind him, so he turned again and lent his ear to the music.

From the back, he saw a slim fellow with slanted shoulders in a sheepskin coat and a dust-colored hat with a peaked crown and a wide brim. The man stopped where Cole Chamberlain and the Dodge boys stood back from the end of the bar in their own little group, and his head went back and forth as if he was greeting them. They did not pay him much attention. He raised his hand as in a farewell and moved in toward the bar a few places down from them. At that moment, Delaine recognized him as Hiram Fitts, one of the men who had helped bring in Chamberlain's cattle.

Delaine returned to his drink. He was in no hurry. The conversation went on around him, and the music continued at the piano. A tune picked up, and a voice began to sing "Green Grow the Lilacs." Delaine turned to watch and listen. The man at the piano moved his head to one side and the other as he sang out the verses.

The slim puncher in the sheepskin coat and large hat sauntered in Delaine's direction. He did not have much of an expression on his face until he stopped next to Delaine. His eyebrows went up a little, and his mouth tucked back at the corners.

"What do you know?" he said.

"Not much."

"We drove cattle in at the same time, about a week and a half ago."

"I thought I recognized you."

"Hiram Fitts." The young man held out his hand. "F-I-T-T-S."

"Jess Delaine." They shook.

Delaine noticed the fellow's pale blue eyes and straight, untrimmed hair the color of grass in the winter. Fitts had not shaved in a few days, but his stubble was not very visible.

"Been to Chicago and back."

"With the steers?"

"Yep. Workin' at the stable now. Not bad. Stayin' in

the harness room. Got a place to sleep inside, and I don't miss a meal if I don't want to."

"We were in the stable yesterday, and I dropped in for a minute again today, and I didn't see you."

"I just started. I worked part of the day today, and I'll work all day tomorrow. Give Kent some time off. Then I'll work some nights."

"That's good." The song ended, and Fitts did not speak. Delaine had the impression that he had been snubbed by Chamberlain and his men after coming back to town, maybe broke or close to it, and was looking for a friend. "Buy you a drink?"

"I could take one," said Fitts. "Just one."

Delaine signaled to the bartender, found a dime, and put it next to his change. He handed the whiskey to Fitts.

"Thanks."

"You bet."

Fitts drank half of the whiskey and smiled. "What do you do?"

"I'm workin' on the corrals right now."

"Nothin' wrong with that."

"Not that I've seen."

"I guess you worked with Caswell."

"For a couple of days was all."

"Kent said he found him right there in the straw. Too bad about that."

"Seems to have some people worried."

"I s'pose so." Fitts had a half-smile on his face as he looked around. He tipped up his glass and made short work of the rest of his drink. "Thanks," he said.

"You're welcome."

Fitts had not been gone more than a minute when Paul Hensley came into the saloon. Areas of his black hat appeared as a dark brown in the lamplight, and he had the dusty, filmy texture about him that Delaine had noticed on the earlier occasions. He came to a stop next to Delaine.

"I was wondering if I'd see you," he said. He put his hands in the pockets of his denim jacket.

"How have you been?"

"All right."

"Ready for another?" asked the bartender.

Delaine was aware that his drink was almost gone. "Let me finish this," he said, and he drank the last of it. He glanced at Hensley. "One for you?"

"Why not?" Hensley took out the makings and began to roll a cigarette.

Delaine nodded to the bartender and put a silver dollar on the bar. He did not like to be cheap, but he told himself he had to watch his money.

He handed Hensley his drink as the man shook out a match from lighting his cigarette.

"Thanks."

"You're welcome." Another song had started, but Delaine did not recognize the words. He was not sure of what kind of conversation to make. When he did not know someone very well, he did not ask questions that he thought were forward, such as where the man worked or where he was from. There was always the weather.

Hensley took a drink and then spoke. "You said you worked at the corrals."

"That's right."

"I thought you did." At that moment, Hensley's eyes went to the side. Delaine recognized the slender man in a grey wool jacket and pants and a dull-black hat, with a thin scar on the left side of his face. He walked past them in the direction of Chamberlain and his men.

"Do you know this song?" Delaine asked.

"I don't know very many." Hensley tipped his head to one side and another, as if his neck had stiffened. "This fellow sounds like he learned to play in a whorehouse."

"Maybe he did."

"There's always someone who thinks he knows how to sing." Hensley hunched his shoulders. "This ain't quite like a night at the opera."

"I've never been to one."

"Neither have I, for that matter." Hensley took another drink. "Maybe I'm not in the mood to listen to this kind of stuff. Sounds like he's cryin' about the milk cow that died."

"Sometimes you can hear lovely melodies in a whorehouse, if you know the right place to go."

"Long ways from here." Hensley tossed off the last of his whiskey and set the glass on the bar. "Thanks again for the drink. I'll pay you back when I'm in a better mood." He patted Delaine on the side of the shoulder and headed for the door.

Delaine tried to pick up the thread of the song, and it came to a close. At the end of the bar, the man in the grey suit and dull-black hat was holding a drink and facing Chamberlain and the Dodge boys. They seemed at ease with one another, three men with their guns in plain view and a fourth who might have one under his jacket.

The music picked up again, this time without any singing. It was a tune that Delaine thought he had heard from the street in a dozen towns. None of it seemed to do any harm.

A grubby-looking man wearing a battered hat, a collarless work shirt, overalls, and brogan shoes came stepping along behind the men at the bar, from the direction of the door toward Delaine. He had a stubbled greying beard and a pink face, and he was smiling as he stepped from side to side and waved his hands to the music. He opened his mouth and sang.

> *She's the sheep queen of the Badlands,*
> *And she's got a thousand sheep,*
> *And she keeps a cowboy prisoner*
> *In a dungeon dark and deep.*

He stopped in front of Delaine and said, "And good evening to you, sir."

Delaine nodded and said, "Good evening."

"Have I seen you before in our fair city?"

"I don't know. That is, I don't know what you've seen. But I do know we haven't met."

"A precise man. My kind." The stranger took off his hat, revealing a pate the same shade as his face, and said, "My name is Pinky." He put on his hat and held out his hand.

Delaine shook and said, "Jess Delaine."

"And how are you this fine evening?"

"All right. And yourself?"

"Not bad for an old musker."

Delaine was sure he heard the word as it was pronounced, but he did not know any meaning to attach to it. He did not want to promote the conversation or invite familiarity with this fellow who seemed to style himself as an original character.

The man ordered a whiskey, took a drink, and let out a long "*Ahhhh*," followed by "That's the stuff." He smiled and faced Delaine. "A few of these make you strong, and then it goes the other way. Ha-ha-ha. So where do you work?"

Delaine tensed and relented. "At the shipping pens for the time being."

"I thought I saw you there. Are you a friend of Sundown?"

Delaine frowned. "I don't know who you mean."

"It's that fellow you had a drink with and were talking to. The one in the sheepskin coat."

"Oh, him. He said his name is Hiram Fitts. He even spelled his last name for me."

"Yeah, but they call him Sundown. Because when he's in town, he's drunk every day by that time."

"He didn't seem to be drunk yet this evening." Delaine reflected that Fitts hadn't wasted time on his drink, but he chose not to say any more.

"It's early yet. He might be broke. Spent all his money on the one night they lay over in Chicago."

"I wouldn't know."

The man in the dark hat and grey jacket walked by on his way to the door. The clear side of his face was showing, as was his prominent Adam's apple, and he had a dry quality about him.

Pinky paid him no attention. He raised his glass and said to Delaine, "Here's to it. It's a good life if you don't weaken."

Delaine resisted the temptation to say something in return. He lifted his glass.

Pinky said, "So I was in the café, and the waiter asked me how I liked my eggs. I said, 'Mighty fine.' And he said, 'How do you like 'em cooked?' And I said, 'I like 'em that way best of all.' Ha-ha-ha."

Delaine put on a smile. He had heard the joke more than once before.

The older man moved on. The man at the piano continued to play. Chamberlain and his men were standing by themselves near the end of the bar. Nobody seemed to pay any attention as Pinky danced a strange little jig by himself.

Delaine finished his drink, looked up to see the woman in the blue dress sitting on the white mule, and walked out into the night.

———

DELAINE MET the schoolteacher at the livery stable at nine in the morning. Hiram Fitts was on duty. He brought Delaine his brown horse, and a few minutes later he returned with a stout grey horse for Gresham.

"This one shouldn't give you any trouble," he said. "I worked here last winter, and I know most of the horses."

Delaine brushed, combed, and saddled his horse. Fitts did the same with the grey, with very little comment, as the schoolteacher looked on. The two of them led the horses out into the sunlight.

Fitts handed the reins to Gresham and stood by. He rolled a cigarette as Gresham draped the reins over the saddle horn and put his foot in the stirrup. The grey horse moved away, and Gresham hopped.

Fitts put the unlit cigarette in his mouth, moved forward, and took the horse by the headstall. Gresham pulled himself up and into the saddle.

"Thanks," he said.

"Sure." Fitts lit his cigarette.

Delaine checked his cinch and swung into the saddle. "Ready?"

"I think so," said Gresham. He was not wearing a hat, and he wore plain shoes instead of boots, but he did not look as if this was his first time in the saddle.

"Let's go north, then," said Delaine. "There's a good trail for about four miles until we come to a 'Y.' We can go that far and decide whether we want to go on or come back."

Energy emanated from the two horses as they climbed the grassy slopes north of town. Gresham put on a pair of grey wool gloves, and Delaine put on the leather gloves he used for riding and for ranch work. The sky was clear overhead, and the country stretched out for miles around.

Delaine had a comfortable sense of leaving the town behind and with it the unresolved death of Tom Caswell. He recalled the would-be entertainer who gave his name as Pinky, and he wondered what the man's place was in town. Almost everyone had a place in relation to others, even the outcast and the scapegoat, as he had seen such people. Some of them seemed to volunteer for their roles. At least Pinky had paid for his own drink.

A *scree*-ing sound caused him to tip his head back and look up.

"Is that a hawk?" asked Gresham.

"It's some kind. There are quite a few."

"I plan to get a bird book. Then I can look them up."

"No harm in that. There's been times I wished I had one."

"The students could use it as well. I keep most of my books in the schoolhouse so they can have access to them. It always gives me pleasure to see them looking up something on their own."

"Have you got good learners?"

"Some. One thing you see in a group of pupils is a range of abilities and aptitudes. Also, not everyone learns in the same way, and some of the textbooks are rather rigid."

"I remember when I was in school, there were some kids who hated it."

"There's always that. There are also those who live it. And then there are those in between. And they aren't the same, either. Some of them do their work because they're told to, and they put in enough effort to get by. Others work harder for the same average results. And there's a kind of reserved attitude I've noticed here, from some of those who come from comfortable families, in town and in the country both, who seem as if they are a little better than a school-teacher who doesn't make any more than a person who works for their father."

"That sounds familiar, though I don't remember anyone in school ever saying it."

"I've heard it, but not from any pupils."

"Oh, yes, in places like the White Mule."

"The saloon?"

"Places like it. I haven't been in there that much."

"Neither have I. A time or two. I suppose you've noticed the painting."

"Of the lady and the mule? Yes, I have. It's pretty."

"It is. It comes from a poem called 'My Last Duchess.' Written in the early 1840s by a British poet named Robert Browning. It's in the form of a speech, or monologue, set in Italy, with a Duke telling a visitor about his Duchess, who died. In the course of the poem, it becomes evident that he had her done away with because she had an independent spirit. He makes an innuendo that she might have been unfaithful, but the white mule, being white and not being sexual, suggests that she didn't do anything wrong. It's a subtle poem, with many interesting features to it."

"Seems like quite a bit of poetry for one small town, what with the café just two doors down."

"As I understand it, both businesses were once owned by a man who came out from Rhode Island, made money in the mines of Colorado, in the Leadville area, and stopped here to help build the town and become some kind of a civic leader. Until he died of tuberculosis. Not without irony, the same disease killed a few well-known writers in this century."

"Is the town named after him?"

"No. It's named after a town in the East, in Ohio, I think. Quite a few towns are named that way, for others. Buffalo, for example, is named for Buffalo, New York, not for the monarch of the plains. Perhaps you knew that."

"Buffalo, Wyoming? No, I didn't."

"Sorry if I got off into a lecture. One leads to another, sometimes."

"Not at all."

They lapsed into silence and rode along for a while. Delaine recalled one person and another from the evening before. He half-expected to meet up with Hensley or the Dodge boys or even the man with the gravelly voice who was looking to buy cheap horses. Sometimes when a fellow was miles from anywhere, another rider appeared out of a swell in the landscape, as Hensley had done a few days earlier. Delaine recalled once on a Sunday morning, many years earlier in this same cow country, when he was fifty miles from town and came over a rise and almost ran into a horse-shoer from town. They said hello as they rode past each other.

When Delaine and Gresham reached the main fork in the road, they dismounted to walk around for a couple of minutes. Delaine would not have been surprised to see someone from the Silver Pine, but no one appeared.

Delaine waited for the schoolteacher to mount up. When the grey horse moved away, Delaine said, "Try snuggin' the reins. If he wants to walk forward or walk out from under you, snug the near rein, and turn his nose in toward you. Then he won't go forward. If he wants to move away from you, try snuggin' the other rein, bring his nose in a little on that side."

The schoolteacher adjusted the reins and put one hand on the saddle horn and one on the cantle.

"And one other little thing, if you don't mind. You'll do better if you don't put your right hand on the back of the saddle. Put it on the saddle horn. Other-wise, you have to move it when you're halfway up and over, and that's when a horse can pop you off balance if he wants to."

"I was holding the saddle to try to keep him from moving away."

"And you see you can't keep him. You can do more with the reins. You'll see old, slow, and heavy people grab on the back of the saddle, and beginners, but you'll do better if you don't have that habit."

Gresham put both hands on the saddle horn and let out a breath with the increased strain. "Do it the hard way, then."

"It becomes the easy way."

Gresham got set again, put his foot in the stirrup, and swung up. He landed in the saddle without the horse moving.

Delaine swung aboard. "Are you ready to go back, or do you want to ride out farther?"

"I think this is a good time to turn around."

They rode back the way they came, seeing the country from the other direction. Town was not visible, just the rangeland and the cottonwoods along the river and a row of bluffs a few miles beyond.

"There's an antelope," said Gresham.

"Plenty of them."

"I'd like to hunt a deer."

"Shouldn't be so hard."

"I don't have much to start from," said the schoolteacher. "I've got a rifle, and I suppose I could rent a horse again, but I don't have a place to go. Some of my pupils who stay in town during the week live out on ranches where, from what they say, there are deer and antelope. But they aren't very forthcoming with invitations, and I find it hard to get up the nerve to ask."

"There's plenty of public land out here," said Delaine. "It's just that some of it is a ways out, and a fellow would have to organize things, like the two of us today, with maybe another horse to pack something if you shoot it."

"It takes some know-how to take care of it. Clean it and all, and then load it on."

"You don't have to learn it on your own. I can help."

"That's very good of you to offer."

"I don't mind. Depending on the weather, we might think about next Sunday."

"Very good. Count on me to buy the beer afterwards, whether we get one or not."

———

DELAINE FOUND a message waiting for him when he returned to the rooming house after work on Monday. He broke the seal and unfolded the sheet of paper. It was written in ink in a legible hand.

Delaine:

If you are interested in work prospects you can come to the ranch and talk to me.

Sincerely,
George Mace

Delaine folded the letter. He did not want to ask Al Portman for time off to go see about another job. If Mace knew where he was staying, he knew where he was working as well. Better to ride out there this evening and see how desirable the prospect was.

Delaine saddled his horse in the stable and rode out on the familiar trail as the sun went behind the mountains in the west. Dusk was gathering when he reached the pine ridge, and night had fallen when he rode into the ranch yard.

He tied up in front of the ranch house and knocked on the door. Mace's voice called for him to come in.

Delaine went inside, crossed the front room in dim light, and paused at the doorway to the office. He took off his hat as the boss stood up behind the oak desk. Mace was dressed as before in a brown wool jacket, vest, and pants with a white shirt. Behind him, a hat hung on the wall, with the portrait of the president on one side and the painting of a deer in front of a canyon on the other.

The boss held out his hand as he said, "Delaine. Thanks for coming."

"Thanks for the note." They shook.

"Have a seat."

Delaine sat down.

Mace took a pipe from his desk drawer, stuffed it with tobacco, and lit it. "I assume you had a safe ride."

"Yes, sir. The weather is holding out well."

"You never know when it'll change." The boss puffed out a cloud. "I'll tell you what I have in mind." He brushed his hand over his mustache, and he spoke in a steady tone. "You know we lost Tom Caswell, and with that, I need someone to take his place, to ride the range and check on cattle through the winter. I won't mince my words. There are some low-class people around, and they're not all in town, though there's enough there." He puffed. "I think I've lost stock here and there, now and then, and I'd like someone who can keep a sharp eye, remember what he sees, and tell me straight." He held the bowl of his pipe in the palm of his hand. "Tell me what you think."

Delaine felt himself resisting some aspect of the offer. The purpose seemed honest and open enough, but something felt disagreeable, as if he would be brought back into contact with practices or ways of doing things that he would rather not have anything to do with, even if he was on the law-abiding side. Though Mace didn't say it outright, Delaine was being asked to spy on people, or if not quite that, to report someone who might be doing something questionable.

Delaine winced. He would be expected to be on the lookout for people and things to suspect, and he would be expected to report on the basis of suspicion.

The line of thought took but a few seconds. "I thank you for the offer," he said, "but I don't think it's quite the perfect situation for me."

The boss waved the stem of his pipe. "That's all right. I appreciate your taking the trouble to come out. While I have you here, I'd like to ask you a question, if you don't mind."

Delaine tensed. He wanted to say that it depended on what the question was, but he did not feel that he was tied to where he sat, so he said, "Go ahead."

Mace puffed on the pipe. "I wonder if, in the time that you got to know Tom Caswell, whether you had any indications of him having any kinds of dealings with others."

Delaine shook his head. "I didn't have any specific indications, to use your word. He didn't ever say anything definite about things he might have done or people he might have done them with."

"That's all right. I wouldn't ask a hired man to talk about another, and I know there's a kind of code for one man not to tell on another, but since he's no longer alive, and he seems to have died under suspicious circumstances, I didn't think it was improper to ask."

Delaine still did not feel that he was being put on the spot. "There's no harm in asking, but I'm new here, and I haven't had any knowledge of anything that goes beyond, or I guess you could say beneath, the surface." Delaine was sure that Mace's question was related to his earlier comment that he thought he had lost livestock, but Delaine did not want to show his recognition or further the conversation. He said, "I don't think I have anymore. I should be going. I hope things go well for you and your ranch over the winter."

"Thanks. I know cattlemen are prone to thinking that someone is making off with their stock, but I'm not one to speak without some basis, and every man has got to look out for his own interests."

"Of course. And I don't feel that any of it is personal."

"No reason you should." Mace's tone became lighter. "Would you like to have something to eat before you ride back to town? I'm sure Ambrose could rustle up something."

Delaine recalled the bunkhouse cook, and the prospect of a meal was agreeable, but he said, "Thanks. I think I'd better start before it gets any later."

"Thanks again for coming out."

"Thanks for thinking of me."

———

IN THE DARK, Delaine found the trail easier to follow from the "Y" on into town. Various moments from the ride the day before came back to him, and with those thoughts came a clear image of the woman on the white mule in the painting, young and pretty and far away. The story behind it, as the schoolteacher had told it, was interesting. In a fanciful way, it reminded Delaine of the story of the girl who worked in the laundry, two doors down and on the corner.

7

———

DELAINE WAS FINISHING A MEAL OF BREAD, CHEESE, AND dried apples when a knock sounded on the door. He rose from his chair, covered the short distance to the door, and opened it. An unfamiliar man stood in the hallway. He was about thirty, with dark eyes and a full face with the shadow of a beard that he must have had to shave every day. He was dressed in shades of light brown, with a clean hat, a herringbone wool coat, a clean shirt and leather vest, and creased pants. A dark-brown gunbelt seemed to support a full upper body.

"Good evening," he said. With his left hand, he drew aside the lapel of his brown herringbone to reveal a shining brass star. "I'm Deputy Cavanaugh Erskine with the Laramie County Sheriff's Office, and I'd like to ask you a few questions."

"Come on in." Delaine stood aside to let the deputy into the narrow room. "Please have a seat."

The deputy took off his hat and sat in the only chair. Delaine sat on the bed.

"I came by yesterday evening, but I didn't find you here."

"I rode out to the Silver Pine Ranch to talk to George Mace about a job possibility."

"Didn't you work there before?"

"Yes, I did."

The deputy kept his dark eyes on Delaine. "Are you going back?"

"I don't plan to."

"I was given to understand that you work at the shipping pens."

"I do."

"It's my preference not to question a man at his work if I don't have to."

Delaine did not have an answer.

"My purpose in talking to you is to ask if you know of anyone who had a reason to do harm to Tom Caswell."

Delaine settled. "No, I don't."

"Did you know of anything he might have done that might have caused someone to want to do harm to him?"

"No, nothing in particular. Nothing specific."

The deputy's eyebrows went up. "Something?"

"No, nothing more than a general sense that he thought that someone might not like him."

"Someone?"

"He didn't name anyone. He didn't even say that someone had it in for him. I don't remember his exact words, but it was something to the effect that he might have done something out of line and another person didn't want to let him out of it."

"No names?"

"No."

"And no indication of what kind of activity he participated in with this other individual?"

"No. Like I say, it was not specific at all. Vague in a deliberate way, it seemed."

"I was just wondering," said the deputy. "I was given to understand that you two worked together and had some kind of a friendship."

Delaine noted the second use of "I was given to understand." He said, "I didn't know him that well. And even when you think you know someone, you can learn something that surprises you."

The deputy gave a solemn nod. "I see it more often than you would think." His upper body expanded as he took in a breath through his nose. "It is suspected that he was involved in the transfer of cattle that were not his."

"George Mace as much as told me the same thing, but he's the only person I've heard it from, except you. Tom Caswell was never that specific with me as to why he was in too deep with someone who didn't want to let him out."

"In too deep?"

"I think he might have used that expression."

"There must have been something, then. And I would bet that there's more than one other person, somewhere, who knows what it is."

"Well, I hope you find out."

"So do I." The deputy stood up and put on his hat. "Thanks for what you were able to tell me."

"You're welcome."

———

DELAINE CROSSED the street in the early morning. It had been a few days since he had seen Rachel, and he hoped not to find Herbert in the café again.

He was glad to see no other customers, and his spirits improved even more when Rachel came out from the kitchen. She smiled as she saw him.

"Good morning," she said.

"Good morning. Good to see you."

"Coffee?"

"Yes, please."

She went to the kitchen and came back with the pot and a cup. As she poured the coffee, she said, "I didn't see you for a few days, but I assumed you were all right."

"Oh, yes. Just a few other things to take up my time." She did not seem to be in a hurry, so he said, "On Monday after work, I went out to George Mace's ranch to talk about a job, which I didn't take, and I had a visit yesterday evening with Deputy Erskine."

"I know him. He comes to town on a regular basis."

"He's asking questions about Tom Caswell."

"Maybe he will do something."

Delaine thought he heard a hint of skepticism. "He seems to be trying, but he also seems to have the tendency that some of them do, which is to follow the ideas they've already formed."

"He has a high opinion of himself, or that is how he seems to me. But if he does something with this case, that is good. It doesn't always happen, as you and I have talked about."

Delaine had an image of the young woman who worked in the newsstand. "I know what you mean. I've heard from a couple of other people as well about the girl who worked in the laundry and disappeared. Someone like the deputy, or whoever was here at the time, could say they weren't sure a crime had been committed. But in the present case, there's no doubt."

"That's true. And he wasn't here at the time the girl disappeared. They say someone else was." She smiled. "I hope that the other things that take up your time have been more pleasant."

Delaine felt a soft glow, a closer familiarity than on his earlier visits to the café. He said, "I went on a ride with the schoolteacher. It was all calm and pleasant, as you say. Pretty in the small ways that the rangeland can be."

"I like that, but I don't get out much. Do you miss being out in the country every day?"

"I work at the corrals, which is at the edge of town, so it's a little like being in the country. Much better than working in a factory or a warehouse in a big city."

"I haven't seen much of cities," she said. "But I am not attracted to them."

"Neither am I."

The bell on the door tinkled, and Deputy Erskine came in. His herringbone wool coat was closed up with leather buttons, and he was wearing leather gloves. He came to a stop, took off his gloves, and put them in his left coat pocket.

Rachel's eyes met Delaine's for an instant, and she went to meet the deputy at his table as he sat down. Without looking straight at her, he said, "I'll have an order of ham and eggs."

Rachel smiled to Delaine on her way to the kitchen.

In a faint voice, mouthing the words, he said, "See you later."

—————

DELAINE AND BENNY were working on a pen close to the main thoroughfare when a rider came in from the east. Delaine recognized the dark hat, denim coat, and dark horse all together. It was Paul Hensley. Delaine let up on his hammering as the rider drew near, and Benny did the same.

The horse's coat shined as a very dark brown in the sunshine, though from a distance it looked black. The animal's mane and tail were solid black. The horse was short-coupled and not tall. It tossed its head as Hensley brought it to a stop.

"Still workin' on the pins," said Hensley.

Delaine had reacquainted himself with that pronunciation since he had come back north. He had even heard people use "pit" for "put." "It's work," he said.

Hensley looped the reins once around the saddle horn, took the makings from his coat pocket, and began to roll a cigarette. "Wouldn't be surprised if we see snow within a week."

"I know a fellow who wants to go hunting. Should be good for that."

"Should be good for somethin'. Makes it easier to track."

"Seems to bring the deer out."

"That, too. They get hungry." Hensley licked the paper seam. He put the cigarette in his mouth, struck a match, and cupped his hands as he lit his smoke. He shook out the match, and after a couple of seconds, he dropped spittle onto his thumb and forefinger and rubbed the head of the dead match. Rather than drop it on the ground, he put the match in his coat pocket.

Delaine had known other men who disposed of their matches that way. He did not ask why, but from the men he knew, he deduced that with some, it was taking care not to start a fire, while with others, it was taking care not to leave a trail. He noticed that Hensley was wearing spurs today.

"I heard there's a deputy in town." Hensley blew away a stream of smoke.

"I've seen him."

"Who knows if he'll do anything."

"Just wait and see, I guess."

"I imagine." Hensley took another drag. He seemed to be deciding what to say, until he asked, "What do you think of the women in this town?"

Delaine was startled by the jump in topic. "I don't know that I've seen enough to have an opinion. Seems to me that women are women, pretty much the same wherever you go, unless you go to a big city, where you meet more different kinds."

"Hard to keep track of."

"Or if you go among a different kind of people. Like Chinese or Indian."

"Don't know much about that."

"Even at that, women are women."

"Sure. They've all got that thing."

Delaine did not know if he had run right over the topic or whether Hensley was just making talk, as men liked to do about women in the company of younger men. But Hensley seemed to ignore Benny, and his comments about women were curt, as if he was saying as little as he could rather than expanding on a familiar topic. Delaine waited.

Hensley said, "Didn't get to talk much the last time

I saw you. I don't like talkin' in places where people have big ears."

To make sure Benny understood that Hensley was not referring to their meeting out on the range, Delaine said, "That's the way saloons are. After you left, I met a fellow who talked all over the place. Didn't care who heard him. Calls himself Pinky."

"Oh, him." Hensley frowned and took another drag on his cigarette. "I wouldn't mind talkin' to you sometime when you have the chance. When there's not a lot of people around."

Delaine felt again a resistance to becoming too confidential with the type of fellow he thought Hensley was. Mace and the deputy already had Delaine characterized as a pal of Caswell's, and even if they did not associate him with Hensley, he did not want to be drawn in to hear things he would then wish he hadn't. On the other hand, Hensley seemed to have something he wanted to talk about, and from his odd comments about women, Delaine thought it might be about more than the transfer of cattle.

"It would be all right with me," he said. He recalled talking to Caswell the last time, outside the lit doorway of the livery stable. "How about right here, this evening? Say about six or six-thirty. It's dark then, out of the public eye. Let's say six-thirty."

"I can do that." Hensley put his cigarette in his mouth and adjusted his reins. "I won't keep you from your work anymore. I'll see you then."

As he rode away, Delaine wondered if he would put his cigarette butt in his pocket when he had smoked it down and pinched it out.

———

Delaine had almost an hour to kill before his meeting with Hensley. He had made short work of his cold evening meal, and he was feeling edgy. He was doing well on saving money, and he was halfway to his next payday, so he thought he would allow himself a drink to calm himself.

There were more patrons in the saloon than he would have expected in the middle of the week. The piano sounded tinny through the sea of voices, and a cloud of tobacco smoke had gathered by the lamps overhead. The woman on the white mule held her repose and seemed to be in her proper place, above it all.

Delaine found a spot at the bar and signaled for a drink. The bartender served him, and he took a drink of whiskey. The notes from the piano sounded irregular, and Delaine turned to see a different man seated on the little bench. He wore a shabby, dull-black suit, and he had a pasteboard suitcase by his feet. When he finished the tune he was playing, he turned and smiled in the direction of the bar. He had wavy, mouse-colored hair, a pointed nose, and a mustache that could have been clipped from the end of a paintbrush and glued onto his upper lip. His lower lip and jaw were recessed, and his upper teeth showed through the bristles of his mustache.

"Thank you," he said. "All generosity is appreciated."

An upside-down bowler hat came into sight as it was passed among men standing away from the bar. The man played a melody that did not sound much different from the previous one. When he finished, he stood up and bowed, and leaving his suitcase by the piano, he walked to the bar. The bartender poured him a glass of whiskey and held up his hand in a gesture saying there was no charge. The man in the shabby suit smiled and kept an eye on the progress of the bowler.

Another man stood by the piano. Like the previous man, he did not wear a hat. He was balding and clean-shaven, and he was wearing a brown corduroy suit with a crossed ribbon for a tie. He held a hat in his hands, and he spoke in a clear, smooth voice.

"Good evenin', folks. Some of you know me. For my turn, I'm goin' to do just one song. I don't play the piano, so here it is. It's called 'One More Winter.'" He sang in the same smooth voice.

He was just a bunkhouse cowboy,
A little older than the rest.
He sat close to the cookstove
With his hands out from his chest,

And he said, "Just one more winter,
Checkin' cattle in the snow,
And I'll go back to the country
Where the plums and peaches grow.

"Where it hardly ever freezes
And the flowers bloom year round,
Where a man don't catch pneumonia
Just from sittin' on the ground.

"Where the roosters crow at daybreak
And the cows come in at three,
And a blue-eyed girl named Helen
Is still waitin' there for me,

"In a cabin in the sunlight
On the banks of Cherry Creek,
Where she bakes hot bread and biscuits
And an apple pie each week.

"Just another year of workin',
Playin' nursemaid to these cows,
And I'll have me a bundle
I can take back to the South."

With his hands held to the fire
And a glow upon his cheek
He appeared to be contented
With his thoughts of Cherry Creek,

In a world all soft and sunny
Far away from ice and snow,
Where the flowers bloom in winter
And the plums and peaches grow.

When he finished, he nodded to the applause, and with his hat still in his hands, he made his way to the bar.

A voice at Delaine's elbow said, "Not bad for a ranch cook, eh?"

Delaine was taking a drink. He lowered his glass and divided his attention to recognize the speaker as the coarse old man named Pinky and to verify that the man who had just sung the song was not Ambrose, the cook at the Silver Pine. "I don't know him," he said.

"You haven't been around here for long." Pinky took a drink from the glass in his hand. "How go the wars?"

"As usual."

"Diggin' holes and poundin' nails. I saw you at it with your young com-pan-yero."

"It's work."

"Sure. And you're not like these others, done for the year." Pinky waved his hand at the piano.

"Is the fellow in the black suit a cook as well?"

"You might not think it to look at him," said Pinky, "but he's a cook's helper. Says he was a sigh-cologist."

"Maybe he was."

"Maybe I was the king of Prussia."

"Everyone has to work."

"Except for kings and criminals."

Delaine took a sip from his glass.

"Tell you a little story. There was a fella had trouble with his wife, was sure she was foolin' around on him. One night the devil came to him in a dream and told him that if he put this ring on his finger, his wife would be faithful to him as long as he never took it off. So the devil helped him put it on, and he woke up, and he found out he had his finger inside his wife. Ha-ha-ha. Ha-ha-ha. Ha-ha-ha." Pinky hunched his shoulders and danced to each side as he laughed another round.

Delaine wanted to laugh at the joke, but he was held back by his sense of the man's vulgar presence and of the grotesqueness of the man's celebration of his own joke.

Pinky settled down and said, "Looks like your friend Sundown isn't holdin' up as well this evening." He motioned with his head toward the far end of the bar.

A couple of men who had blocked the view earlier had cleared out, and Delaine had a back view of Hiram Fitts standing with a drink in his hand and his hat tipped back. He was swaying as he faced the two Dodge boys, who had their heads raised and were regarding him with downturned mouths. Fitts lurched and stood up straight.

"What do you think of that?" asked Pinky.

"It's sorry to see someone drunk like that, but it's none of my business. And there's worse things in the world."

"Oh, yeah, by a damn sight."

Fitts set his drink on the bar and pivoted in an uneven motion.

Delaine looked away, and Pinky said, "Look out. Here he comes."

Fitts had his hat still tipped back and was taking unsteady steps. He brushed against one man who stood back from the bar, and he straightened up for a second and moved on. As he approached Delaine, his face lit up, and he stopped.

"Hey, there. D'ya remember me?"

"Sure I do. How are you doing?"

Fitts swayed. "Drunker'n seven hunnerd dollars."

"Can you make it all right?"

"Oh, yeah. I'm on my way home. T'th'stable. I stay there."

"Are you sure you can make it?"

"Oh, yeah." Fitts smiled and moved on.

Pinky said, "It'll be a wonder if he doesn't fall down in the street."

"I'm going to leave in a few minutes myself, when I've finished my drink. I'll keep an eye out for him."

"Somebody had better."

Delaine turned to the bar, and he was glad to see in the mirror that Pinky was moving away. To be sure, he stayed facing the back of the bar for a couple of minutes. He took a drink from his glass, waited for a minute, and finished off the last bit of whiskey.

He turned from the bar and saw that the cook's helper was taking a seat at the piano again. A few notes sounded. Delaine glanced to see that the way was clear, and he stepped away from the bar.

Someone jostled him on the left side and shoved him with both hands. A voice that might have come from Texas said, "Look where you're goin', fella."

Delaine gained his footing and turned to see the Dodge boys, one standing in back of the other. The near one had darker hair. He would be Earl.

"Sorry," said Delaine. "I didn't see you."

"I guess you didn't. You got all the attention of a pack mule with his nose in the ass of the one in front of him." Earl stepped closer. "I don't like it."

"I said I'm sorry."

Earl's two hands came up fast and pushed Delaine in the chest, knocking him off balance again. Earl stepped forward and pushed once more, with enough force to send Delaine to the floor.

Delaine got his hands under him, then his feet, and stood up. Earl moved close enough for Delaine to smell bay rum.

"I don't like it," Earl said again, with a scowl.

The bartender called from in back of the bar. "Everyone knows we don't have any of that in here. Take it outside."

"I was leaving anyway," said Delaine.

"Put your tail between your legs." Earl had his hands at his sides with his fists half-closed.

"I said I was leaving anyway."

"Well, maybe I am, too." Earl smirked.

Delaine was aware that the music had quit and at

least a dozen men were looking at him. He knew he was being goaded, and he expected Earl to follow on his heels, but he had said he was on his way out, and that was what he had to do.

The door was open, so he headed for it and walked on through to the sidewalk, where he stepped down into the street. Boot heels sounded behind him, and he kept walking.

Earl's voice came to him. "Hold it right there."

He kept walking.

"I said stop."

He thought he heard the click of a gun, so he stopped and turned.

Earl let down the hammer on his .45 and slipped the gun into his holster. With his hands out at his sides and his shoulders swaying, he stepped up to within two feet of Delaine. "You must not be much of a man to let someone push you around like that in front of everyone in town."

"What else did I do wrong?"

"You stepped in front of me."

"We've already been through that. I said I was sorry."

"Was."

Delaine tried to keep his eyes on Earl's hands without letting the man stare him down and make him look aside.

"Where do you come from?" said Earl.

"Here."

Earl's right hand came up fast, and his fist was like a club on Delaine's cheekbone. He stepped forward, whiskey on his breath, and hit Delaine on the other side of his face.

Delaine went back in two short steps and was

raising his fists when Earl hit him one more time and caused his feet to go out from under him.

He landed on his rump, and he heard a tweeting sound he had heard once before when he had been hit hard. The scene in front of him was mixed and wavy, with spurs jingling and men muttering as their boots took them back into the saloon.

Delaine found his way to his feet and stood for a moment to get his bearings. He was not surprised that Earl Dodge had picked a fight with him. Caswell had said that either of the brothers would punch a man for stepping on his shadow. But there could have been more to it. He wondered if the Dodge boys knew he was conversant with Hensley. They had seen him talking to Hensley on an earlier occasion, and there did not seem to be any friendship between them and Caswell and Hensley together when everyone had gone to the saloon the time before that, after eating roasted pig. Delaine did not think they could know he was on his way to talk to Hensley now.

Delaine shook his head. There was Fitts to consider. The arrogant brothers seemed to regard him with contempt, and if Pinky saw Fitts as a friend of Delaine's, the Dodge boys might see him that way as well. Maybe Earl just wanted to punch Fitts, but seeing no glory in picking on a drunk, did the next best thing.

8

—————

DELAINE STOOD INSIDE A PEN NEAR THE MAIN thoroughfare. A dim light showed in the land office across the street. Horse hooves clopped and wheels creaked as a wagon rolled out of town. Smoke from stoves and chimneys drifted on the air.

The sound of hooves and a horse's snuffle drew his attraction to the left. Against the faint glow from town, a horse and rider moved. No white marking showed on the horse as it came close to the corrals.

Delaine spoke in a low voice. "Is that you?"

Hensley's voice came back. "Yeah." He stopped the horse, dismounted, and came forward on foot without the sound of spurs.

"Let me climb over," said Delaine. He was conscious of scraping a boot on a corral plank as he let himself down on the other side. "Quiet night," he said. He was glad it was dark. He was standing within three feet of Hensley, and he did not know if he had a bruise where Earl Dodge had hit him.

Hensley's voice was restrained. "Moon's not up yet, but it will be."

"We ought to be able to talk without being bothered."

Hensley did not speak for a couple of seconds. "Not sure where to begin. But if there's some way we can do right by Tom—well, I'm not one to go to the law, and I don't live in a place in town where the deputy's likely to come to me."

Delaine felt the familiar resistance. He did not want to be on confidential terms with Hensley to the extent that someone would be justified in thinking that he, Delaine, was on Caswell's side or in his group, if there was one. On the other hand, he was interested in having more knowledge, and he was open to doing right by Tom if there was a clean way. He said, "Go ahead. If you tell me more than I want to know, I'll say something."

"Well, I'll say this to begin with. Tom didn't complain."

"Uh-huh."

"So if he did something, and it came out now, he wouldn't whine. I don't know how much you've heard, but it seems like the deputy is trying to get people to say that Tom was moving cattle."

"He may have heard it from someone—not from me, that's for sure, because I didn't know."

"We could say a certain cattleman. And he might not even be wrong. But the thing was, it wasn't all Tom's doin'."

"I don't know who else he had contact with."

Hensley seemed to hesitate, and he let out an audible breath. "What I think I know is that he was tangled up with a rough customer and wanted to make a break with him but was afraid he might not get free."

"I had a faint impression of that, but I don't know if I want to know who it was."

"Tom tended to get in a jam."

"Seems like."

"Well, here's another thing. He might have been more than friends with the wife of a certain fella that has an eatin' house not far from here, on this side of the street."

Delaine felt the air go out of him as he had an image of the interior of The Knight's Table. "Do you think that could be a reason—?"

"I don't know how likely a suspect he is, himself. For one thing, he had a solid alibi for that night and morning. He ate supper at his own business and went home to drink whiskey and keep an eye on his wife. From what I understand, he hired a girl to help with the housework and the kids in the daytime, so she isn't ever alone. And then he goes home and sits on her lap at night. Makes her use a chamber pot and won't let her go to the outhouse in the dark."

Keeping the ring on his finger, Delaine thought.

Hensley took another breath. "He's put on weight since he took to runnin' an eatin' house, so he looks soft, and he might not have the nerve to do his own dirty work, but he knows crooked people and he's not so straight himself."

"Do you think he could have gotten someone else—?"

"Not that by itself is what I'm thinkin', but like I said, Tom made the mistake of helpin' a certain rough customer move maybe a steer or a calf here or there that might have missed bein' branded by a certain outfit."

The Silver Pine Ranch. Delaine thought that the two strands of Hensley's story crossed. He had just told Hensley he didn't know how much he wanted to know, and now he had to reconsider. Hensley was not the first person to refer to a rough customer, and as before, the term brought up an image of a burly character like a stevedore or a freighter. Delaine did not want to ask, but he thought he would listen to what else Hensley had to offer.

"Damn it. It looks like someone's coming."

A speck of light was moving in front of the land office, as if someone was carrying a lamp or a lantern.

"It does."

"Well, there's no need for me to stick around. I'll catch up with you later, if you want. We can talk again."

"All right. You can find me here."

With a rustling of cloth and leather, Hensley swung up into the saddle, and his horse took off on a fast walk to the east. Within a few seconds, horse and rider were absorbed into the darkness.

The speck of light came closer, moving in little jerks. Delaine made himself be patient. He thought it would be worse if he, too, took off.

The light turned out to be a shuttered lantern that cast a beam in front of the person who carried it. The person was Ed Herbert, the busybody land agent, which was no surprise to Delaine.

The man came to a stop with a long sigh. His soft face and drooping nose were visible in the glow behind the lantern, which he now lowered.

"I thought I heard something over here, so I

thought I'd come see what someone was doing at the pins at this time of night. You work here, don't you?"

"Yes, I do."

"Are you doin' night work?"

"No, I'm not. I decided to walk out this way, you might say to cool down. I was in the saloon, and another chap followed me out and saw fit to knock me down."

Herbert clucked. "Too much of that these days." He raised the lantern.

Delaine wondered if he had any bruise showing, but he did not see any reaction in Herbert's face. "When I was here, a fellow on horseback stopped. Said he wanted to find his way to the Moomaw Ranch."

"Never heard of it."

"Me, neither. But I'm new here. I don't know much."

Herbert made a fizzing sound, like a laugh. "I'm old here, and I don't know much. Are you goin' home now?"

"I'm cooled off."

"So am I." Herbert looked to the east. "Whoever that was, he might find himself out on a cold night, wandering like the Jews in the wilderness." When Delaine did not respond, he added, "In the Bible. Book of Exodus." His voice chirped as if he was about to announce the hymn number to be sung.

"Good enough," said Delaine. "I think I'll go home. Good evening to you."

"Same to you. and be careful where you go."

"It's just to the rooming house."

"I know. I meant the dins of iniquity."

Delaine let him have the last word. As he walked toward the center of town, he thought, *din, den, pin, pen.*

———

In his room, Delaine inspected his face in good light. The area around his left cheekbone was red, but he had no bruises or black eyes. He remembered the smirk on Earl's face, and he wished he had gotten in at least one punch in return.

———

Delaine felt as if he had Herbert's eyes on him as he and Benny worked on the corrals the next morning. The sun was weak in a pale sky, but he kept warm with the work. Just before noon, Al Portman came to watch for a few minutes.

When they finished tamping in the post they were working on, Al spoke. "There's an outfit gonna bring in a herd of about a hundred steers sometime after noon today. This may be the last bunch, but I don't know. I'd like to see everything shipped before the snow, but there's always one more outfit out there somewhere." He rubbed his gloved hand across the bottom of his nose. "When you get done eating, you can come to the office, and I'll give you each a cane. As far as that goes, you can eat in the office. I don't think it's going to get any warmer today."

———

The office air was heavy with the heat of a wood-burning stove, the fumes of a kerosene lamp, and the smoke from Al's cigarette. The room was not large, and the walls seemed to close in with ropes, quirts, bullwhips, chaps, and slickers hanging on hooks, while buggy whips, poles, and long canes leaned in corners and in open spaces.

"Do you miss Skip?" Benny asked.

Al said, "I sure do. I don't know if I'll get another dog. But I've said that before. I 'magine I will, maybe in the spring."

Delaine was picking crumbs off his lap when hoof-beats came to a stop outside the door.

"That'll be them," said Al as he rose from his chair. "Each of you take a cane, or a stick if you want. I'll be at the main gate. You fellas just help 'em put the cattle in pens however the foreman wants."

Benny selected a cane about five feet long and more than an inch thick. Delaine took a stick of about the same dimensions, maybe a little thicker. If something was going to break, he did not want to be responsible for losing a good stockman's cane.

The cattle were not far beyond the outrider. They came down the slope east of the land office, crossed the main thoroughfare, and crowded outside the first large pen as well as inside. The foreman was on his horse at first, then put it in a pen by itself and stood on a catwalk as he gave orders. He knew his herd, and he knew how he wanted the animals sorted. Two of his men held the bulging herd outside the corral, while two men rode inside and cut out the steers as the foreman ordered. It was slow work. The foreman was grouping the stock in numbers of ten to fifteen per pen so that they would go into the cars as he wanted, and Delaine and Benny were opening and closing gates to herd one steer at a time into its designated pen. The cattle bellowed, and the pen riders yipped and hep-hawed. Delaine had done his share of all the tasks, and the smells of farm animals, manure, and dust were common to him. The work would last as long as it took, so there was no need to be in a hurry.

The sun was poised in the west, just before it began to slip in late afternoon, when the last steer went into a pen and Delaine shut the gate. The riders put their horses into a pen and loosened their cinches, then walked in the corral dirt, their bowlegged stride accentuated by their chaps. They were headed toward the main gate.

Al came up to Delaine and Benny with a cane in his hand and said, "Let them go first. We're all gonna eat at the regular place. You both know where. Let the railroad hands eat before you, too. The trains is bound to come in at any time, and they may have to wolf their grub. We won't need you two to help load."

Delaine and Benny put their herding tools in the office and made their way to The Knight's Table. The aroma of roasted meat wafted out through the doorway as they stood in line.

When they moved inside, the air was warm, and a row of lamps shed golden light down on the tables. Some men were moving around, some were talking and laughing, and some were eating.

Two baskets of sliced bread were being refilled, and two pans of boiled potatoes sat steaming. A large tray of roasted beef ribs sat where the pig had been on the earlier occasion.

As he waited in line, Delaine saw again the sign with the name of the establishment in red letters above the illustration of a helmet and a long-handled axe.

Goodwin was giving orders to the man named Griggs. The man named Andrews was cutting the ribs into portions. The knife blade glistened, and the meat steamed as it separated.

Delaine wondered if anyone present knew of his humiliation the night before, when he was knocked down in the street. He did not think so, as no one paid him any attention.

His eyes rested for a moment on Goodwin, and he recalled what Hensley had told him. The man was a bit heavy and soft, with his full face and ruddy cheeks and wide apron, and he had a displeased, almost resentful expression. His blue eyes blazed. Any man would be unhappy if his wife was carrying on, if that was what happened, but what he did about it would tell what kind of a man he was. Even that, Delaine admitted to himself, was easy to say about someone else. Goodwin struck him as the type who would see it all in terms of something happening to him, with great injustice, irrespective of anything he may have ever done.

Delaine had his plate filled and took a seat across the table from Benny. "Good grub."

"Oh, yeah," said Benny. "It's always good here. Plenty to eat."

The conversation went up and down the tables in cheerful tones. Delaine was glad not to see the Dodge boys striding to the serving table for another helping of ribs. This was a civil bunch, stacking the picked bones and wiping their hands on plain cloth napkins.

Delaine's sense of well-being faded when he saw Ed Herbert in his dull brown suit and small hat, making his way down the food line and heaping his plate. Delaine recalled Caswell's comment about others coming to the trough.

A minute later, Herbert was standing next to a nearby table where the ranch foreman and riders sat. His hair the color of old straw stuck out beneath his hat, and his stomach pushed forward in his loose-fitting suit. His voice rose on the air as he spoke to the foreman.

"Well, Frank, are you glad to get 'em shipped?"

"Oh, yeah. We beat the bad weather."

"They'll go out tonight, then?"

"They should."

"That's good. You can never be too careful. Had some get out of a pin a few nights ago. You never know who might be around, on the lookout."

"Well, I secured a good count, and I'll make sure every last one of 'em gets loaded onto a car."

Herbert tucked his chin and smiled so that his nose almost touched his chin. "That's just fine. I'll let you go."

"Thanks, Ed."

Herbert made his way to a table where Goodwin had taken a seat. He bobbed his head with a comment Delaine could not hear, and he sat down, smiling, across from the proprietor of The Knight's Table. Delaine did not think he looked like a rough customer, but he might be one of the crooked people that Hensley said Goodwin knew, all very amiable.

———

Night was falling as Delaine left the eating house and headed home. He stopped in to check on his horse at the livery stable, where Kent was talking to a customer who had his back to the door. From the conversation, which Delaine did not make an effort to listen to, it appeared that the man was returning a horse he had rented and might come back the next day.

As the man turned around, Delaine recognized him as the investigator named Richards, wearing the drab clothes he was wearing the first time Delaine saw him, plus a canvas jacket of a similar dusty hue and a hat of stitched heavy canvas such as surveyors and field scientists wore. As he did in their meeting in the bakery, Richards gave Delaine a glance of recognition, said good evening, and passed by.

Delaine walked through the stable to the pen outside where his horse was eating hay. Seeing that his horse was all right, he went back through the stable, where Kent was busy forking hay into mangers. Delaine did not see Fitts, and he wondered if the man had slept off his drunk. Fitts had not been out late, and Delaine had not seen anything to suggest that he had any delay in going to the harness room and falling into bed.

———

DELAINE HAD NOT BEEN in his room very long when a knock sounded on the door. He opened it to see the dark eyes, clean clothes, and shining star of Deputy Erskine.

"Good evening," he said.

"The same to you. I imagine you remember me. Deputy Cavanaugh Erskine, Laramie County Sheriff's Office."

"I do."

"Mind if I come in?"

"Not at all." Delaine stood aside as before, let the deputy pass through, and closed the door.

Erskine took off his hat and sat in the chair. He

fixed his eyes on Delaine, who was seated on the bed, and said, "I've been looking for you."

"I was having my evening meal."

"I didn't find you at the café."

"We helped sort a herd of steers to be shipped out. We worked later than usual, and we went with the rest of the crew to eat at The Knight's Table."

"Oh, that place. I haven't been inside."

Delaine thought, *You might find your kind of fish there.* But he said, "I've eaten there twice. Good food for a work crew."

The deputy drew himself up in the chair with a breath. "You get along well with everyone you work with?"

"No reason not to. We've all got a job to do, and no one wants to get run over by a steer."

"And you've been working there since you finished working for George Mace?"

"Pretty much. There was one day in between, and I did some work at the livery stable."

"Uh-huh. That's where Hiram Fitts works, isn't it?"

"That's what he said. I was just there, and I didn't see him. He may have been working outside, or he may be on night shift later on." Delaine assumed that the deputy had come to ask more questions about Caswell and was making small talk. He wondered how much of Hensley's commentary he should repeat, as it was all on the level of gossip and hearsay, not anything he had known or heard at first hand.

The deputy said, "I have been given to understand that you know Hiram Fitts."

"In a small way, I guess."

"Did you work with him on that day when you worked at the stable?"

"No. I believe he was on the train with a load of steers going to Chicago."

"I see." The deputy took a deliberate breath. "What I would like to ask is, do you know of any connection between Hiram Fitts and Tom Caswell?"

Oh, thought Delaine. They were going to talk about Caswell after all. "No, I don't," he said. "I can't imagine what it would be. They worked for two different outfits, and I didn't see them ever talking together. The fellow who seemed to know Fitts, who went on the train with him before as well as this time, was a puncher named Bloom."

"I know him." The deputy folded his arms across his chest. "I don't think it's a big secret that George Mace thinks that Tom Caswell might have been skimming a few head of stock from his herd. I think you said in our last meeting that George Mace intimated something of that nature to you."

"I believe I did."

The deputy raised his chin and made a mild back-and-forth motion with his head. "The suggestion has come to me that Hiram Fitts, this cowhand they call Sundown, who is known to be broke most of the time, might have been on the lookout to make a few extra dollars and might have collaborated with Tom Caswell."

"I haven't seen or heard anything that would even suggest such a connection, but I don't know much about either of them."

"Yet I think you may have heard or seen quite a bit."

"I've seen little, and as for what I've heard, it's all gossip, which I'm sure you could hear in any of the places you go. I'm sure you've heard more than I have, because this is the first I have heard of any association between Tom Caswell and Hiram Fitts." Delaine was glad they were within the confines of his room as he said it, and as he did so, an image of Fitts came to mind, and it did not match any idea he had of a rough customer.

"I have to follow up on what I've heard, but I did hear that you were friends with both of these men."

"Not very much. In the case of Fitts, I've talked to him in passing twice, and on one of those occasions, he was dead drunk."

The deputy nodded.

Delaine reflected on the earlier wording of "The suggestion has come to me," and he wondered where the suggestion came from. He said, "It seems to me that someone might be going out of his way to cast suspicion on Fitts, just because he's an easy target and doesn't have many friends."

"That seems to be speculation on your part, about someone going out of his way." The deputy shifted in his seat but kept his eyes on Delaine. "Do you have a grudge against someone?"

Delaine took a moment to measure his response. "I wouldn't say it's that much, but I guess you may have heard that one of the Dodge brothers went out of his way to pick a fight with me and knock me down in the street. That's not speculation, and I didn't mean to imply that I thought the same person was saying things about Fitts."

"Well, that he went out of his way to hit you might be speculation. It's your interpretation, or at least your version."

"I was there." Delaine told himself to cool down. The deputy might be provoking him to see if he could get a rise out of him. "But enough about that. Do you have any other questions?"

"Maybe one. Are you planning to leave town in the near future?"

"Not as long as I have work. I *am* planning to go out with a friend to see about getting a deer. Mr. Gresham, the schoolteacher. Don't know if you know him."

"I know who he is. You don't have to tell me if you're just going out on a little excursion with him. I meant whether you were going to *leave town*, in the sense of packing up and going somewhere else, such as to look for work or just to relocate. I would want to know that."

"Well, I don't have any plans in that respect."

"Very well. I don't think I have any more questions at the present time. Do you have any questions for me?"

"Now that I think of it, yes. Did you ever hear about a girl named Nora Peele, who disappeared from this town a couple of years ago?"

The deputy's face tightened. "Yes, I've heard of her. That was before I came. There was never anything definite to suggest that a crime had been committed."

"That's what I heard."

"It was what I was told. Do you have any other questions?"

"Not at the present." Delaine realized he was speaking the deputy's language.

"Good enough, then. Thanks for your cooperation." The deputy stood up and put on his hat, then held out his hand.

Delaine was on his feet. He shook, and he showed the man out.

With the door closed, he walked back and forth in his room. He had let the deputy get under his skin, and he wished he hadn't. The deputy was just going about his work in his own way, which was annoying but not pigheaded, as far as Delaine could see. There was something going on in the aftermath of Tom Caswell's death, and it did not seem as if the deputy was being drawn in to cast blame. He was repeating what he heard in order to get a reaction. He was smug and condescending, but he had to play his cards close to his chest.

Delaine wondered if half the town had heard of Earl Dodge knocking him down, and he wondered if people were laughing at him. He had a notion to go to the White Mule and look the world in the face.

He checked himself. That was what people did when they had a dose of guilt or shame. He didn't feel either way. But he wouldn't mind having a drink, just one, to take the edge off and to get a hint at what people thought of him.

He put on his hat and coat, went downstairs, and stepped out into the chilly air. Across the street and down a couple of doors, men would be laughing and talking in the White Mule. He didn't need to go there. If he saw the Dodge boys and had a confrontation, it would be something he could have avoided.

The Three Hermits lay close at hand, here on the same side of the street. One drink. When he had the choice, he preferred whiskey over beer, but this was any port in a storm.

Inside, he found Butch by himself, standing behind the bar in a heavy flannel shirt of gray and black plaid, the kind that some people would call a lumberjack shirt, which fell straight down, untucked.

"What would you like?"

"A glass of beer."

"Comin' up." Butch turned his back and drew a mug of beer from a tap. He made a smooth pivot to the bar and set the drink in front of Delaine. "Just ten cents."

Delaine put a dime on the bar. "What's new?"

"Nothin'," said Butch. "Not since you were in here last. You know what they say. Nothin' ever happens here except the weather."

Delaine drank from the mug. Either the news had not traveled or Butch was being polite. "Could be worse."

Butch slid the dime toward himself. "Oh, yeah. No matter how things are, they can always be worse. And that goes for the weather, as well."

9

THE SKY WAS OVERCAST, AND THE TEMPERATURE WAS cool. The steers had been shipped, and the pens had an empty feeling, with the odor of manure and stirred-up dust lingering from the day before. From time to time, Delaine kept an eye out on the main trail in and out of town, as he expected Hensley to drop by to arrange for a continuation of their conversation. A few men on horseback and in buckboards came and went, but Delaine did not recognize any of them.

In the morning, his attention was drawn to the area outside the corral, where a man on foot had come to a stop. Delaine recognized the battered hat and stubbled face of Pinky, who was wearing a checked brown flannel overshirt in addition to his regular work shirt, overalls, and brogan shoes.

"Still at it," he said. "Dig, dig, dig."

Delaine rested the iron bar. "Still glad to have work."

"Yon stripling with the shovel reminds me of the story of the two Irishmen who were workin' in the sewer. One of 'em, Pat, says to the other, 'I say, Mike, what are you muckin' about in the crop for with your shovel?' And Mike says, 'It's me coat. I'm tryin' to get it out.' And Pat says, 'Ah, Mike, you know that coat's not any good anymore.' And Mike says, 'Of *course* it's no good. I know that. But me lunch is in the pocket.' Ha-ha-ha." Pinky slapped his knees and gave another round of laughter.

Benny pushed on the post to loosen it, and Delaine gave another hard jab with the bar. He moved a few inches to the left and drove the bar three more times. Seeing a few chunks of dirt loosened, he pulled the bar up onto solid ground and took a breath.

"I guess they had a little excitement in town," said Pinky.

Delaine gave half his attention to Benny scooping out the loose dirt with the shovel. "Is that right."

"Yep. They found a fella dead in his hotel room."

The shovel stopped.

Delaine looked at Pinky, who may have enjoyed being the matter-of-fact bearer of news. "Someone from town?"

"Not anyone I know," said Pinky, stretching his chin as if to see how the digging went. "A fella who's been in town about a week, from what they say, name of Richards."

Something tightened in the pit of Delaine's stomach. "The hell. I just saw him yesterday, in the stable."

"Then you know him."

"I can't say that I know him. He stopped in here, I'd say it was a little more than a week ago. Looked as if he had just come into town, carrying a knapsack."

"Did he tell you what he was up to?"

Delaine did not want to lie, but he did not want to

give Pinky more to gossip about. "He didn't say a great deal." Delaine glanced at Benny. "But the little he did say, I think maybe we should save it for Deputy Erskine. I'm sure you know him better than I do."

Pinky gave a little laugh. "Oh, yeah. Jealous sort. Doesn't like to have someone else tell him something that he thinks he should have heard first. But what kind of a fellow was this Richards?"

Delaine knew that if he ever hoped to hear information from Pinky, which he thought he might, he couldn't hold out on him all the way. "Mild-mannered," he said. "He was on foot when he stopped here. I don't know if he came into town that way or caught a ride in a wagon. When I saw him yesterday, it sounded like he was turning in a horse he had rented and he might go back out again. So he was still on foot, in that sense."

"He was. He told Baird at the hotel that he might want to go to another town to send a telegram. Baird told him there was a telegraph office right here, and he said it was a mooshy message and he didn't want to dictate it to someone who would repeat it."

"Mooshy?"

"Yeah. Sweetheart stuff. Did he strike you as a Romeo?"

"I didn't know him that well. Not enough to make much of an impression."

"Well, he made one now. Or, rather, they made one on him."

"They?"

"Whoever choked him. Has Baird worried, that someone could get into one of his rooms and lock it on the way out. The dead man's key was still there in the room."

"I think anyone should find that…unsettling."

"I should say so. It could happen to you or me." Pinky opened his eyes wide. "If someone had a reason."

"Try not to give 'em one," said Delaine.

"That's my creed." Pinky raised his hat and lowered it. "I'd better let you gentlemen tend to the fine art of diggin' in the dirt."

"Thanks for sharing the news."

"Just happened to be passing by."

Delaine went back to punching with the iron bar. When he saw that Pinky had crossed the street, he spoke to Benny. "Sounds like a bad thing that happened."

Benny worked with the shovel on his side of the post. "That's two, in a little more than a week."

"Hard to say whether they're related, but that's for the deputy to figure out." Delaine glanced at the retreating figure of the old gossip. "I didn't want to tell him anything that wasn't already public knowledge. I haven't told anyone what Richards told us that day."

"Neither have I."

"I'm sure we'll have a chance to tell the deputy before long."

"Oh, yeah. Pinky will tell him we know something."

"I hope I wasn't too short with Pinky. He's a little more forward than I care for."

"He puts his nose in everything. You know, they call him the pig man. He has pigs, and he goes around to the businesses to collect scraps. Any place that sells food, he has buckets, for them to put in food they want to throw away. He changes the buckets every day, and he comes in the back door whenever he wants. They're used to it, but someone working for the first time, they get a surprise to see him."

Delaine glanced again in the direction where Pinky had gone. "He doesn't seem dangerous to me. Nosy, like you say. But you never know."

"They tell the little kids to stay away from him, but I never see him trying to talk to them anyway. Not like some old men. There was one, he said he liked to play with kids because he never had any of his own, and they made him leave town. He was cleaner than Pinky, and he always had candy. Like you say, he was a little too forward. But he's gone."

"There's always one kind or another." Delaine jabbed with the bar. "I feel sorry for this fellow Richards. I wonder if he told many people what he was up to."

———

DELAINE CROSSED the street after work. He passed the general store and came to the barbershop. A small crowd inside the barber shop drew his attention, and he stopped. A man who looked like a businessman, standing near the door, told him that the body was in the back room. The coroner was with the body, and anyone who knew the deceased was welcome to go back and confirm the identity. Delaine hesitated, and a feeling came to him that he owed it to the man to stop in for a minute.

He walked through the crowd and went into the back room, where a man in a white jacket was writing in a notebook. The barber, whom Delaine knew by sight, said that the other man was the druggist and the coroner.

The deceased was lying on a table with his hands folded on his chest. He was wearing the drab clothes he had been wearing the day before, with the addition of a yellowed white handkerchief draped across his throat.

The coroner looked up. "Did you know him?"

"Only in passing. I spoke with him once, and I saw him a couple of other times."

"Did you hear his name?"

"Richards. I think he said his first name was Jerome."

"That's what we have. Anything else?"

"Not as far as identifying him."

"Your name?"

"Jess Delaine. I work at the shipping pens, and I stay at the rooming house."

"Anything more?"

"I don't think so."

"Thanks for stopping in."

Delaine felt as if he had been holding his breath when he stepped out into the fresh air. He reminded himself of where he had been going. The newsstand next door.

As he was about to reach for the door handle, the door swung inward, and Deputy Erskine walked out, settling his hat on his head.

He flicked a glance at Delaine and said, "Evenin'."

"Good evening." In the few seconds it took for Delaine to go inside, he wondered what the deputy was doing in the newsstand if he had a new case to add to the one he was working on. Maybe he was buying candy.

Marian stood behind the counter. She was wearing her striped grey apron over a dress of a subdued blue.

Her light-brown hair was pinned in place, and her blue eyes were clear. She had a serene expression on her face as she smiled and said, "Good evening. Is there something I can help you with?"

Delaine gave a smile. "I'd like to buy another small package of chocolate like the one I bought last week."

"Wasn't it this one?" She pointed at the candy with the illustrated wrapping.

"That's it."

"It must have met with approval."

"You made a good recommendation."

Her face relaxed in a smile, and she set the package on the counter between them. "Five cents."

He handed her a nickel.

"Thank you. You don't need it wrapped?"

"No, thank you." He felt that she was comfortable with him, a man out of her age range who had an interest in another woman. Not that age mattered to some men. Delaine did not want to look too long at her, but he observed her for a couple of seconds and wondered how much she resembled her lost sister. In that same instant, he felt a pang of sadness that no one had done anything toward finding the girl named Nora. He imagined Marian must be feeling the loss in a new way as people murmured about one more death in town, with the body right next door.

"Thank you for coming in," she said.

"And thank you for your help." He put the package in his coat pocket as he walked out. At the edge of his vision, she turned to some other aspect of her work. He thought she did a good job of being businesslike and positive, tending to her customers, while she carried her sadness and kept it from public view.

Outside, he crossed the street to stop in at the

stable as he did every day after work. The image of the young woman stayed with him. He felt that he should do something if he could. He did not have an idea of what it would be. It had not been so hard to stop in and do what he thought he owed it to Richards to do. He had known the man. He had seen him in the stable just the day before. He felt that he knew Nora Peele in some way as well. He did not owe her anything, but she deserved something.

———

THE FIRST HINT of pink was showing in the eastern sky as Delaine crossed the street on his way to the café. He was glad once again to see no customers inside.

The sound of the doorbell faded as Rachel came out of the kitchen. Her face brightened as she saw him, and she turned around and went back. She returned a minute later with the coffeepot and a cup.

As she poured the coffee, he set the package on the table near her. "This is for you."

"Oh, how nice." She withdrew the coffeepot and pursed her lips. "I didn't tell you how much I enjoyed the other one. I made it last three days."

"I'm glad you liked it." He did not delay, as he did not know when someone else might come in. "What would you think if I visited you at the place where you stay?"

"With the little Dutch boy?"

He laughed. "I had forgotten about him. Is he in honor of the little Dutch boy who put his finger in the dike and was stuck there until the others could get him out?"

"I think so." Her face took on a serious cast. "I'm

sure you heard about the man they found in the hotel room yesterday."

"Yes, I did."

She glanced at the door. "We had better not talk about it now. Shall I take this?" She put her hand next to the wrapped chocolate.

"By all means. It's yours."

"Thank you."

"You're welcome. I'll see you this evening."

She put the package in her apron pocket and took the coffeepot into the kitchen.

The bell on the door rang as two jaunty young fellows came in joking with each other. They wore caps, pullover work shirts, suspenders, loose trousers, and laced-up work boots.

One of them said, with cadence, "All the way to Santa Fe."

The other one laughed.

Delaine was glad to see young people without many worries. He was also glad he hadn't wasted any time in speaking with Rachel.

———

DELAINE DID NOT HAVE any items in his hands as he stood third in line at the general store. The woman at the front of the line set a couple of items on the counter as the previous woman walked away.

The storekeeper said, "Good afternoon, Mrs. Goodwin. Or I should say, good evening. What else would you like?"

"Just a couple of things," said the customer.

Delaine took half a step to the left to see the woman who had been addressed. She was of average height, with dark hair gathered under the collar of a grey-and-black houndstooth coat, with a black beret-like cap on top. She did not look remarkable to Delaine, but he knew that she was someone he should talk to if he could.

He left his place in line and walked without hurry to the front door. A middle-aged man in town clothes was coming in, so Delaine stepped aside, let the man pass, and walked outside before the door closed. He stood on the right side of the door, facing the street with his back to the window. After several minutes, the door opened, and the woman in the wool coat and cap walked out and turned to the right in front of him.

His heartbeat picked up, and he knew he had to speak. "Excuse me, Mrs. Goodwin," he said. "I would like to talk to you for a minute if you don't mind."

She had her hands together with the loop handles of her shopping bag over her right forearm. As she turned to look up at him, he saw caution and worry on her face. She was not a pretty woman, as she had a rough complexion and a tooth that was visible over her lower lip. Her coat was open, revealing a close-fitting, dark grey dress with a modest bosom, and he could see that she retained something of her figure at thirty-four or thirty-five.

"I don't think I know you," she said.

He took off his hat. "My name is Jess Delaine. I worked for a short while at the Silver Pine Ranch, and I got to know, in a small way, a ranch hand who is not with us anymore, and I thought that if there was anything I could do to help his cause, such as it is— that is, to bring about better knowledge—"

"I'm sorry. More than I can tell you. I was sorry to hear what happened, and I am sorry that no one, as far as I know, has found an explanation. But if there was ever anything I knew, it is in the past." Her tooth went out of view when she finished speaking, and she had a pretty mouth. Her eyes moistened, but she did not break. "I appreciate your concern for your friend."

He moved back half a step. He admired her ability to address him, a stranger, in a calm and clear way. She had to look out for herself. He could not blame her. She seemed to have herself under control, but at the same time, she had a defeated air about her, as if she had had to grovel to her husband at some point. She may have been affected by the more recent death in town as well. Still, she had not given Delaine the abject response she might have, that she did not know what he was talking about. "Thank you," he said.

"I wish you well."

"And the same to you." He watched her walk away, a person alone in her troubles, it seemed. He came back to his own concerns, remembered that he needed to buy something for his evening meal, and went back into the store.

———

DELAINE WALKED past the little Dutch boy and knocked on the door. The lock moved, and the door opened.

"How do you do?" said Mrs. Vanderhoven. "Come in."

Delaine took off his hat as he stepped into the room. He reached into his coat pocket, drew out a pint of brandy wrapped in newspaper, and handed it to the landlady. "A small gift," he said.

"Why, thank you," she said. "Rachel must have said something."

Delaine smiled and nodded, then turned as Rachel entered the room. Her eyes were bright, and her hair hung loose at her shoulders. She wore a brown jacket and skirt with a cream-colored blouse. The jacket had dark embroidery, and it reminded Delaine of styles he had seen in the Southwest and along the border. "You look very nice," he said.

"Thank you."

Miss Vanderhoven turned the lock on the door and withdrew into the kitchen.

"Shall we sit down?" said Rachel.

They sat in the same places as on the previous visit. Rachel folded her hands in her lap and said, "Isn't it terrible that we've had another person die in town?"

"It is. No one seems to have made much progress with the first one, and now this. I haven't heard anything about whether they might be related."

"Neither have I. They say the man who was found dead in the hotel was a detective. He was looking for a missing girl from Colorado."

"Eastern Colorado, from what he told me."

"Oh. You talked to him?"

"He stopped to chat with Benny and me when he first came to town, I believe. He showed us a picture of a blonde girl, and he told us her name. I don't know how many other people he was that forward with. He more or less suggested to us that we not tell anyone, and I haven't. Benny says he hasn't, either."

"He came into the café, but he never asked me anything."

"I don't know how good he was at what he did. I would think he wouldn't tell the first people he met and then try to keep it under his hat."

"I think he told several people he was looking for a missing girl. He just didn't say anything to me."

"Maybe he came up against some difficulties or sensed some kind of danger. It seems as if he might have been onto something. I heard he wanted to go to another town to send a telegram."

"I heard that, too."

"It's too bad he didn't get any further than he did."

Rachel moved her lips before she spoke. "It's good to know that people will go to that much trouble to look for a lost girl. He came all the way from Colorado."

"My guess is that the family had enough money to pay for an investigator—if not an agency, an individual detective."

"That might be the difference, the money. There was this girl in town that you and I have talked about. Nobody seems to have done anything about her. But she was of a lower class. I don't mean that in a bad way. But she didn't have money, or a family that had money. All she had was her sister."

Delaine assumed that Rachel knew in what other way Nora Peele had a lower status in town. He said, "I asked the deputy about the girl, and he said what you and I had already said, that nobody did anything because there was no proof that a crime had been committed. They could say that about the girl from Colorado as well, but they can't about the man who said he was looking for her."

"Having a man die in the hotel is very clear, or plain to see. It can't be denied."

"I thought the same about the man who was found in the livery stable, but it took a while for anyone to move on that case. But the deputy is in town, and he was asking questions about it." Delaine recalled the incongruity of seeing the deputy walk out of the news-stand. "I'm sure he'll be asking questions about this one as well."

"I think he has been." Rachel gave him her full attention. "What do you think?"

"About—?"

"About either the first one or the second one."

Delaine took a breath. "Well, with the first one, people seem to think the fellow was caught up in crooked dealin's with someone else's cattle and that one crook turned on another, or something like that. Maybe that seems like a blunt way to put it. I feel kind of sorry, because he was a friend of mine, in a way. But I also heard, and I wouldn't want to be quoted as the source of this, that he might have had something to do with someone else's wife but that it wasn't enough for someone to have something done to him."

"I heard something like that, too."

"Than I imagine the deputy has. But he hasn't asked me about that aspect. He's questioned me twice about Tom Caswell, and both times, he has seemed focused on the angle about, to use his words, the transfer of cattle."

"And the other?"

"Richards? I don't have any ideas past the story that everyone seems to know. He was looking for a missing girl. I would guess he got too close."

"Do you think they have anything to do with one another?"

"That's hard to say. When two deaths come together close in time, and they seem to be similar, it's natural to think that they might be related. But I don't see it. Not yet. That could change, of course. I don't like to make light of any of it."

"Neither do I." Rachel smiled. "But let's talk about something else. Has anything else happened that was interesting?"

Delaine had already decided not to tell her about the altercation with Earl Dodge until it became more pertinent. "Not much. I've run into a fellow named Pinky a couple of times. He seems to be quite a gossip, on top of considering himself an original character."

Rachel shuddered. "Oh, him. He collects scraps of food for his pigs. The first time he came into the kitchen when I was there, he scared me. I wasn't expecting anyone, and he came in from the alley without knocking. I don't like him. I don't ever go close enough to let him talk to me, and thank God he doesn't come in as a customer."

"Do you think he's dangerous?"

"No. Just…dirty."

"I didn't see him as dangerous, either. He seems to like to be known as a person who is wise about the world, and funny, and who knows many little things."

"Maybe he does."

"He might. But enough about him."

"Yes. Tell me more about yourself. What do you think you will do when your work ends at the corrals?"

"Well, I hope it doesn't end tomorrow, but it's bound to before long. Another week or two, maybe. I guess I'll look for more work here."

"That's good."

"I hope so. You get to know somebody, you think maybe there's mutual interest, and you don't want to pack up and leave." He observed her, and he did not think he had said too much.

"Work is sometimes hard to find in the winter."

"I know. Maybe I'll go to work delivering coal. I've never gone without work for very long. I just don't like to worry about it too far ahead of time."

She smiled. "Neither do I. The past is in the past. And we don't know what is in the future."

Delaine took it as a good sign that she wanted to know if he planned to stay around. He was thinking of what to say next when she spoke again.

"What do you like to do in the winter? Do you play cards?"

He gave a light laugh. "Just about anyone in a bunkhouse learns to play cards in the winter. And everyone knows how to play checkers. We do other things, like braid rawhide—make halters and lariats. And yourself?"

"I don't play cards much. Or dominoes or checkers. Sometimes I sew, but not much since—well, I told you about my earlier sadness. Maybe I'll take it up again."

"Maybe there's a card game that doesn't have much at stake, like seven-card rummy. When I get all cleaned up from delivering coal, we can play for matchsticks, or beans."

"We'll think of something," she said. "As you know, I don't stay up late, anyway."

"Now that you mention it, I shouldn't keep you up late now."

"Oh, no. I didn't mean that."

Mrs. Vanderhoven appeared at the doorway. "You can't leave yet. I just got the water heated for a hot toddy."

Delaine sat up straight. "I don't know if I'm—"

"Just one," said the landlady. "To fortify you on your long walk home."

"It's all of three blocks."

"Just one warm little drink. I'm going to have one, and I think Rachel will. You're not going to leave us to ourselves, are you?"

"I don't know how I could."

———

DELAINE WAS warm but not tipsy as he turned the corner at the end of the block. He had two blocks until he came to the main street and then another half-block until he reached the rooming house. The night was chilly but normal.

He saw his breath in front of him as he walked. His hands were comfortable in his gloves. His footsteps sounded on the hard ground. He had the presence of mind to keep his eyes and ears open, and he saw a faint glow in the main street well ahead.

When he came to the next corner, he reminded himself that this was Elm Street. Rachel lived on Green Street. He was on Sterling. As far as he knew, the main street did not have a name. He yawned, then took in a deep breath and reminded himself to stay alert.

At the next corner, still on the west side of Sterling Street, standing by the laundry, he paused. Across the street, two doors down on the north side of the main street, light spilled out of the front of the White Mule Saloon. He did not need to go there tonight.

He was about to cross the main street when movement caused him to stop and watch. A man was going into the saloon. The shape and the details registered. A slender man in a dull-black hat and a grey jacket and pants was almost gliding, silent at this distance. Delaine could not see the prominent Adam's apple or the thin scar on this side of the man's face, but he knew the dry-looking man of the sallow complexion who had eaten roast pig with Herbert and had had a drink with Chamberlain.

Delaine tensed his upper body against the chill, and when he was sure the man had gone inside, he walked onward, across the street and then to the left, keeping his eyes ahead until he came to the rooming house.

10

Movement on the main street picked up through the morning as people came into town on horseback and in wagons. Delaine had been in town a little over two weeks, and the activity seemed to be normal for a Saturday. He had it in mind that he was going to go deer hunting with Gresham the next day, so he kept an eye on the sky.

Late in the morning, Hensley stopped by on his dark horse. He had a somber tone about him, as he most often did. He stayed in the saddle and did not take out his tobacco and papers.

"Looks like you have a bunch of short posts left over. The part that wasn't buried is still good on most of those."

"There's always a use for 'em," Delaine said. "They make good cross braces. Even the ones that are split don't go to waste all the way. They make good firewood."

"Cedar posts are good for that."

"They are. Some of these are pitch pine and other

stuff I'm not sure of—like pine, but harder and heavier. Interesting things to cut and burn through the winter."

"Yuh." Hensley nodded. "I was wonderin' when we might pick up on the conversation we left off the other evenin'."

Delaine gazed off in the distance for a second. "Today's better than tomorrow. I agreed to go out and help a fella try to get a deer. So sometime this evening after work, or into the beginning of next week."

Hensley glanced across the street in the direction of Herbert's office. "You want to meet here again?"

"Might as well. We can move somewhere else if it looks like we're going to have company."

"This evenin', then? Same time as before?"

"Sounds agreeable."

Hensley clucked, and the dark horse raised its head. Hensley gathered his reins. "See you then."

———

Delaine waited in the general store as the customers ahead of him made their purchases. A couple of them looked him over. He thought they were trying to see if he was wearing a gun beneath his jacket. He could feel a tension in the air; he could hear it in the people's voices.

He went over the list in his mind for the excursion the next day—crackers, cheese, canned peaches. He heard another customer ask for canned sardines, and he decided against them for himself. As he had heard a hunting guide in New Mexico say, the deer can tell who uses eau de cologne, who smokes cigarettes, and who had sardines for lunch.

A woman at the head of the line gathered her bag and turned to leave. Delaine expected to see Mrs. Goodwin, while at the same time he knew better.

———

NIGHT HAD FALLEN when Delaine showed up at the shipping pens. He was glad to see that no light glowed in the land office. Faint sounds came from the middle of town as the day's commerce came to a close. Delaine envisioned patrons going into the White Mule, and he imagined a tune playing.

The footfalls of a horse sounded as the animal moved toward him from the east. He could not see the horse at first, and then he saw a dark shape moving.

"I'm here," he said, in a plain voice, not loud.

Hensley's voice came back in the monotone syllable of "Yuh."

Delaine heard the horse breathing. The hooves came to a stop. Saddle leather creaked as Hensley dismounted, and his boots made a soft thud on the ground without the sound of spurs.

"Looks like the old snoop isn't around," he said.

"I haven't seen him."

"I don't expect to be here too long anyway." Hensley stood close. "There was just a thing or two I thought I might pass on, in case it would do any good."

"I understand." Delaine waited.

"I was about to tell you about this same old son of a bitch when he showed up."

"I don't follow you."

"Last time. The fellow who has his office over there."

"Oh." Delaine was becoming used to Hensley not mentioning names.

"He's a go-between, you know."

"Somewhat. I don't know in what ways."

"He would set things up for Tom to turn over a head or two at a certain time and place. Another party would have someone take the stock from there."

"I see."

"And all of that was just normal business, you might say. But then this old son of a bitch offered to let Tom in on another line of business. Tom didn't tell me what it was. He just said it was something else, something he didn't want to have anything to do with, but once this old fool let him know about it, he was stuck. He couldn't get out because he knew too much and they had it on him."

"But you don't know what it was."

"It was better for me not to know, and it still is. And even if I ever did know something, or thought I did, I don't."

"Let me back up and get something straight if I can. You say Tom turned stock over to another party. Is that the rough customer you referred to the other time we talked?"

"It is."

"And that's the one Tom thought he was in too deep with. He wasn't afraid of this fellow over here."

"Not in the sense that he would do something to him, no."

"I see. And how far back do you think this goes?"

"Maybe a couple of years."

"And this rough customer, if I wanted to make sure I steered clear of him, how would I know him? What does he look like?"

"You may have seen him. He's older than you or me—over forty, I'd say. He's got beady eyes and a thin face. He's lean himself. Doesn't dress like a workin' man, more like someone from town who's got a business. And that's what he is. He doesn't get cow shit on him himself. If you saw him not too far away, you could know him by a thin scar he's got runnin' down the side of his face." Hensley's hand made a downward motion next to his own ear.

A chill went through Delaine. "I think I know who you mean. He's a friend of this fellow over here, and he might be some kind of friend to a tall cattleman with a red beard."

"Might be."

Delaine felt as if the breath had gone out of him.

Hensley made a small noise in his throat and then spoke. "Like I say, there's things I don't know. But I'd like to see someone answer for what they did to Tom. I might be able to take you somewhere and show you something, even though I don't know a thing about it."

Delaine found himself tiring of Hensley's indirectness. He did not think the man was leading him on as much as he was sounding him out. Hensley wanted to be sure before he took someone further into is confidence, and it was the same kind of confidence that Delaine was reluctant to be drawn into. Whatever else there was to be known about, it had to be more sinister than rustling cattle. Even with the simpler crime, Delaine had wanted to keep his distance. Still, he had an indefinite sense that there was something here that he should know. "When do you think we would do that?" he asked.

"Not tonight. And not tomorrow if you're goin'

huntin'. I'll look for you here at the beginnin' of the week."

"All right."

Hensley mounted up and rode off in the darkness in the direction he had come from, and Delaine walked in the direction of the rooming house. He felt as if he would be leaving things in the air when he went out hunting with Gresham, but on the other hand, he did not feel burdened with knowledge he did not want to have, at least for the present. He was not overwhelmed by the one piece of new knowledge he had gained. Knowing who the rough customer was, even if Delaine did not yet have a name to go with the person, could help him avoid confrontations. He did not need to go to the White Mule Saloon tonight, anyway. He remembered what came his way when he went in there just to pass a little time in the middle of the week. It was Saturday now, when more people were bound to be there, and he had things to do early in the morning.

———

THE SKY WAS dark as midnight as Delaine and Gresham walked to the livery stable. Lantern light was showing through the crack of the door, and once inside, Delaine saw that Hiram Fitts had three horses tied. Delaine's brown horse stood by itself, while the stout grey horse that Gresham had ridden before was tied next to a sorrel with a thin blaze and no other markings.

"Kent said you wanted this grey horse to ride and a packhorse to go along."

"That's right," said Delaine. "If you have a scabbard for his rifle, that will help."

The schoolteacher had a lever-action Winchester .30-30 that he carried in his hand. Delaine had his .45-70 and scabbard, which he had carried along with a ditty bag holding food and a few small items he thought he might use, such as a sheath knife, a folding saw, and twine.

Fitts tucked back the corners of his mouth. "I'll get the saddle horse ready first and put on a scabbard."

Delaine went about getting his own horse ready as Fitts brushed and saddled Gresham's. He came out of the harness room with a small, dark scabbard that was dry and had a curl at the tip. After sticking the .30-30 in to see that it fit, he strapped the scabbard on in what he called northwest position, on the left side with the stock pointing forward.

For the packhorse, Fitts brushed and combed the animal, picked its hooves, and laid the pad on its back. Next came the wooden packsaddle with its cinches and breeching, which he called "britchin'." Fitts poked at the animal, pulled on straps, and shook the wooden frame by its crossbucks. "Should be all right," he said. "We'll put the panyards on."

He came out of the harness room with two canvas panniers, stained and discolored with patches and sewed rips. He draped one on each side, hooking the leather loops on the crossbucks. Each pannier also had a strap and buckle across the top to keep it closed.

"Put a little weight in 'em, and they won't fall off. With luck, you'll have plenty of weight comin' back." Fitts smiled.

Delaine said, "If I could have a length of thee-eighths or half-inch rope, I'll have something to tie the packs if I have something to put in 'em."

"Good idea. I thought of that earlier and forgot." Fitts hurried into the harness room and came back with a manila rope that had a few wraps around a bundle of curled coils. He put it into the near side of the pack as Delaine and Gresham put in their small bags, one on each side.

"One more thing," said Delaine. "I'd like to have another halter as well. I've got one for my horse, but I'd like one for his. I'd rather not tie these horses with reins when we tie them up to go hunt on foot." The packhorse would have a halter the whole time, so there was no need to mention it.

The faintest light was showing in the east as they led the animals outside. Fitts held the grey horse as Gresham climbed aboard. When Delaine saw that Gresham was ready, he turned his saddle horse so that he could hold the lead rope clear, and he swung aboard. The packhorse fell into place alongside, and the small group headed out onto the main street. The morning was quiet except for the sound of three sets of hooves hitting the earth.

Delaine did not speak until they had ridden the three blocks north out of town. "My hunch is that our best chance of finding deer is along the pine ridge. I think that the country to the east of the 'Y' is a little more open."

"Will we get there in time?"

"First light is good if you know a place where the deer show up, but even then, it depends on the moon. In a full moon, they graze more at night, but with the moon like it is right now, they're more likely to graze through the morning. If you know where to be, some deer go to water in the late morning and in the early evening. Even at that, deer are where you find them. You can see them every morning at seven, for example, on a hayfield, and then the morning you go down there to get one, they don't show up. Little things can make 'em change their patterns through the day. Some kid ten or twelve years old can walk smack into a big buck at ten-thirty in the morning."

"Success favors the prepared mind."

"That's right. When you're on the hunt, you want to have it worked out in your mind what you would do if you saw one."

"Rehearse it."

"Yes. You also want to practice the actual motion of getting into position and lining up your sights. It doesn't hurt to line up on a deer you don't plan to shoot, just to practice holding steady. Have you hunted before?"

"A little. But it was more shooting than hunting. Where the deer came into the haystacks. Then two or three of us would shoot at once, on the count. I missed more times than I hit, and you'd get only one chance per day."

"I know people do things that way," said Delaine, "and they get some results. But for me, I don't like to shoot when it's not the perfect time for me, that tiny part of a second when I know everything is in the right place. If I shoot before or after, things aren't right. That's one thing you practice, knowing when it's the perfect spot in time. Sometimes you go past it and have to get set again."

Daylight was spreading when they reached the main fork in the road. Delaine took them to the right. Before long, more cedar trees appeared in the draws.

The horses moved at a fast walk, huffing and blowing, and the individual trees on the pine ridge became more visible.

The trail went down through a wash that was dry at present. Delaine stopped at a thicket of chokecherry bushes, which had shed their leaves. "I want to try something," he said. "I won't be long."

He took the folding saw out of the bag and found two straight, dry chokecherry branches less than an inch thick. He cut each one in a length a little more than a yard and put the two branches in the pannier close to him.

Back on the trail, he said, "When we find a place for you to watch for a little while, I'll see about makin' you a shootin' stick."

The sun had cleared the hills to the east when Delaine saw an area that looked like a good one to watch. They tied their horses to a couple of low pines, and Delaine set Gresham in a place where he could sit behind a rock outcropping and rest the rifle for his aim.

Back at the horses, Delaine cut the longer stick to match the shorter one for length. Saving the edge of the sheath knife for skinning, he used his pocketknife to cut a notch around each stick about two inches from the narrow end, or top. He tied the twine into one groove, looped the twine tight into the other, and continued to tie the crossed tips together into a series of figure-eights. He cut the twine, tied it off as tight as he could, and spread the two sticks so that they made a small crossbuck at the top.

He turned the sticks around and went to work on the other end. Still using his pocketknife, he sharpened the point of each leg so it would stick in the ground. He spread the legs and tried them. They worked.

Walking in a crouch, he came up behind Gresham. "See anything?"

"Not yet."

Still in a low voice, he said, "You can try this. They call it a shooting stick. You use it when you don't have a tree or a fence post to take a rest on, which is most of the time in open country. You spread the legs like this, and that's how you adjust for height, you see? Raise it or lower it as you want. Now, you hold the cross here with your left hand, and you lay the forearm of your rifle in the notch. You've got to hold it snug, or it'll jump when you fire. So you hold the rifle and the crossbuck together with your left hand, keep your right hand on the grip near the trigger guard, and pressing with both hands, you hold the butt of the rifle into your shoulder. You get the feel of the angle you want, holding the rifle across your chest, so everything lines up right. Then when you've got that perfect point in time, you fire. Go ahead and give it a try. Without firing, of course. That's right. You use it kneeling."

The schoolteacher, who was larger than Delaine, shifted and adjusted a few times as he experimented with the position of the rifle. At length he relaxed and said, "This is pretty good. You can hold steady with it."

"As a fellow told me, it'll make you better than you are. With a smaller-caliber rifle like yours, you can't expect to hit a deer just anywhere and knock it down. That's not a good way to hunt anyway. You want to hit your deer in the heart and lungs. That's right behind the front shoulder, a little more than halfway down. Don't shoot too far back, or you've got a gutshot mess to deal with, and sometimes the animal gets away.

Antelope are good for that. Seems like they're easier to gut-shoot, and they can run forever on three legs."

"I don't plan to shoot an antelope today."

"I know. But it all comes together to help you make a good shot. You concentrate, shoot at the right time, and don't flinch. Don't take a bad shot if you can keep yourself from doing it. Some fellas, they start shootin' at animals on the move, and then they're ruined for the rest of the day. Better to pass up a bad shot. There's always another animal and a fresh chance somewhere, even if it's not the same day."

The schoolteacher heaved a sigh. "That's quite a bit to think of all at once."

"It's not all that much if you concentrate. Just think about makin' a good shot. If he takes off running before you shoot, don't throw lead at him. Wait for another opportunity. A lot of these mule deer, if they start to trot away on you, will stop. Some of them look back. You follow and try to get things to come together. If you don't, like I say, at least you have the peace of mind to know that you didn't take a bad shot."

"All right. Let me practice this part again. Getting set."

"Sure. Go ahead. No one's in a hurry."

When Gresham was done with his practice, they mounted up and rode about another mile. They came to an area where larger draws ran not quite perpendicular to the pine ridge. It all looked like good deer country, with grass and cover.

Delaine shifted in the saddle and spoke. "Let's tie the horses again and hunt some of this on foot. I haven't seen any deer yet, but when we do, we want to be ready."

With Gresham holding the horses, Delaine

exchanged bridles for halters on the two saddle horses. He put the bridles in the panniers and tied each animal to a separate pine tree.

"Tie 'em up high," he said. "Four feet or a little higher, and not much slack, so the horse doesn't put a foot over the rope. These boys will just stand here and doze most of the time."

He put the sheath knife on his belt and pulled his rifle from the scabbard. Gresham stood ready to go as well, with his rifle in the crook of his arm and a small knapsack on his back. His short-brimmed hat shaded his eyes from the sun.

"Don't forget the stick."

"Oh, yes." Gresham pulled the bipod from the panniers. "Just carry it, then?"

"It'll be like a part of you."

They set off with the sun in their eyes, then shifted direction with the contours of the land. From time to time, Delaine waited to let Gresham practice getting down into position with his rifle and the shooting stick.

They crossed a couple of draws, and Delaine saw something that made him kneel. Gresham hunkered down next to him.

"What is it?"

"Looks like two does and two fawns." Delaine pointed to the south.

"I think so."

"Have you decided what you want to shoot at and what you don't?"

"I'd like something with antlers, but I don't expect a trophy."

"That's what we'll think of, then. It's part of being prepared, like we said."

"Uh-huh."

"Let's not spook these if we can help it. You never know if there's something else nearby."

They waited as the deer moved away from them, and they crossed over the next rise. They came to an area where the pine ridge tapered down and gave way to the grassy slopes. Delaine led the way to the edge of the small timber, where he thought their shapes would be absorbed by the tree growth.

"You can go first if you'd like," he said.

"I don't mind following. If you see something, just signal, and I'll come up beside you. As far as that goes, you're welcome to shoot first."

"I just brought my rifle to back you up. I don't care to get anything for myself today."

They moved on. Delaine's mind was adjusting to the lay of the land. Each time he came to a rise, he slowed so that his eyesight went over the crest little by little. Gresham followed his example.

At one little ridge, he saw something that caused him to draw back even as the image registered. A small group of deer was crossing the next rise. He signaled for Gresham to come up close.

"I just saw the last of a group go over. I don't like to chase deer, and we don't want to run up that next hill and be out of breath when we see them and want to take aim. We could go up into the trees and try to move around, but it might take too long, and some-times you find rough going when you get into the timber. So let's try this. Let's move ahead like we've been doing. We don't want to shoot into the sun, so if we come up on them with the sun in back of them, we may have to move down the slope and peek over again."

They set off with the land taking them in a southeast direction. They went down and up, slowed, and moved in a crouch as they approached the crest. Delaine saw shapes and sank back.

He whispered, "Let's move down the ridge a little. Try to get set for a good shot. If there's one with antlers, let him get in the clear so you don't hit something else."

Gresham nodded.

Delaine led the way for about two hundred yards along the grassy slope. He edged up to the crest again and dropped back. The whole little scene had registered in shapes he recognized. "It looks like five," he said. "One looks like he has horns, not real big. I could tell better if they were in full sun, but I think you can pick him out. He's in the middle, but they're not close together."

Side by side, they inched their way up, then lowered to their knees. They moved on their knees, in laborious motions, until the deer came into view. They settled back.

Delaine whispered, "Be as quiet as you can when you put a shell in the chamber. Hold the rifle down here, so the ridge will block the sound, then bring it up and around when you load it. Don't point it at me."

Gresham nodded and did as he was told. He brought the loaded gun around and settled it into the crossbuck. He shifted and shifted again. The deer grazed, taking a step at a time, so they were not always the same distances apart.

Delaine watched the deer. He did not want Gresham to feel himself being watched.

The rifle blasted, and Delaine flinched. At the same time, the deer with antlers contracted, drawing up an inch or so, and bolted. It moved on a dead run, with its head lowered, then turned as if it was trying to dig into the earth, and spilled over. The other deer scattered and were gone.

"He's down," said Delaine. "You made a good shot. Wait a minute, though. Sometimes they get back up."

Gresham let out a heavy breath. "Whoo. I didn't know if I hit him well enough at first. How far was that?"

"Between a hundred and a hundred and fifty yards. It looks like more when you're tryin' to get a bead."

"My mouth is dry."

"That'll do it. Let's go make sure of him."

They stood up, walked down the slope into the bottom of the draw, and angled up the other side. The body of the deer was in view, but the head was behind a clump of sagebrush.

Closer, Delaine saw the antlers. The deer had two points on one side and three on the other. It was an average-sized deer, neither large nor skimpy. "Not bad at all," he said.

Gresham stood looking over his deer. "This is good," he said. "Nothing went wrong." He looked at Delaine. "I suppose we have to clean it now."

"That's right. The hard mental part is over, and the physical work begins. If you want, I'll dress it."

The schoolteacher put his hand to his jaw. "I suppose so. I can watch and refresh my memory. I've helped before, but I haven't done it myself."

"I don't mind. We can decide first how we want to do it. I can gut him, and we can heft the whole thing onto the packhorse, but I don't think much of tyin' it on that way. It's hard to balance the load, and you carry back more weight than you need. Do you want the head?"

"Well, I don't know. I don't think I need more than the antlers."

"I can cut them out with my little saw. And we'll cut off the lower legs. How about the hide?"

Gresham drew a breath. "Again, I don't know. I don't like to see it go to waste, but I don't know how to tan one. If I wanted to keep it as a souvenir, I'd have to pay someone to tan it, and not to put too fine a point on it, I've already spent quite a bit of my resources, or will have, on the horses and gear."

"Well, here are the options. I can gut it and quarter it with the hide on. It's not my favorite way, because you get hair all over the meat, and it can give it a bad taste. And the hide goes to waste anyway, plus you have to skin the quarters when you get back. With the other way, I can skin it here on the ground first and then gut it. That's the cleanest. You get just about no hair on the meat, and you get the guts out in good time. Then you just take back the quarters of meat, half the carcass in each pannier, with your antlers tied on top."

"That sounds like an efficient way to do it."

"It's all work. You just do the hardest part first, which is skinning it on the ground. When it's clean, I can leave you to keep the magpies and coyotes away, and I'll go for the horses."

"I feel bad about having you do all the work."

Delaine smiled. "We'll get it done, and then you buy the beer."

"That's right."

It had been a while since he had skinned a deer bent over for an hour, getting at one awkward angle and another, but Gresham helped by tipping the body, and at last Delaine had the carcass free from the hide. Next came opening the abdomen, spilling out the entrails, and trimming the cavity clean. He had drying blood up to his elbows, and his back ached, but now he had the hard part done.

"I'll leave my rifle here," he said. "I should be back with the horses in about an hour."

"What about the antlers?"

"I'll quarter the meat first, while the saw is clean, and then I'll cut them out of the skull. My saw's in the panniers, anyway." Now that he thought of it, he had some more hard work ahead.

———

THE SUN WAS warm on his back when he reached the horses, and he was glad to have a drink of water from the canteen. He put the bridle on his horse, stowed the halter, untied the other two animals, and held the lead ropes as he mounted up.

———

GRESHAM WAS STANDING in a position to shade the dark-red carcass when Delaine returned to the site.

"No visitors?"

"Nothing at all."

Delaine handed him the lead ropes and slid from the saddle. "I've got nothing to tie these horses to, so I think you'll have to hold them while I split that carcass by myself. But I can do it."

He took out his folding saw and did his best to cut the backbone all the way down the middle. It was much easier to skin, clean, and split an animal if it was hanging, but it would have been a separate job, taking them into later in the day, to drag the deer with a horse, and even then, it might have been hard to find a pine tree big enough to hoist the deer in the clear. So he had decided to skin it on the ground to begin with, and now he was following through.

His back was stiff again as he finished with the carcass, cutting across each half to make quarters. He knelt by the head of the deer, still attached to the hide, and skinned the area around the base of the antlers so he would not have to saw through a hide that would slip back and forth. After another small struggle, he sawed through the skull plate and twisted the antlers free. He handed them to Gresham.

"Thank you. I'm feeling worse by the minute."

"Not all. I do have the hardest part done now. Just hold this packhorse still, and I'll get it loaded. I have to overlap the quarters a little on each side in order to get them in. That's why I cut 'em across."

As he went about his work, he kept the process in mind. Load the left side first with a hind quarter. Balance the load with one on the other side. Do the same with the next two quarters. Tie to the horse when possible, which was to the cinch rings, and not just to the wooden frame of the packsaddle. Tie everything tight to keep things from shifting.

Delaine took another drink from the canteen and put it away. He did not want to waste water by washing his arms. The palms of his hands were clean by now, from all of the other work.

He was summoning his strength and thinking of the ride back when Gresham spoke.

"Who's this?"

Delaine followed his line of sight to the north,

where three riders came angling down the slope. Delaine recognized them not quite in the same way that he picked out deer, but he knew them. The taller rider in the middle, dressed in brown with a reddish tint, was Cole Chamberlain. The other two, a matched pair in lighter colors, were the Dodge boys.

Delaine swallowed. "I'll talk to them," he said. He let Gresham continue holding the three horses as he stepped out into the clear and waited.

The riders did not hurry. Their horses approached at a walk, swishing their tails. Delaine had no doubt about who they were. Before long, they were close enough for him to determine that Earl was on his right and Cal was on his left.

Wisps of grass and small clouds of dust rose from the horses' hooves, and the riders drew to a stop. One horse snuffled.

Chamberlain's voice, not very deep or commanding, came out of the center of the group. "Where did you get that deer?"

The gutpile, hide, and plundered head were in plain view, and Delaine wondered where else they might have brought it down. "Right here," he said.

Earl's voice came up in a drawl and a sarcastic tone. "What makes you think you can go anywhere and shoot where you want?"

"I had the understanding that this was all open range."

"Some of it is," Earl answered. "But that's for cattlemen. It's not for any old person to do any old thing."

"I should have said public domain."

"You should have stayed home. People can't come out here and do as they damn well please. They can't come out here and cut hay, or open up a coal mine, or set up a factory."

"We're not doing any of those things. On public domain, people can hunt, camp, catch fish, or gather firewood if they want."

Cal spoke from the other side, in a voice just like his brother's. "Don't tell us what you think you can do out here, partner."

"I thought your place was quite a ways farther out."

"This is cattle country. Cattlemen look out for one another. So don't get smart with us." Cal smirked. "You ought to remember what happened the last time you smarted off."

"I remember someone pickin' a fight. I didn't have to do a damn thing."

"And you didn't. You just stood there and took it like a girl. Let's see what you do this time." Cal swung down from his horse, led it across in front of the boss, and handed the reins to his brother. With his hands now free, he tipped his hat back and swaggered up to within four feet of Delaine. "Did you hear what my brother said? About you havin' no business here?"

"I don't think he was correct."

Cal took on a menacing expression. "Are you calling my brother a liar? You, a two-bit day laborer? Huh?" He stepped forward, and his right fist came out of nowhere.

Delaine felt the force on the left side of his head, just below his temple, as his hat fell off. He went back a couple of steps, trying to keep his balance, as Cal stepped forward and hit him twice more. He landed on the ground on his hip and shoulder.

Cal stood over him with his fists at his sides. "Don't

try it, partner. Don't even think of it. The best thing you could do would be to go somewhere else." Cal kicked at the ground, but the grass was too good in that spot, and all he raised was a little spurt of dust.

He strode back to his brother, took his reins, and stabbed his foot in the stirrup as he sprang up into the saddle.

Earl was the last of the three to turn his horse. He looked down over his shoulder and said, "Don't come back."

Delaine found his feet and stood up. He had been conscious all along that Gresham stood by watching. He said, "Maybe we should have thrown the whole deer on and gotten out of here sooner, but it's not as if we're poachers or anything like that."

"It was obvious to me that they were just looking for a reason."

"I don't know why."

"I know who they are. They're bullies. From what I've heard, they look for fights."

"I wish they'd look somewhere else."

"Well, I'm sorry things went the way they did. I don't mean to make light of it, but it could have been worse." Gresham looked at the sky. "We'll get back to town before dark, and I'll make good on my word to buy the beer."

11

———

On the way into town, Delaine asked Gresham what he planned to do with the meat.

The schoolteacher said, "I'd like to offer you any amount you'd like."

"I don't know that I could use any. Even if we could cook where we live, there's only so much I could eat before it spoiled. And we don't have a place to make jerky."

"I've thought about all that, of course. I know of a family in town, one of my pupils. They have the shoe repair business, and they don't take in a great deal of money. The father does other leather and canvas repair, but he tries not to step on the business of the saddle and harness man at the other end of town. The mother does sewing. They raise a few chickens and sell eggs. They can use the meat. The father told me he would make as much jerky as I would like, as well as for you. I believe he has a grinder and knows how to make sausage, so I don't think anything will go to waste."

"That's good to know."

"So I think we can go by their house and leave off the meat before we take the horses back." After a minute, he added, "In another year, if I set up house-keeping in my own place, I can learn to manage the meat. This year, I'm learning about the first two parts, going after the animal and taking care of it in the field."

"Then you're not doing this for sport."

"No, that's for other people. When you grow up having to meet your basic needs, you don't change much. At least, I haven't. Even if I were more affluent, I don't think I could go out and shoot for sport."

"There's money in it for people like guides and outfitters."

"Oh, yes. There's a clientele." Gresham looked behind him and said, "There are people you meet who say, 'Everything's for sale.' Now that's a view of life that goes along with others that seem almost foreign to me. When I say foreign, I mean a different kind of person, not just a different nationality."

"I follow you."

"It's like people who say that life is competition. I've always had enough to do to try to manage circum-stances, and I'm not interested in trying to take some-thing from someone else."

"Same here."

"Well, enough of that. If I get too wound up, I'll forget to enjoy the scenery."

"And now's the time to do it. These sunny days are bound to change."

———

DELAINE'S WORDS came back to him at work the next day when a cold wind brought in a cloud cover and flung grains of dirt in his eyes. The crowbar was cold as he pried planks from a post that he and Benny had to take out. The temperature did not warm up through the middle of the day, and not many people stirred on the main thoroughfare.

At about three in the afternoon, Paul Hensley came by. He had his head bent down so that his dull, dark hat blocked some of the wind. His horse had its head turned at a similar angle. Hensley's spurs sounded as he stepped down from the saddle and stood in the lee of his horse.

"Thought I'd stop and see if you're interested in what we talked about last time."

"About—?"

"Thought I might take you to look at somethin'."

"I could. I don't know if this weather is going to get any better by the end of the day."

"This evening's no good anyway. Tomorrow would be."

"We could try that."

As usual, Hensley did not pay any attention to Benny. In a low, almost mumbling voice, he said, "Let's meet somewhere else, and maybe a little earlier. Say at six. North side of town. By the schoolhouse. There's no one there at that time."

"I know where it is. I can be there."

"See you then." Hensley turned his horse away from the wind and climbed on. He seemed sluggish in his movements, as if he had two more layers of clothing underneath.

———

BENNY WAS DIGGING with the iron bar when Deputy Erskine made his appearance half an hour later. Delaine thought Hensley would be glad to know he left when he did.

The deputy had his herringbone coat fastened all the way up with its leather buttons, and he wore lined leather gloves, which he patted together before he spoke. He stood with his hands in his coat pockets and his back to the wind.

"I said before that I didn't like to bother a man at work, but I thought I'd catch the two of you at once."

"It's all right with me," said Delaine. He deferred to Benny, who nodded.

The deputy summoned a breath and kept his dark eyes on the two workmen. "What I came for today is to ask you about the man who was found dead in his hotel room. Name of Jerome Richards. I have been given to understand that he might have come by here and talked to you two."

"He did," said Delaine. "He told us that was his name."

"And did he tell you…the nature of his business or rather the reason for his being here?"

Delaine glanced at Benny to let him speak.

"Go ahead," said Benny.

"He said he was looking for a girl who had disappeared in eastern Colorado. He didn't give a town or a locality."

The deputy nodded. "Anything more?"

"He showed us a picture, a photograph of not very high quality, of a blonde girl. I believe he said she was seventeen years old."

"What else?"

Delaine felt himself becoming impatient with the

deputy, who wouldn't let him speak at his own pace. "He gave us her name. As I recall, it was Evelina Ralston." Delaine looked at Benny. "I don't remember anything more than that, except that her parents were worried sick."

Benny said, "That was it."

"Did he tell you not to tell anyone?"

"Not in so many words," Delaine said. "But he implied that he would rather we didn't. He said it was a risk to tell people things but he had to if he was going to get anywhere."

The deputy kept his clear-eyed gaze. "Did he say anything more about the girl or the nature of his mission, such as where he planned to look?"

Delaine shook his head. "No, it was just the basic information."

The deputy sniffed. "It's the same as I've heard from everyone else."

Delaine shrugged.

"It's to be speculated that he would have told someone more than that."

"Well, he didn't here. Sometimes I wonder why he told people as much as he did."

The deputy's chest went up and down as he kept his hands in his pockets, and he breathed out through his nose. "I don't think I have any more questions at this time. If you think of anything else, if you remember something, be sure to let me know."

"We will."

"Very well. Thanks for this." The deputy patted his gloved hands together, then put his hands in his coat pockets again as he turned and walked away.

When he had crossed the street, Delaine said to

Benny, "That's the way he's been every time he's talked to me. For all I know, he may be effective."

Benny shrugged.

"I asked him about the case you mentioned, about the girl from town here who disappeared."

"Nora."

"Yes. He said it happened before his time here, but there was no strong evidence that a crime had been committed."

"That's what they all said."

"I saw him coming out of the newsstand, though, the same day they found Richards in his room."

"Oh, he likes Marian."

Delaine sank. "No wonder. I couldn't make the connection. Now that I think of it, he didn't seem to appreciate the schoolteacher."

Benny laughed.

"You'd think he would have taken an interest in helping her find out about her sister, but maybe he accepts it as a lost cause."

"I think so. He's like everyone else in that way."

Delaine and Benny did not talk much more until quitting time. As they were putting their tools away, Benny spoke.

"I don't know if you want to, or if you have time, but the people in my family are having a little party for my cousin. It is her saint's day. There will be food, and a cake, and people to talk to if you want."

Delaine brightened at the idea. "I don't have anything to do, except go back to my room and eat a cold meal. So your invitation sounds good to me. If you give me a time, and directions how to get there, I'll be glad to go."

"You can just go with me right now."

"Are you sure?"

"Yes. When it's for little kids, they do these things early. And everyone has to work tomorrow, so it won't go late."

Delaine had not sweated in the cold wind, but he felt as if he had a film of dust on him. "Let me rinse my hands and face at the pump, then." After a thought, he said, "Should we stop and get some candy for this little girl?"

"She's going to have plenty. We can just go straight there."

Benny took them to the first cross street and then north for two blocks. The house was near the edge of town and not far from the house where Delaine and Gresham had left the deer meat the day before.

The house had been a small one to begin with, but it had been added onto in a couple of places, so it consisted of various rooms, including one long room with tables and chairs. People were already gathered, and conversation flowed in Spanish. Benny introduced Delaine to a series of people who all spoke English.

The house belonged to a couple older than Delaine. Benny introduced the woman as his aunt, who was the grandmother of the little girl. There were other cousins, aunts, and uncles, and Delaine renewed his familiarity with Mexican families, in which generations overlapped in age, and distinctions were not made right away between aunts and great-aunts, cousins and second cousins.

Delaine was given a plate and a spoon, and one of Benny's aunts showed him to a serving table, where another smiling woman served him beans and a portion of cut-up beef and red chile. All of the younger people were standing up to eat, so he found an area of floor space out of the way, and he ate as the others did.

He bided his time until he saw where people were putting their plates and utensils. He had not been idle for long when the cake was brought out, accompanied by a large metal punch bowl and a ladle.

Benny appeared by his side and said, "Be sure to get some cake."

"I'll wait."

"No. You can't wait too long. You know, the women have an order for serving things. The older people first, and the men. Then the children, and then the women who are serving."

"Oh, yes. I remember." Delaine took his place in line for cake and punch.

The gathering became more fluid when everyone had eaten and a couple of the tables had been taken away. A woman offered Delaine a warm glass of punch with brandy, and he accepted. Having heard Spanish all around him, and hearing this woman speak in uncertain English, he did not hesitate to answer and thank her in Spanish.

"*¿Ah, usted habla español?*" asked the woman. Oh, do you speak Spanish? She was about sixty, smiling and hospitable, and she seemed to be pleased to address him in her language.

"*Un poco,*" he said. A little.

"That's good," she said, still in Spanish. "To be able to speak two languages. Where did you learn?"

"In New Mexico. I worked with many people there, and I enjoyed learning to speak."

"How nice. And you are here in town?"

"Yes. I work with Benny."

"Oh, yes. Benny. He is a good worker."

"He invited me."

"That is proper."

"And you are…"

"We are all friends. His family and mine."

"And you live here in town."

"Yes. I work at the laundry."

It had been a while since Delaine had heard the word *lavandería,* but an image came up right away. He remembered the business with the sign and the picture of an iron with its goose-necked handle. "Oh, yes. The iron like a goose." The words came to him, *plancha* for iron and *ganso* for goose.

"Like a goose."

"Yes. Sometimes they call the iron a goose. The man who makes suits."

"*El sastre.*"

"Is that the word? I didn't know it." He realized he had been showing off the words he did know, and he came up short. Still in Spanish, he said, "And so you work at the laundry."

"Yes, at your service there."

"Thank you."

"Very well. Excuse me." The woman went on to serve warm punch to others.

A familiar voice at his elbow said, "I didn't know you spoke Spanish."

He turned to meet Rachel's smiling eyes and bronze complexion. "Well, good evening. How good to see you here."

"And you. So, tell me. Where did you learn Spanish?"

"In New Mexico."

"Oh, yes. You told me you lived there. And worked there. Your accent is not too bad."

"Thank you. I try not to say *carny* and *kameeduh*."

She laughed.

"It didn't occur to me that I might see you here," he said.

"Things didn't work out with the family I was helping, but we still get along. And I know the other families, of course."

"Benny invited me."

"I thought so. I saw him talking to you."

After a second, he said, "Well, it's good to see you."

"Oh, yes. I was wondering if I was going to have to ask someone to walk me home. After these things that have happened, no one wants to walk alone after dark. Not a woman, anyway. She shouldn't."

"I'll be glad to. Just let me know when you want to leave."

"In a little while. I don't want to be the first one to leave, but as you know, I don't stay out late. And this is not a wedding, where people are going to dance all night." She was quiet for a moment. "And you? How have you been?"

"Well enough. I went out with the schoolteacher yesterday, and I helped him with a deer."

"That's good."

"Quite a bit of work, as it turned out, but sometimes things go that way."

"And the meat?"

"He knows a family that can use it, and they're going to make jerky for him. Neither of us can cook where we live, of course."

"I didn't think so."

"And yourself?"

"Everything as usual. Work goes on." She glanced

away. "Excuse me. They're going to sing to the little girl. You can listen if you want. Or sing."

He walked with her to a part of the room where people were gathering around a beaming girl about ten years old. The crowd settled, and the people began to sing. The song sounded very much like the birthday song, *Las Mañanitas*, but he caught the words *"el día de tu santo,"* the day of your saint. When the song was finished, Delaine asked Rachel which saint it was.

"*Santa Leticia*," she said.

"So that's her name, Leticia?"

"Yes."

"And what day is yours?"

"November 1. *Santa Raquel.* What would be yours?"

"Oh. My name, Jess or Jesse, translates to *Jesús*. You know, in English, people don't name their babies after Jesus. Not that I know of. Not like in Spanish."

She smiled. "We can give you San Juan, June 24. Everyone knows that saint's day. It is in songs." When he did not answer, she said, "That was just a joke. I don't want to change your name. But it is like a joke in Spanish. You know, in some places, there are still many people who don't read or write. A couple has a baby, and they take it to the *registro civil*, like the county clerk, and they say they want to name him *Víctor*. The clerk says, 'Is that with a *B* or a *V*?' They say, 'Then we'll call him *Héctor*.' The clerk says, 'Is that with an *H* or without an *H*?' They say, 'Well, then, let's call him Carlos.'" After a pause, she said, "Well, it's better in Spanish. There aren't as many spelling errors as in English, but there are a few."

"I see."

"And the clerk didn't know, either."

"Oh. That *is* funny."

"It's terrible to have to explain a joke, isn't it?"

"That was just because it came from Spanish, and it depends on spelling, so I didn't get it right away. If there was an equivalent joke in English—well, there are plenty of people in English who aren't very good with the alphabet, also."

"Here's Benny. What do you think of leaving pretty soon?"

"It would be all right with me."

They took leave of Benny and of the people who hosted the party. Rachel wished the little girl a happy saint's day once again, and they walked into the chilly night.

"The weather is changing," he said. "You can't quite smell snow yet, but it's not far away."

Rachel drew her coat close. "There is always good in snow. Like rain, if it's not too much at once."

Delaine thought of his meeting the next evening with Hensley, and he wondered if there would be snow on the ground.

Rachel spoke. "Have you heard any more about these things that have happened? I didn't want to talk about it very much at the party. Everybody there is aware of it, too, of course, but it wasn't the right time."

"I can't say that I've heard much more. The deputy came by the corrals and asked Benny and me some questions, but he didn't tell us anything." Delaine reflected on his conversations with Hensley, which tended to be vague and roundabout. One aspect that was more definite, the purported affair between Caswell and Mrs. Goodwin, seemed like something he should mention later if at all.

Delaine walked along, looking ahead in the dark. The outer world seemed distant enough that he thought he could tell her of one aspect that he would rather mention now than in Mrs. Vanderhoven's parlor.

"There's one thing that has happened, not something that I've heard, that I could tell you about, though I don't have a good explanation for it."

"Go ahead."

"There's a couple of fellas by the name of Dodge, brothers, who seem to like to pick fights."

"Oh, yes. I know who they are."

"One night when I was in the White Mule Saloon for just one drink, one of them went out of his way, it seemed to me, to bump into me and start a fight. I didn't want to go along with it, but we went outside, and he knocked me down. He didn't do anything worse, and I was just trying not to get hurt. I thought that if I got into it too far, I might have both of them jump in, so I let things be. But he hit me pretty good."

"Sometimes it's better that way, not to make things worse."

"Then it happened again. After the schoolteacher and I had his deer all cleaned and packed and ready to go, and I was good and tired, the two of them showed up on horseback with their boss. This time, the other brother took the lead, after they picked an argument about us hunting out on the public domain. He got off his horse, came right up to me, and knocked me down like his brother did. Both times, they seemed satisfied with that much and walked away."

"They do things like that. They have a reputation for picking fights."

"I know. But I don't know why they pick on me. Maybe I'm nothing special. But this second time, the one named Earl told me I'd be better off if I just left. So I don't know if they're trying to run me off, or if so, why. But I've had enough of being pushed around."

"I don't know."

"The only thing I can think of is that they have me identified as a friend of Tom Caswell, and they may have some grudge against him. Both the deputy and George Mace have me identified the same way." Delaine chose not to mention that Hensley treated him as an ally as well. He did not know if she knew who Hensley was, and again, he preferred not to bring Hensley into the conversation yet.

"They may not need that much of a reason."

"I know. But I also know that they might try something again. If they do, I'll do what I have to. I can't just let them knock me down and walk away every time."

"You're right. You have to stick up for yourself. Those two are like roosters. They think too much of themselves."

"I would rather they leave me alone."

"It would be better. But as we say in Spanish, they put stones in your road. We have another saying. He throws the stone and hides his hand. They don't do that."

Delaine laughed. "No, they don't. They're a lot more outward about it."

They came to a street crossing, and he gave her his arm. She did not let go when they reached the next block, so they walked along in unison.

"Do you know this fellow named Goodwin?" he asked.

"I know who he is."

"I don't suppose he comes into the café very much, as he has his own business."

"He doesn't come in at all. He and his friends keep their company at his place."

"How about George Mace?"

"He doesn't come in much. They say he is saving his money for a wife."

"Good for him."

"You think that's a good thing to do?"

"As long as he doesn't have his eye on you."

She tugged at his arm. "Of course he doesn't."

He walked her to her doorstep, and they drew apart. "Please don't feel that you should ask me in," he said. "I think it's late enough to say good night here."

She turned to face him. "Very well. Thank you for walking me home." She leaned toward him and kissed him on the cheek.

He felt himself glow. "It was a privilege."

He waited until she went inside. He heard the door lock as he turned and walked away.

The thought had been at the edge of his mind that he had not stopped in to check on his horse that day, as he had gone with Benny straight from work. He felt he should go by the stable on his way home. In order not to walk past the saloon, he went east on Green Street until he came to the main street leading north out of town, Center Street. He turned right and walked two blocks south to the main intersection. He crossed over east to the bank and angled across the main street to the stable.

A lantern hung from a rafter inside, and Hiram Fitts stood in the doorway of the harness room.

"Just came to look at my horse," Delaine said.

Fitts nodded.

Delaine crossed through the area of stanchions and stalls and went out to the pens. He left the door open to let the soft light fall outside. His horse was in a pen with three others, and the animal came to him without his having to speak. He reached across the rail and patted the horse on the neck.

Movement from inside the stable caught his eye, and he moved out of the faint light to a spot where he could still see what he thought he saw at first glance.

The slender man in the dull-black hat, grey jacket, grey pants, and black boots, the one he had come to understand was the rough customer, was talking to Fitts. Delaine could not hear words. He waited for a long minute until the man left.

Delaine walked into the lit area of the stable.

"Everything all right?" Fitts asked.

"Oh, yeah." Delaine lingered for a moment. "A small thing," he said, "but could you tell me the name of the fellow who was in here a minute ago?"

Fitts glanced at the door and said, in a low voice, "Mull."

"Is that his last name?"

"It's all that anyone calls him."

"Thanks. No need to mention it. I wouldn't want anyone to think I'm that curious."

"Think nothin' of it." Fitts tucked back the corners of his mouth in a closed smile.

"Thanks again for your help yesterday."

"I was glad he got his deer."

———

DELAINE WAS PLEASED to be able to think about Rachel through the day as he worked. It was better than thinking about recent events and missing people. As the day wore on, however, and he began to anticipate his meeting with Hensley, a sense of dread crept into him. It was the same old feeling of not wanting to become too familiar with an element he wanted to keep at a distance, combined with an interest in knowing things that would help him be careful about where to step but that, at the same time, he might wish he didn't know.

At the end of the day, he checked on his horse and went home to eat a cold meal. Hensley in his usual way had not specified whether they would go somewhere on foot or on horseback, and clouds had been gathering all day, so Delaine decided to leave his horse at the stable and to go for it on short notice if he needed it.

He walked north on Center Street, crossing Elm Street and then Green Street. The school was ahead on his left, and not far beyond it, the street became the main trail north out of town.

Snow was beginning to fall, and he hoped Hensley did not have a long excursion in mind. In the short while since he had left the center of town, the tiny, mist-like flakes had given way to larger ones that melted on his face and tongue.

The night was dark, but light was moving around on the other side of the schoolhouse. Delaine did not expect Hensley to make his presence visible, but maybe he had brought something to show. Delaine could not imagine what it would be. When he tried to imagine something unexpected, he came up with a donkey or a child in clothes too big for him—something improbable but not out of this little world.

Past the schoolhouse, Delaine walked onto a scene where more than one man stood. Three of them. One was holding a lantern.

Delaine stopped, and he heard his foot on the ground. So did one of the men, who turned and said, "Who's there?"

It was Deputy Erskine's voice.

"It's me, Delaine."

"Come over here, if you would. I'm Deputy Erskine of the Laramie County Sheriff's Office."

Delaine swallowed hard and did as he was asked. The three men were standing around a shape on the ground. The deputy was wearing his hat, gloves, and wool coat. The other two men were dressed in the hats, overcoats, and everyday suits such as were common with the owners of businesses in town.

The shape on the ground was the body of a man, face down. He wore a denim coat, and a dark hat lay on the ground nearby.

The deputy said, "I had a report that there was a lurker here, and not long after that, that there was a body. So I asked these men to come with me. What are you doing here?"

"I was out on a walk, and I saw your light."

"Why would you be walking out here?"

"Sometimes I walk this way because there's a person I know on Green Street?"

"Not this one?" The deputy pointed at the body.

"No, I don't know where he lives. The person I visit is a woman."

"Do you know him?"

"It looks like a man I know named Paul Hensley."

"That's who it is. A friend of Tom Caswell. I never got a chance to talk to him. They're both in the same place now." The deputy looked at the sky. "I don't like this snow. If it had fallen earlier, it would have given us tracks. Now it looks as if it's going to cover things up."

12
____

Snow was falling when Delaine went to work in the morning. About six inches had accumulated. Tracks at the office door showed where Al Portman had gone in, and the door opened as Delaine approached.

Al had his hands in the pockets of a long, ash-colored wool coat. His light-brown eyes were steady as he said, "I think you can take a day off until this lets up. It stopped once in the middle of the night and then started again, so I don't think we're in for a long storm. But it's easy to be wrong."

"I'll see you tomorrow, then."

"Sure. Take it easy. Get caught up on your letter-writing."

"I might." Delaine took it to mean that he should not spend the day in a saloon. He put his gloved hands in his coat pockets and followed his own tracks toward the center of town. Sound did not travel much when snow was falling, so the morning was quiet.

In his room, he set his war bag on the bed and

went through it to see if he had anything to mend. This kind of weather was good for tasks like sewing on a button or stitching a rip. In the bottom of the bag, he found something he had almost forgotten about, the lower legs of a pair of denim trousers he had worn out. He had cut off the bottom fourteen inches or so because the cloth was not worn much at all and the hems were good. By sewing across the cut end of each, he would have a couple of small bags for items like his folding saw and sheath knife, so that they would not rub against one another. He turned the two lengths inside out, threaded a needle with a double-double strand, and went to work.

He took his time, trying to keep a straight stitch. As he worked, he had plenty to think about, and his thoughts went from one topic to another. They were like strands of a rope that had been taken apart and sat each one by itself in a crooked little heap. The death of Tom Caswell had been there almost from the beginning. Then came the case of Richards and the missing girl, Evelina, which was a strand in itself but might be separated again, as one of the principals was dead and the other might still be alive. And there was the death of Paul Hensley, whose body had still been warm enough to melt the first flakes of snow. Delaine had no doubt that Caswell's end and Hensley's were related. A hunch told him that Richards's death might be related, but the caution of logic told him not to make any assumptions.

Another thought rose, like a piece of something boiling in a pot—like a piece of swollen bacon rind or even like a puffy garment in a laundry cauldron. Nora. It seemed as if, all along, there might be some connection between what happened to her and what happened to one or more of the others, who were men, except Evelina. Delaine had seen a picture of the blonde girl, but he did not have much feeling for her. He did for Nora. He had talked to people who knew her and to people who didn't but thought her case still mattered. And he had observed what had seemed like a re-embodiment of her in her sister. He admitted to himself that he might be sentimental and a fool for women, but he knew that Nora mattered to him at least as much as any of the deceased people he had known in the town. The thought of Nora, more than anything, made him feel as if he should do something. Or so it seemed. At the same time that he felt sentimental, he had tinges of resentment. As he let his feelings flow, actual anger welled up.

He told himself he had to keep his thoughts clear. He couldn't let the bullying of the Dodge boys agitate him. He had to keep things separate.

The shining point of the needle came pushing through the lighter-colored underside of the denim. He pulled the needle through, drew the thread, and pushed the needle in for the next pass. What he needed to do was to think things through and make no assumptions. Any of these aspects could be related, and any one or more of them could be unrelated. But at the two ends, or outer edges, Nora and the Dodge boys, he had to leave the possibilities open. Caswell and Hensley had both seemed uncomfortable around the Dodge boys—or, rather, it might have been Mull. The needle stopped. Of course Mull. He was the rough customer.

Delaine worked on with the stitching. He had to sort things out, take things in order. They were all in a jumble. He had to start at one end, or, as it seemed, the bottom. Start at the beginning and work up to the top, the present, where people were still walking around.

———

ONLY A LIGHT SNOW was falling as he walked to the laundry and the sign of the goose, as he had once heard the phrase. The windows were fogged up, but the inside did not feel humid when he walked in. A lamp overhead shed light on the woman he had met at the party, who was standing at an ironing board about four feet from a cast-iron stove, where one of two goose-necked irons was heating. The other was in the woman's hand. Tiny wisps of steam arose from the white shirt she was ironing.

She looked up and said, in an automatic tone, "Gude morning."

"*Buenos días,*" he answered.

"*Ah, buenos días.*" Still in Spanish, she said, "How good to see you again."

"Likewise. This is a good day to be working inside, near a fire." He used the word *lumbre* for fire, hoping it was the best of the three words he knew.

"Oh, yes. Did you bring something to wash? Or to iron?"

"Some work clothes." He took the bundle from under his arm.

"You can put them in the basket there," she said, pointing at a hamper on the end of the counter. "And write your name on the paper."

He used the pencil to write his name on the top slip of paper.

"And how do you find yourself today?" asked the woman as she continued ironing.

"Very well. There is no work today. So I am doing little things."

"One needs to have clean clothes, even for work."

"It is true. It appears to me that you like your work."

"Oh, yes. To help the people."

Delaine saw a man in the work area in back. He wore light tan clothes like a uniform, and he had thinning hair and a pair of spectacles. Delaine imagined he was the proprietor and was used to hearing the woman talk in another language, for he paid no attention.

"You have worked her for a while?" Delaine asked.

"Some years. Seven. I am going to complete eight."

"That is good." Delaine paused. "I imagine you know the girl who used to work here. Benny talks about her at work."

"Oh, yes. Nora. Poor girl, she was not that bad. A good worker."

"But she had difficulties."

"She did not earn much money, and she lived alone until her sister came."

"It is difficult," he said, using another easy generality he knew. "And that was how she fell into friendships with working men."

The woman sighed. "I think so. It is not a good thing to do, but who can say what the life of another is like."

"I have become interested in her story. Because of what Benny has said, and I have met her sister, who seems to be very sad for her."

"Oh, yes, it is a sad thing to lose a sister."

"When she was working here, did men come to see her?"

The woman gave a light shrug and met Delaine's eyes as if in understanding that he was not just making small talk. "Sometimes. As if they were in love. But she told them not to come here."

Delaine hesitated, then went ahead. "Did she ever seem to have business relations with any men other than…the clients?" He knew that the word *cliente* meant customer.

The woman's eyes went to the work area in back, and she lowered her voice even though she continued to speak in Spanish. "There was a man, and I think he managed that business. He came and went when he did not have any clothes to wash."

"I understand."

"Yet it was not the strangest thing, for he goes into most of the businesses in town and is very *metiche*."

"*¿Metiche?*"

The woman touched her nose, and still speaking in Spanish, she said, "Always wants to know things, always looking for gossip."

"Oh. It is possible that I know who that is."

"I think they call him in English *Sombrerito*." Little Hat.

"Perhaps his last name begins with an *H*." Remembering Rachel's joke, he said, "The *H* is pronounced in English."

"That is how he writes it." She glanced at the pencil and paper.

"A little bit disagreeable."

"Some things."

He raised his voice a little as he said, still in Spanish, "Thank you very much. A pleasure to speak with you."

"*Igualmente. Que le vaya bien.*" Likewise. May it go well for you.

———

DELAINE OFFERED to share a growler that evening with Gresham, who had no objection.

"I'll go down to The Three Hermits and get it," said Delaine.

The snow had stopped falling, and footprints were abundant. Some of them were muddy.

Inside, Delaine saw a man standing at the bar. As his eyes adjusted to the dim light, he recognized the heavy build, ruddy face, and sullen expression of the proprietor of The Knight's Table. He and the bartender, Butch, had quit talking when Delaine walked in, and they had the air about them of having been talking about something they did not want to share.

"I'd like a bucket of beer," Delaine said.

"Comin' up." Butch reached down for a pail, turned and filled it, and set it on the bar. As he settled the lid in place, he said, "Twenty-five cents."

Delaine put a quarter on the bar. "Thanks."

"Thanks to you."

Delaine exchanged a nod with Goodwin and left with the beer.

In the schoolteacher's room, Delaine mentioned the person he had seen in the tavern. "I didn't expect to see him there, although I don't know who I would expect."

"Neither do I, but I think he goes in there, out of

the public eye, to have one or two while his employees are cleaning up. Then he goes home."

Delaine recalled Hensley's comment, and though he was tempted to repeat it, he reminded himself that he did not know the truth even though Mrs. Goodwin's response seemed to confirm it. "I had the occasion to drop off some clothes at the laundry today," he said.

"Oh," said Gresham.

"I happened to have met the woman who works there. At a little party with the Mexican people. I fell into a conversation with her, and it seems that she knew Nora."

"Oh, yes. She's worked there for a few years or more."

"She says that Herbert is a big gossip."

"I believe he is. I've heard it from more than one person, though I've had very little to do with him myself. Which I don't mind."

"She said he used to come by the laundry when Nora worked there."

"I don't doubt it."

Delaine thought about how much he wanted to repeat. "I don't suppose it would be a good risk to ask him what he knows."

"No, I wouldn't trust him."

Delaine thought that if he were to share with Gresham what he thought Herbert had been, he would use the word "procurer," but he also thought it might seem intrusive. He did not feel that he had a right to speak on his own about what Nora did. "I still think somebody ought to be able to find out something about her."

"Maybe so," said Gresham, "but I've become more pessimistic. With the passing of time, I've accepted the probability that no one is going to find Nora alive. I feel guilty for saying it, but I think it's realistic." The schoolteacher had a wistful expression on his face. "It seems as if Marian has passed her up, as if Nora is just a lost person who is yet to have her elegy. Sorry. Another mournful idea, perhaps."

"Not at all. It still seems wrong that no one has done anything, or very little. The deputy, for example, seems to brush it off as something that happened long ago and that nobody had a good case for pursuing."

"That seems to be the way. He doesn't seem to feel responsible for anything that happened before he came here. And to tell you the truth, I think he's afraid of it because he doesn't want to talk about it with Marian, because of the delicate aspect, and because he doesn't want to try and then fail. He likes Marian. I don't know if you know that."

"I think I had gathered that impression."

"At any rate, I think that if anyone wanted to know anything, he'd have to go in another direction."

Delaine said, "I think there's gossip to be had, if a person could put it together. Asking Herbert could spoil it. Who else knows all the back-alley gossip?" A light seemed to go on in Delaine's mind as he said it. "What about this grubby old fellow who goes by the name of Pinky?"

"He's back-alley, all right. In a literal sense. He goes in and out of the back doors of businesses to collect scraps for his hogs."

"I've heard that. And from what I've seen of him, he's quite a busybody as well."

"He is. Sometimes he's brazen about it. But you never know. He might tell you what he wants to divulge, but he might hold back on things you want to know about. You do seem interested in this case."

"It's touched me in a small way, and I think it may be related to one or more of the other things that have happened of late. In the middle of these three deaths in town, there's a story of another missing girl. And for all I know, one of those things might be connected with the Dodge brothers' going out of their way to pick on me."

"What do you think the connection is there?"

"I can't say for sure, but I think either they or someone they know had it in for Caswell and maybe his friend Hensley, and at least in an outward way, they were both friends or friend-like with me. Hensley would stop and talk to me for a minute at work, and with the land office across the street, Herbert may have seen it and passed it on. This stuff goes back and forth until I get dizzy."

"You don't want that. They'll take your beer away from you."

"Hah. What I want is to know more. I want to know why in the hell these cock-of-the-walk cowpunchers want to push me around. That makes me mad. And I want to know why some of those other things happened. I don't think I would risk much by sounding out Pinky."

"Not if you were careful. Being a bearer of gifts might help."

Delaine frowned.

"A pint of whiskey or something like that. A universal language."

"That's an idea. Do you know where he lives?"

"Yes, I do. It's not very far from the place where we took the deer meat the other day. Just keep going north and turn right on the last street. He lives in a place on the left, by itself. If you know what hog sheds look like, you can't miss it."

Delaine nodded. "I think I'll give it a try."

———

THE SNOWFALL HAD LET UP, so Delaine and Benny scraped snow away from the places where they had to dig and pile the dirt. They took care not to lose any nails. On a couple of occasions, they followed the spot where a bent nail left its shape in the snow. Delaine fancied that it was alike a body falling off a barn, in miniature.

In the time since he had come to this town, the days had shortened by about half an hour in the evening, so dusk was drawing in by the time he checked on his horse and bought a pint of whiskey. The sky was overcast, and the snow was trampled on both sides of all of the streets until he reached the edge of town where he looked for the dark shapes of hog sheds. He followed two sets of tracks that appeared to have come and gone a couple of times. In the fading light, he could not tell if the marks came from light wagon wheels and a horse, but he doubted that Pinky collected the food scraps on foot and carried them this far. He followed the tracks into the yard where the odor of hogs hung in the air.

No light showed in the house or in the low barn. The three hog sheds and what looked like an abandoned chicken house were also dark. Delaine was walking back onto the street when he saw a horse and a cart approaching.

Pinky sat on a small seat atop the cart. He spoke to

the horse and stopped it. "Well, it's you, my young friend. What brings you to the hallowed halls of Hobbes Hollow?"

"Curiosity."

"To see how the philosophers live?"

"I wasn't thinking of that."

"Hobbes was a philosopher. He said life was nasty, brutish, and short."

"I thought it might have been your last name."

"It is, but we are related only in our beliefs. Let me take this cart into the yard, and we'll see what spur has been pricking your side. Ha-ha."

Delaine followed the cart to the spot where Pinky stopped the horse and climbed down.

"We can leave the vittles here for a few minutes. Let us go into my carriage house." Pinky led the way into the small barn and lit a lantern. The interior was cluttered with a broken-down wagon, scrap lumber, and odds and ends of scrap tin and iron.

"I brought you this," said Delaine. He handed him the unwrapped bottle.

"Oh, that's like candy for a baby." Pinky took the bottle and admired it in the light, then slipped it into the pocket of his coarse woolen overcoat. "It looks like a bribe, but I'll take it as a token of friendship, for which my thanks." He looked Delaine up and down and said, "What's on your mind, that you're willin' to throw your money away like this?"

"The same thing as anyone else in town."

"People I know have two things on their mind. Whiskey and women."

"Close."

"Well, I'll let you ask the questions."

Delaine took a breath as he thought of how to

frame his words. "You seem to know as much as anyone else in this town, and more than most."

"You seem to think I'm a fool, if you're trying to butter me up that way."

"Then I'll be more direct. I'm tired of being pushed around by a couple of parties, and I want to know what the hell's going on in this town."

"Oh, that's a tall order."

"Let me scale it down. There's a fellow who has a land office."

"The one they call Little Hat?"

"The only land office in town, I think."

"We both know his name, so go on."

"I'd like to know what else he does in addition to helping people buy, sell, and locate land."

Pinky raised his eyebrows. "Well, he buys and sells other things. Horses and wagons and the like. He'll buy something when someone's up against it and needs the money, things that are portable, and then he'll sell 'em for a good profit. As you would expect."

"What else?"

Pinky shrugged. "He may buy cattle. I don't know. I don't think he buys grain or other warehouse goods."

Delaine recalled hearing that Herbert might have bought and sold beans, but he decided it didn't matter. "I'd like to know what else he trades in."

"I'd like to know what you're getting at."

"Then I'll be more direct again. I'd like to know what he had to do with the girl who disappeared a couple of years ago. The girl who worked at the laundry."

"Oh-h-h. She worked at the laundry, but she did tricks on the side."

"I've heard that."

"She was a crib girl. He had the crib."

"Then he should have had an interest in her well-being."

"Like the goose that laid the golden egg. Sittin' on a pot of gold."

"So he's a kind of middle man."

"I'd say so. He's a busybody."

Delaine let the comment pass. "Did he ever get in the middle of other dealings, do you think?"

"Such as what?"

"To borrow a phrase from Deputy Erskine, the transfer of cattle."

"I don't know. He may have set up a deal here or there, but he wouldn't ever get his hands dirty handling the stock himself. He's not much of a buckaroo."

"I wouldn't think so." Delaine hesitated and went on. "He's friends with a fellow that some people would all a rough customer, isn't he?"

Pinky held his mouth in a closed circle for a few seconds. "They're friends, all right, but I wouldn't venture to say what-all they've done."

"Because you don't know well enough to say?"

"You could put it that way. Everyone knows they have dealings."

"Let me put it this way. Do you think the rough customer would do things beyond what our land agent would do?"

"He's got more nerve, if that's what you mean."

"Or less principles."

"Don't underestimate Little Hat in that respect."

Delaine assumed that Pinky had told the deputy what Delaine told him about Richards stopping at the pens to talk. He did not think Pinky would blab to one of these others, but he did not think a pint of whiskey would keep him from doing so if he were inclined. Still, it was worth a question.

"Do you talk very much to those two?"

"With them, I speak when I'm spoken to, which is just about never. You don't see them talkin' to me in the White Mule, them or their friends, but you don't see their minions pushin' me around, either."

Delaine wondered if Pinky was referring to Delaine's comment earlier or if he had heard at least about the incident with Earl. He figured it didn't matter. "Thanks for telling me what you did."

"I don't believe I said a thing."

"Not that I recall."

"And thanks for the token of friendship." Pinky touched his coat pocket.

"You're welcome. I'll leave you to your chores."

"Before you go, here's a story for you. There were two friends who studied philosophy together. One of them went on to be a well-known philosopher and college professor, and the other went back home to raise pigs in Missouri. After several years, the professor went to visit his old friend. He said, 'What about this? I turned out to be a professor, and you became a pig farmer. What's it like?' His friend said, 'It's interesting.' 'Interesting?' 'Yes. I'll show you. It's just about feeding time.' So he called in his pigs, 'Sup, sup, sup,' and a whole herd of pigs came running into the yard. The farmer leaned over and said, 'Come here, Hubert. And he picked up a little pig and held him up to an apple tree, where the pig went chomp, chomp, chomp and ate an apple.' He put that pig down and called to the next one. 'Come here, Bertram.' And he picked up that little pig and held him up to the apple tree, and it ate an apple just like the first one. At this point the professor says, 'That's interesting, all right. But isn't it time consuming?' And his friend the farmer says, 'Hey, what's time to a pig?' Ha-ha-ha!"

"That's a good one," said Delaine. He had heard it before, and he thought the second pig's name was Herbert in that version.

———

DELAINE WENT into the café early the next morning and was glad once again to see no one else there.

As Rachel poured the coffee, she said, "You look serious today."

"I think I am. And not to lose time before someone else comes in, I'll tell you what's on my mind. I've decided to do something on my own about something that no one else is looking into and that to me is a starting point for other questions." He waited for her to nod, and he continued. "Not to mention names, but I think that the fellow who has a land office and a fellow who is called a rough customer may have had something to do with something that you and I have talked about, the disappearance of a girl from town. They've got a little circle with a party who has an eating house, but I think that if I tried to work my way into that circle, I would do worse than no good."

"So what do you want to do?"

"I would like to try to get a woman to help."

"Me?"

"Only in a preliminary way. I have a hunch that the wife of the man who has the eating house might say something if it was in private and if she thought it wouldn't come back to her."

"I don't know." Rachel looked away for a second

and came back. "I don't know her, but I don't think she is all bad, and I know someone who knows her."

"It there was a way to talk to her, out of view…"

"I can try. You can come by the place where I live, in the early evening when you leave work, when they are still serving food at that place. If she can't come, or doesn't want to, I should know that by then."

"Very good. Thank you. I was hoping you could help."

"I can try."

———

Dusk was on the way once again when Delaine walked past the little Dutch boy and knocked on Mrs. Vanderhoven's door. The lock clicked, and Rachel opened the door.

"Come in," she said.

She closed and locked the door behind him as he took off his hat. "Mrs. Goodwin couldn't come," she said. "I think it was too much."

Delaine's spirits sank. "Thanks for trying."

"But I think another girl will come. A girl who works in her house and goes with one of the men who work for her husband."

Delaine recalled the men's names. Griggs and Andrews. "I didn't expect that," he said.

"Neither did I. It was my friend's idea. But I think your idea to get a woman to help, about a woman who disappeared, is a good one." Rachel smiled. "Let's sit here in the front room. If this person comes, she will knock on the back door, and I will answer. Mrs. Vanderhoven knows, and she will stay out of the way."

They sat in their accustomed places. Rachel began

the conversation in her easy way. "And everything is all right at your work?"

"Yes," he said. "We lost one day to the snow, but we're back at it. Al wants to finish, and it seems like we're pretty close to the end." He felt restless about the interview he was waiting for. "And you?"

"The same. From time to time, someone new comes in, but for the most part, it's the same people every day."

Silence fell again. He was trying to think of something else to say when a knocking sound at the back door made him jump.

"That must be her." Rachel stood up and walked to the kitchen.

The latch sounded, and the two women exchanged greetings. After a short exchange, Rachel returned to the living room with a woman in a dark- grey shawl and ulster.

Delaine stood up as the woman took off her shawl. He was expecting a girl, but he saw a woman almost his age, above medium height and not slender, with a flushed, full face and blondish-brown hair.

"How do you do?" he said.

"Good enough, thanks."

"I appreciate your willingness to come here."

"I don't know how much I'll have to say, but we'll see."

"Thanks. Would you like to sit down?"

"I would just as soon stand."

"Very well. Let me think of where to start. I might as well tell you my name. It's Jess Delaine. I worked for a few days with Tom Caswell, so some people see me as having been a friend of his. I'm sorry that no one has done much to find out who was responsible for what happened to him. At one point, I tried to talk to a person who I thought knew him, but she preferred not to talk."

The woman said, "I think I know who you mean. I do housework for her."

"I hope I don't do any harm by saying that I have sympathy for her."

"I don't know how much she wants sympathy, but I feel sorry for her, too."

Delaine nodded for her to go on.

"Being kept like a bird in a cage."

Delaine sensed a hesitation on her part. He said, "I want to reassure you that this conversation is confidential. And it's not for any gain of mine. It's in someone else's interest—we'll just say another woman."

He thought she regarded him for a moment in a personal way, as if he was a physical specimen and not a bad one.

Her eyes met his as she came back to the matter at hand.

"It's been humiliating for her. And ugly." The woman had a firm expression on her face. "It has turned me sour on him, the way he gloats about what happened to Tom. I don't think he had anything done, and everyone else seems to think Tom got it for something else, but it was a dirty deal, and there doesn't seem to be any clear way to pin it on anyone."

Delaine wondered if she thought she had come to talk about Caswell's death in spite of what he had just said. He continued with his own thread. "What I was interested in knowing about was something I think is related."

"Oh?"

"This may seem roundabout, but it's the way I

heard it. A friend of Tom's, who is no longer with us, told me that he might be able to take me somewhere to show me something about someone's murky dealings that Tom knew about without wanting to."

"Oh. That's something different."

"I imagine it might be, but I think it's related."

"Then I'm not sure whose dealings you might be talking about."

"No one likes to name names, but I've heard him referred to as a rough customer, and he's not your husky roughneck kind of fella."

The woman's face was motionless for a few seconds. "I thought that might be what you meant. He's a bad one. He has no feelings for other people or what happens to them, women least of all. I don't think he cared about anything between Tom and Jo."

Delaine took in a breath to fortify himself. "To get back to something I said earlier, and to state it in plainer words, I'd like to know where a person might look for a woman who disappeared."

The woman's eyes opened a little. "Oh, I think I know what you're getting around to. You didn't hear this from me, but if someone was going to look for something, one place to go would be a place called Lost Canyon."

"Uh-huh."

"I don't know if I should have said that much."

"Well, you didn't say anything at all. I didn't hear a thing from you."

"I guess I didn't. Is that all, then?"

"I think so."

"Then maybe I'll leave. I should get back to Jo. I help her out, you know."

"Thank you."

"It's all right." She looked him over as if for the first time. "Good luck. And be careful."

"I will."

Rachel let the woman out the back door and returned to the living room. "Did you find out what you wanted to know?"

"As much as I was going to, I think. Thanks for your help."

"You're welcome. What do you think you'll do?"

He met her eyes. "I think I have a hunch about who lives at Lost Canyon. I'll find out."

"Be careful."

"You can bet I will be. Like I said before, I've had enough of being pushed around, and I'll be prepared."

"Good. Sometimes you have to be ready to make the first move."

13

Delaine and Benny finished the work on the corrals in the afternoon, and they spent their last hour and a half cutting the unusable posts and planks into stove lengths and stacking the wood in the office. Al Portman paid them at the end of the day and thanked them for their work.

All day long, Delaine was needled by the question of where Lost Canyon was, although he thought he had a general idea. He had not heard of it as a local place name, but he had not talked to that many people who worked out on the range or traveled it. For reasons of discretion, he did not ask at work.

After checking on his horse and eating his solitary meal, he knocked on the door of the schoolteacher's room. Gresham let him in and must have read his face, for he asked, "What's on your mind?"

Delaine took a chair and spoke in a low, confidential tone. "I've heard of a place where someone might be holding a girl."

Gresham's eyes opened wide. "Are you sure?"

"I'm sure of the name of the place. What I asked for was where a person might look for a woman who disappeared."

"Oh." Gresham's attention wandered for a second and came back. "What's the name of the place?"

Delaine kept his voice low but his pronunciation deliberate. "Lost Canyon. Do you know where it is?"

"I believe it's north of town, out on the other side of the pine ridge. There's a pass that goes through there."

"I am imagining there is a ranch there."

"I believe so. I don't have any students from that place, but I've heard of it, and I've been out that way once. I think it belongs to a cattleman we met last Sunday."

An image came to Delaine's mind. "A man with a red beard."

"That's right."

Delaine felt a tightening in the pit of his stomach. "I thought it might be something like that. I don't have a clear idea of whether it's the girl that this fellow Richards was looking for or the girl who disappeared from here."

"Nora."

"Yes."

The schoolteacher scratched the side of his head. "I don't think Nora is there. As I suggested the other evening, I don't allow myself the false optimism to think that someone will find her alive. But I would be interested in knowing if there is anything to be seen or anything to this...I don't know what to call it, a report?"

"That's good enough. Well, I'll tell you, I'm sure enough interested. I'd like to take a ride out that way, just to see, as you say, whether there's anything to be seen."

"Just to observe?

"That's my idea. Unless someone tries to push me around again."

Gresham's eyebrows went up and down.

"Do you think you would be interested in going along?"

Gresham said, "I don't know. It sounds like a good way to get into serious trouble."

"That's all right. I can go by myself."

"No, I'll go with you."

"Don't feel that you have to. No one owes anyone anything."

"I would do it for Nora, though I never knew her. Maybe I feel that I owe it to Marian."

"What would you think of tomorrow, about noon?"

"Another Sunday ride? We might get back late. It's a ways out."

"I wouldn't want to get there too early."

"I understand. Noon should be fine."

———

HIRAM FITTS RIGGED the grey horse for Gresham while Delaine brushed, combed, and saddled his own horse. The sun was pale and not very warm as they led the horses outside.

"Should be a good day," said Fitts. He held the bridle as Gresham mounted up.

Delaine swung aboard, and the two of them thanked Fitts. He smiled and began to roll a cigarette as they turned and rode away.

They followed the trail out to the fork in the road. Most of the snow was melted. Drifts remained on the north side of ridges and low swells, now that the sun was farther south. At the "Y," they took the trail to the right, traveling northeast and covering some of the same area where they had hunted.

The trail turned north, and the land had a greater distribution of pines and cedars. At about four miles from the "Y," they began to enter the pass that went up and over the pine ridge. Trees grew on both sides of the trail, and most of the ground between the trees had snow. The trail also had snow on one side or another as it turned, while in other places it was muddy where the snow had melted.

The climb was slow and gradual. When they came out on the north side, the trees ended sooner than Delaine expected. A broad, rolling grassland stretched away with a dark, timbered rise in the land many miles away in the north.

"That's Rawhide Mountain," said Gresham.

"Have you been there?"

"No, but I know where it is, and I've seen it on a map. And like I said, I've been this way once before."

"From the other side, where we see it every day from town, it looks as if this ridge runs east and west. But out on this side, you can see that the hills run in different directions. That must be how you get a lost canyon."

Gresham pointed to the east. "It should be over this way, and back in."

The shadows were beginning to stretch, and Delaine estimated that they had been on the trail between two and a half and three hours. "You're not getting tired, are you?"

"No. I've gotten my riding legs a little on these other Sundays. I might begin to feel it on the way back."

The trail took a wide turn, and before long, the dark form of Rawhide Mountain was on Delaine's left. The shadows did not give a perfect orientation, as the sun was now in the southwest. The closest trees were more than a mile away, where breaks in the hills appeared. Delaine had the sense of being in a wide, interior country higher than the place where he had been working for the last three weeks or so.

The trail turned north, and a lesser trail veered south by southeast. A board attached to two posts had "CC Ranch" burned into it.

Gresham said, "I think this takes us to the place we have in mind."

Delaine felt a nervousness mounting inside. They were going to have to ride through open country, off the main trail. If anyone challenged them, they wouldn't have a very good explanation.

They reached the first breaks when the sun was beginning to slip. The trees and rocks cast shadows on the almost-continuous patches of snow. The trail itself did not have much snow. It was easy to follow, as numerous hoofprints led both ways.

After about a mile, first level and then a gradual descent, Delaine saw a wide area ahead and stopped. He dismounted and drew his horse aside, behind a dull-colored rocky formation. "Let me go on foot," he said. He had not put on spurs, and he would have to take care not to scuff or bump a foot on a rock. With the gathering dusk in an unfamiliar location, it would be easy to bungle and make a noise.

Gresham slipped down from his saddle, led the

grey horse to cover next to Delaine, and took the reins of both horses.

Delaine spoke in a low voice, close to a whisper. "Use your own judgment, but if something happens to me, save your own neck."

"How will I know?"

"I don't know. Don't be in too much of a hurry and leave me stranded on foot. Like I say, you'll just have to use your judgment." Delaine unbuttoned his coat and drew it back so he could touch his pistol. It was too late to wish that one of them had brought a rifle, and he had not wanted the schoolteacher to feel under the obligation of using a firearm. To his surprise, Gresham took a small pistol out of his own coat pocket.

"What's that?"

"A thirty-two. I borrowed it."

"People make fun of them and call 'em a peashooter, but they'll stop someone if you hit him. It's easy to miss, though."

"I'll be careful, and I hope I don't have to use it."

"So do I." Delaine settled his hat on his head as he took light steps and moved away.

The scene opened up in the fading light. In an area of about two acres with rock walls all around sat a normal-looking set of ranch headquarters with a bunkhouse, a ranch house, a barn, and a few lower structures that looked like calf sheds. A trail led out through one opening in the rock wall on the far side of the yard.

A light was shining in the bunkhouse, and a couple of windows were illuminated in the ranch house. Delaine waited to let the dusk thicken. When he set out, he knew he had to keep to the dark spots and not let any of the light from indoors fall on him.

He crept behind the bunkhouse, where a single filmy window allowed him to see bunks, a table, and benches but no people. He went on his way until he came to the ranch house. What looked like the front room was dark. Off to the left, light showed behind a drawn shade in what Delaine thought might be an office or a bedroom. He moved around the right side of the house, toward the back corner, where another shade was drawn with light behind it.

Delaine's pulse jumped when a shadow loomed on the shade and flickered away. He waited until he saw the shape again, still distorted, but he thought it was the form of a woman's head of hair. It was not a man with a hat, and it was more than just the outline of a head.

Ranch houses tended to have a similar layout, and he could guess some of it from what he had seen, but he could not make assumptions. There should be a back door, and it should not be too far away from the door to the bedroom where he had just seen the shadow.

He took soft and quiet steps around to the back of the house. Shadows along a wall showed a doorway. He moved toward it, still in slow movements.

The doorknob was on his right. He drew his pistol with his right hand and cocked it. With his left hand, he tried the knob. When it gave, he turned it little by little until the door relaxed. His heart was beating fast. He drew in a breath, opened the door a couple of inches, and released the door handle by degrees. He opened the door farther and put his left foot in. Shifting his weight, he brought his right foot in, then moved enough to close the door. He had to turn the knob again and release it. The area he stood in was dark.

A mutter of voices came from the far corner of the house where he had the other lit room placed. He wondered how many people were there and how many were in the room where he saw the shadow.

Thin lines of light showed him the door he hoped to find. He took in another breath, trying to stay calm, and took short, silent steps until he stood next to the door. He listened and did not hear voices. He did not hear any other sounds except the scraping of a chair. He took another breath to try to keep his heartbeat down and calm himself. He did not want to barge in on two people, no matter what they were or were not doing.

He put his hand on the white porcelain doorknob and waited before he turned it. The room remained quiet. He turned the knob until he felt the latch come all the way back and the door give, and he waited a moment. When he felt that the time was right, he pushed the door open and slipped in sideways with his gun ready at waist level.

A woman who was seated at a chair in front of a dresser turned and covered her mouth as she let out a sound like a whimper.

Delaine put his left index finger to his lips and said, "Shhh!" He saw her all at once and registered the details. She looked older than a girl, with a cloudy brockle face, large brown eyes, and streaked hair that was neither blonde nor brown. She did not look anything like Marian Peele, and she did not match the image he had of the girl in the grainy photograph.

"Who are you?" she asked.

"Shhh. I came here to help you get away if you want."

She had a lost expression on her face as she looked away. "I don't know."

"Your name's not Nora, is it?"

"No."

"Is it Evelina?"

She turned her gaze toward him. Her lower eyelids were puffy, and her eyes were moist.

"Is it Evelina?" he asked again.

She swallowed and said, "Yes."

The door swung open, and one of the Dodge boys bounded in and landed on both feet with spurs jingling. He had his gun drawn, and a smirk came onto his face.

"Well, it's you, you puky son of a bitch. What a surprise. Well, this is the end." With his face spread in a smile, he drew the hammer on the Colt.

Delaine shot him in the chest and knocked him backward. His boots thumped and clinked as he stumbled against a chair and fell to the floor. His hat fell off, and his blond hair showed.

Footsteps pounded from the other part of the house. Delaine had time to say, "Stay out of the way" to the girl and to get set with his .45 leveled and cocked.

Earl Dodge lunged into the room, sweeping his arm and firing a shot that walloped past Delaine and broke the shaded window. Delaine fired and hit him higher than he aimed, as the bullet hit him at the base of the throat. Earl went off his feet and grabbed at the air as he spilled back into the open doorway.

Delaine turned to the girl. "We've got no time to lose. Do you want to go or not?"

"I don't know if I can."

He could see that she was a prisoner in her mind. "Where's the boss?"

"I think he's in the kitchen. He said he was going to take a bath and then come here."

Delaine saw that she was wearing a housecoat. "Well, you decide for yourself, but we don't have much time."

"I don't know if I can. He'll kill me. If he doesn't, someone else will."

"No one will if you get away from here soon enough."

"And who are you?"

"I'm someone who came to see if someone was being held here."

"I don't have anything to wear. My clothes don't fit me. I wear this most of the time. If I go anywhere, I have to wear men's clothes."

"It would be better anyway. Do you know how to ride a horse?"

She nodded.

"Well, get changed if you want to. If you don't, tell me right now, and I'll get out."

"He'll kill me."

"No one's going to kill you."

Her face clouded darker, and she began to cry. "I can't go, but I don't want to stay here."

"Get changed, then, and hurry up. I'll turn my back."

She was ready to go in a couple of minutes, dressed in a baggy tan shirt and brown trousers and a pair of flat shoes. She sniffled.

"Let's go," he said. He took her by the hand and

hurried outside. "Do you know if they keep horses in the barn?"

"I think they do. I've heard Cole talk about a night horse."

"We're a long ways from town. It would be a lot better if you rode your own rather than ride double."

He ran bent over, pulling her, and lit a match when they stopped inside the barn. He found a lantern and lit it.

A bay horse stood in a stall by itself.

"Hold this lantern for me, and I'll get this horse ready as soon as I can."

Delaine found a bridle, put it on the horse, and led the animal from the stall. He brushed it with his hand, threw on a double blanket, and swung a saddle up and onto its back. He reached down, pulled the front cinch to him, ran the latigo, and pulled it. The saddle had no rear cinch, so he was set.

All this time, he had been working with the horse with the reins in his hand, and the horse had moved. It now stood between Delaine and the barn door. The girl stood behind Delaine part of the time and next to him the rest of the time.

He said, "Hold the lantern here, and let me make sure of that cinch."

As he put three fingers between the woven cinch and the horse's side, a voice came through the doorway. It was forced, not deep, with a tone of command that did not seem to have enough authority.

"Evvie, get over here."

Delaine spoke to the side in a low voice for the girl. "Stay where you are. Stay behind this horse."

Chamberlain raised his voice. "Evvie, I said get over here so I can take care of this son of a bitch."

She burst into a sob and said, "Cole, I can't."

The boss shouted, "Damn it, get over here!"

Delaine had his gun drawn and held the reins in his left hand as he had done all along.

Chamberlain fired a shot that split the air above the horse's hindquarters and sent a concussion wave toward Delaine. The horse lurched, and Delaine had to let go of the reins in order to keep steady and take aim with both hands. His view cleared, and he squeezed the trigger, placing a bullet in the brown coat about a foot below the red beard.

Chamberlain fired a second time, and the bullet sent another forceful wave of air but much higher. He still had the pistol in his hand as he fell to the hard-packed dirt floor.

The light lowered. The girl was holding the lantern, but she had her face in her hands as she cried.

"There's nothing to stay for here," he said. "We can take you to town. There's another fella came along with me. He's out holding our horses. I hope he's still there."

She sniffled.

"Do you still think you can ride?"

She nodded and sniffed and rubbed her nose with the sleeve of the shirt. "I think so."

"Do you need help getting on?" He did not want to be touching her legs or body without her permission, but he was ready to put his shoulder into her buttocks if he had to.

"I think so. I've put on a little weight and haven't gone out much at all."

———

THE MOON WAS at about a quarter as they rode back to town. They did not ride fast, keeping at a walk. Delaine asked the girl at intervals if she was doing all right. She said yes each time, and it sounded as if her nose was congested and her throat was swollen.

———

THE CLOCK in the lobby of the Grange Hotel showed the time to be a quarter till midnight when Delaine asked for Deputy Erskine. The clerk said he would go tell him he had a visitor.

Outside, Gresham said he had school the next day and needed to turn in. He offered to take the horses to the stable.

Delaine agreed for him to go ahead. He gave the girl his hand to step up onto the sidewalk, and he led her into the lit lobby to wait for the deputy to come down.

The girl sat in an upholstered chair, and Delaine sat in a wooden chair with spindles and a cushion. The girl did not look at Delaine or speak. She had a bunched-up handkerchief that she held to the side of her face and daubed at her nose.

Footsteps sounded on the stairs, and Deputy Erskine came into view. He was wearing his hat and his tweed coat, the latter unbuttoned to show his star and his sidearm. Delaine took off his hat and stood up to meet him.

The deputy gave a narrow look at the girl and at Delaine. "Mick didn't say who was here. What's going on?"

Delaine said, "This is Miss Evelina."

The deputy's eyes narrowed again as he gave his

attention to the dismal person sitting in the stuffed chair. "Is that right?"

She nodded.

"Would you mind stating your full name?"

She daubed at her nose.

"I'm Deputy Erskine from the Laramie County Sheriff's Office. If I'm going to help you, I need to know your first and last name." He took off his hat.

She sniffled, and without removing her hand, she mumbled, "Evelina Ralston."

The deputy spoke in clear syllables. "Did you say Evelina Ralston?"

She lowered her hand and clenched it. "Yes! Can't you leave me alone?"

"Not quite yet. I need to know what happened."

"Ask him."

The deputy turned to Delaine. "Did you do something to her?"

Delaine had thought about what he would say, and he was taken aback. "Not at all. I found her at the CC Ranch, in Lost Canyon. She was being held there."

"I see. And did you do this on your own?"

"Mr. Gresham went with me. He held the horses."

"But you went on your own. What compelled you to do that?"

"My main idea was to see if we could find out something about Nora Peele."

The deputy's jaws tightened, and Evelina turned her head toward both of them.

"As I said, I found this person, and we brought her back."

The deputy spoke to Evelina. "Is that right?"

"He just said so."

"Were you being held there?"

"What do you think?"

"I am trying to find out. Before I think about arresting someone, I need to know whether you went there of your own free will or if you could ever have left on your own."

"I was taken there."

"I see. And how long ago was that? How long were you there?"

"I think it was about three months. I lost track."

"Today is October 27th, or rather, October 28th, now."

"Then that's about what it is."

"And during that time, could you have left on your own? Were you under lock and key all the time?"

"I was at first, but what would have been the use? He made it clear to me that I was miles and miles from town and it's easy to lose your sense of direction out there, and they would chase me down if something else didn't happen to me first."

"Something else."

"Rattlesnakes. Wildcats. Wolves. And I couldn't have left. I was broken. I felt helpless. Almost paralyzed. He took it all out of me."

"He broke your will."

She sobbed and cried as she pressed the handkerchief to her face.

The deputy persisted. "What did he do to you? And by the way, when you say 'he,' just to be clear, who are you referring to?"

Evelina's upper body rose and fell.

"Just tell me his name so we can go on."

"Cole."

"Cole Chamberlain?"

"Who else is named Cole out there? But he had

help. Cal and Earl. He said they would help look for me if I ran. And the man who stayed in the bunkhouse. His name was Ike, but I just about never saw him."

"But Cole Chamberlain was the principal one. He was the one responsible for holding you." When Evelina did not disagree, the deputy proceeded. "What did he do to you?"

Delaine felt sick. He could not have asked the question to the girl even if she were in a better state.

"We have to get to this question sooner or later," said the deputy. "What I do depends on it. So please tell me what he did to you."

Evelina held her hand to the side of her face.

"Miss Ralston, just tell me what he did."

She mumbled something.

"I'm sorry. You're going to have to speak so I can hear you. If you say it clearly once, you won't have to repeat it."

She took her hand from her face, and tears were in her eyes. Her countenance was dark. "He used me."

"He used you. You mean—"

"What do you think I mean? He *used* me!"

"I understand. Now, just to give me an idea, how many times do you think this happened?"

She sulked.

"Just tell me how many times, more or less."

Her clouded face was wet, and her hand was clenched on the handkerchief. "How many times? From the very first day. Every day he was there. Three or four times a day when he felt like it. Is that enough for you?"

The deputy's face had a disagreeable expression. "I

have to know these things. Now, this is important, too. Did any of his hired men do anything to you?"

Her face was more placid now, as if she had thrown up her bile. "No, but they would have if they could. They were like dogs. Not Ike. But Cal and Earl."

"When you say Cal and Earl, just to be clear, you mean the Dodge brothers. Hired hands for Cole Chamberlain."

"That's what I mean."

"Well, very good. I think we're getting somewhere, Miss Ralston. I know this is not easy. But I need to know these things in order to proceed. For the time being, I think I have a sufficient idea of what happened at the CC Ranch at Lost Canyon." Deputy Erskine paused. "Now, to give me a fuller picture, I would like to ask you how you got there. You said you were taken. I would like to ask who did that."

The girl stayed mum.

"I think my question was clear, but I'll ask it again. Who took you to the ranch at Lost Canyon?"

She kept her mouth firm and shook her head.

"Very good," said the deputy. "I know it's late. You need rest. What I plan to do is place you under protection. That means I'll arrange for a room for you here at the hotel, and I'll have a man, either myself or someone else, sitting in front of your door at all times. No harm will come to you. I'll see that you get a bath in the morning, and I'll see about getting you a set of clothes. Wouldn't you like that?"

"Thank you," she said, in a flat tone.

"But before we finish, I'd like to ask another question that's been at the back of my mind. Did someone do something to your hair? According to the information I have had, Evelina Ralston has blonde hair."

She made an audible sound of breathing in through her nose. "They colored it with coffee and something else they mixed in. When I asked what else they put in, Cal laughed and said horse manure. I wouldn't have been surprised."

"I think that's satisfactory on that point. Let me say a word to Mr. Delaine, and then I can see to you as I said." The deputy took on his authoritative air as he turned to Delaine. "I think this is enough for tonight. I have more questions for you, but they can wait. Do you think you could come by here at about eight in the morning? Do you need me to talk to your employer?"

"I've finished my work at the shipping pens, so I can be here any time you want."

"Eight o'clock should be fine."

"I'll see you then. Good night to both of you."

14

Delaine met Deputy Erskine in the lobby of the hotel at eight a.m. as they had agreed. The owner of the hotel, Baird, was behind the counter and looked on from a distance.

"Thank you for coming," said the deputy as they sat down. He directed his gaze at Delaine and said, "I'd like to know what happened at the CC Ranch. I'm planning to go out there and make some arrests, and I don't know how much resistance I might meet with."

"I don't think you'll find any resistance," said Delaine. "Cole Chamberlain and the Dodge brothers are dead."

The deputy stared. "The hell they are. Were they dead when you got there? What happened?"

"I was obliged to shoot each of them." Delaine gave the deputy a couple of seconds to collect himself. "Mr. Gresham and I rode out there yesterday afternoon, and we arrived at the ranch at about dark. A light was lit in the bunkhouse, but I didn't see anyone through the window. I am guessing that the man named Ike was there. I made my way to the ranch house, where I saw lights in two rooms, both with the shades drawn. At one window, I saw the shadow of a woman's head, so I went around to the back door. I tried it, and it opened, so I went in and found my way to the room where I thought the woman was."

"You just went in."

"Yes. I didn't know what to expect, but I had been asking questions in town to help me get an idea of what happened to Nora Peele, and the answers I received led me to that ranch. When I opened the door, though, I saw that it must be someone else. I was told that Nora Peele looked quite a bit like her sister, Marian, and this woman had to be someone else. Like you, I didn't know what to think about the color of her hair. But I could see she was being held there, and I offered to help her get away. She was afraid to go, but when she had to decide, she changed into the clothes she was wearing last night, and we were ready to go."

"Did you see her change clothes?"

"God, no. I turned my head."

"I ask because it appears that she might be expectant."

"I imagined as much," said Delaine. "But before we could get out of the room, Cal Dodge came busting in, and he cocked and pointed his gun and said it was the end. I had my gun out, which I don't think he was ready for, and I got the best of him."

"You shot him right there."

"I had no choice. The girl will tell you the same thing. She was there through the whole thing."

"And what happened next?"

"I heard footsteps pounding through the house, and Earl Dodge came rushing in, and he fired a shot that went through the shade and broke the window. So I did the same to him."

"You shot him."

"Yes."

"And where was Cole Chamberlain all this time?"

"That's what I asked her. She said she thought he was in the kitchen, taking a bath, preparatory to making a visit to her room."

The deputy's eyes went up to the ceiling and returned. "Go on."

"She had been dithering about whether she could go. She reminded me of stories I'd heard about women being held captive by the Indians and such."

"Mental bondage."

"Something like that. They form a kind of attachment to the ones who are keeping them that way. Anyway, she decided to come, so I hustled her out to the barn, where I lit a lantern and saddled a horse for her as fast as I could. At about that time, Chamberlain showed up. He ordered her to come over to him, and I told her to stay behind the horse, where we both were. Chamberlain ordered her a couple of times, and then he fired a shot, which made the horse jump out of the way, and I shot him as he was trying to take a shot at me. He did fire a second time, but it didn't do him any good."

"And then you came into town."

"It was a long, slow ride, in consideration of the girl, but we came straight here."

The deputy folded his arms. "I think you took a lot upon yourself to go out there like that."

"It didn't seem as if anyone else was going to do anything about finding Nora Peele."

The deputy's face was rigid. "Well, you didn't find her, either."

"That doesn't mean she's not out there somewhere."

"You mean buried."

"My hunch is that Chamberlain used her like he was using this girl, and when she wasn't of use to him anymore, that was what happened. It might well have happened to this girl as well, before long."

The disagreeable expression returned to the deputy's face. "I think Miss Ralston will be ready for another conversation before long. It seems to me that she is more willing to speak when you are present, but I recommend that you not say anything about that last point, about what might have happened to her."

"She was under fear for her own life the whole time. She said that if he didn't kill her, someone else would. I told her no one would if she got out of there with me."

"And no one's going to. Let me go see if she's ready."

Delaine waited for about ten minutes. The deputy came back with Evelina, who was taking slow steps but looked better than she did when Delaine had seen her last. Her hair was washed and appeared to have regained most of its original color. She was wearing a loose-fitting house dress of a light-blue material with large striped squares.

Delaine rose to meet her with his hat in his hand. "Good morning. How are you doing today?"

"All right, I think. A little sore from riding the horse all that way, but I can walk."

The deputy said, "As I've told Miss Ralston, I've sent a telegram to her family, and someone should be here late tomorrow or sometime the next day. Meanwhile, we want to keep her safe. And ask a few more questions."

They all sat down in the same seats as the night before.

The deputy drew a breath and said, "Miss Ralston, Mr. Delaine has told me about the events that took place at the CC Ranch yesterday. I have a better understanding of what you've been through. At the same time, I still need to know more."

Evelina's face retained its cloudy, swollen quality, and she stared at the deputy with her lips pushed forward in something like a pout.

"I'd like to ask you again who took you to that ranch."

Evelina moved her head to each side in slow motion.

"Nobody is going to do anything to you at this point. I am guessing that Cole Chamberlain did not take you there, or at least he did not take you here from your home in Colorado, or you wouldn't be afraid to tell me."

She remained firm.

"I realize you may be afraid that someone will come for you again when you go back home. If you tell us who it is, we can take steps to see that that doesn't happen."

Evelina swallowed and shook her head.

"Very well," said the deputy. "We'll pass on to another topic."

Evelina waited.

"Did you ever hear of a girl named Nora?"

"Not since I came here."

"Did you ever hear of another girl who had been taken to the CC Ranch?"

"Not right out. But Cal made comments now and then that referred to another girl, and he made comments to me about how no one wanted to end up in the place where the men took horses that weren't of use anymore and shot them. It was another canyon."

"I see. But you never heard a girl's name, and you never heard right out that she was buried in a canyon."

"That's right. But in the sarcastic way he had, and always trying to get close to me, worse than his brother but not by much, I put the things together as kind of a threat. But as long as Cole was there, they didn't do anything. They went places without him, but he never left without them."

The deputy seemed to reflect. "I see. Well, we're going to have to go out there with a wagon and bring in the bodies, and I want to know what else to look for while we're there."

"I've told you all I know."

"About the girl and the canyon. I want you to think about this other part and why it would be best to tell me about it, too. For right now, be assured. No one's going to do anything to you. I'll have a man sitting at your door just like there has been."

The deputy stood up. Delaine did the same, and so did Evelina. The deputy said, "I'll have Mr. Baird see you to your room."

Delaine waited until the deputy came back from the desk. They sat down again, and Delaine moved his chair close. With his lips tight, he spoke in a low voice. "I have a hunch who this person is that she's afraid of."

"Tell me."

"I think it's a man that people refer to as a rough

customer, name of Mull." Delaine's voice dropped as he said the name. "I think he's either the same one who did in Tom Caswell or had it done. Caswell was in on cattle rustling with him, but he got in too deep by learning about something else this fella did. It went back about two years, so I think it was the disappearance of Nora Peele." He waited for the deputy to pass through a rigid phase again, and he continued. "I think Caswell found out or got wind of this more recent kidnapping as well, again without wanting to know, and he was scared to death about what would happen to him, and it did."

"How do you know all of this, and why didn't you tell me before?"

"It was all vague. I never heard names or details. But I heard some of it from Paul Hensley, the vague part, just before he ended up the way he did. The rest, including this rough customer's name, I put together when I asked around about Nora Peele. I found out who her procurer was, and I found out that he was a go-between on various kinds of deals with this rough customer. I figured that either one or the other or both made the deal with Cole Chamberlain, and of the two, I think the rough customer is the one capable of delivering the girl."

"That all sounds credible," said the deputy. "But I need to get his name from her, or at least a description. So far, her and you and me, or you and I, or the three of us, anyway, are the only ones who know what happened at the ranch."

"And Gresham."

"Oh, yes. Him."

"I'm sure he's not telling anyone."

"None of this can be kept a secret anyway. But I

think we have time. I can get a wagon and a couple of men to help, and without telling a great deal of why and where, we can go out there to pick up the bodies and look around. If I can get more out of Miss Ralston at that point, I can arrest this other person. If not, I might have another approach by then. For the present, we can only do one thing at a time. I'll see about a wagon and some help. If you're done with your work at the pens, I'd like to have you along. You have your own horse, don't you?"

"Yes, I do. I'll be glad to go along."

"Then let's see about meeting at the livery stable in about an hour."

———

DELAINE ARRIVED at the stable early to have his horse ready and not cause anyone to wait on him. Hiram Fitts came out of the harness room wearing his wide-brimmed, dust-colored hat, looking tired and taking slow steps.

"I just got up," he said. "I worked the night shift. I was here when the schoolteacher brought in the three horses. He said you would explain where the third horse came from, but I knew the brand and the horse as well from workin' for the CC."

"That's where it came from, all right. The deputy doesn't want to say much about it until a little later on. I'm supposed to meet him here in about half an hour. Has he not spoken for any horses to go out today?"

"Not that I know of. Let me bring your horse in."

Delaine had the brown horse ready to go and was about to lead it out to the street when the deputy walked in.

"I've got a wagon and one man ready to go. I could use another man. If I get one with a horse, I'll ride in the wagon. If I get one who needs to ride in the wagon, then I'll want the horse I have here." He looked at Fitts. "Where's Kent?"

"I think he's in the bank, makin' a deposit."

"We just came from that way. I didn't see him."

Delaine said, "I think he means the outhouse."

Fitts said, "Where are you-all goin'?"

The deputy regarded him as if to decide how much to tell him. "You used to work at the CC Ranch at Lost Canyon, didn't you?"

"That's right."

"Well, that's where we're going. What would you think of going along with us?"

"I'd have to ask Kent. I'm not on shift right now, but I don't know how long we'll be gone."

"Most of the day, at least. I'd say into the night."

"Here he is now."

Kent came in through a separate back door that did not lead to the corrals. His eyes went from the deputy to Delaine's saddled horse. "What do you need?" he asked.

The deputy tightened his brows and said, "I don't need this to get all over town until we get back. But I'm taking a wagon out to the CC Ranch, and I could use another man to go along. Your man here used to work there and knows the country. Can you spare him for the day?"

Kent rubbed his lower lip. "I suppose I could. One of the horses from the CC came in last night. I think it should stay here until I know more. If you want Hi, I suppose I can let him go. And a horse." Kent turned his pale-brown eyes toward Fitts. "You've got your own saddle."

"I do."

"Then go ahead. Take one of those that we rent by the day." As Fitts stepped away, Kent spoke to the deputy. "I 'magine this is something serious. No charge for the horse today."

"We appreciate it."

Fitts came back with a plain-looking sorrel. "I'll throw my saddle on him and be ready in a jiff."

The deputy said, "We'll wait outside."

Delaine led his horse and followed the deputy to the street, where a buckboard with two horses stood waiting. Delaine recognized the driver as Baird, the hotel proprietor, who was now fitted out with a tan cattleman's hat and a wool coat of light and brown plaid. Baird was a slender man of middle height with a narrow face and a clipped grey mustache, and he appeared to have prepared for the weather, as he also wore padded leather gloves and had a folded grey blanket across his lap.

The deputy twisted his mouth and said, "It looks like I'll ride with you." He climbed up and sat on the seat next to Baird. "We have to wait for one more man. He'll be out with his horse."

"Who is it?"

"Kent's hired man. He used to work out there."

"Oh, Sundown."

"He knows the country."

Baird sniffed.

The grey sky was not letting the sun through, and the day was not warming very fast. Delaine put on his gloves and stood by his horse.

Fitts came out leading the sorrel with a cowpuncher's saddle on it, complete with a coiled rope tied on. Fitts was wearing his hat and his sheepskin coat, and he had put on spurs. He tucked his smile and said, "Ready." With his horse clear of the others, he checked his cinch and climbed on.

Baird clucked to the horses and turned them around in the street.

Delaine swung aboard his horse, and when he saw that Fitts chose to ride alongside the wagon, he fell in on the other side. The group traveled to the main intersection, turned right, and headed north toward the open country.

The rangeland looked the same as it had the day before, with unmelted snow in the same places. Delaine had an awareness that Caswell, Hensley, the Dodge brothers, and Chamberlain had all ridden across this land and would see it no more. There would come a time when he, too, would no longer see the grass and sage and stunted trees and grey sky. He hoped that time was far in the future.

Fitts, in the meanwhile, rode along as if he was on a day off. He seemed to be happy to be in the saddle, and he swayed with the motion of his horse. For a while, he had the knotted end of his rope loose, and he tapped the shank of his boot with it.

The two horses pulled the buckboard at a good pace, and they did not slow much as they went up the winding grade and through the pass of the pine ridge. Out on the other side, Rawhide Mountain appeared many miles away in the north, and in less than half an hour, the landmark was on Delaine's left again. The overcast sky did not give a sense of the time of day, and it did not contribute to a sense of direction. Delaine recalled Evelina saying that she had been warned about losing her sense of direction, and he saw how it could happen.

Time wore on, and they came to the turn in the road where the main trail went north and the lesser trail led south to Lost Canyon. The group went past the sign with the name of the CC Ranch burned into it, and Delaine tried to guess where the sun was.

Fitts led the way through the breaks, and the wagon rolled and creaked behind. The scene opened up as it had the day before, but with less delay, and the ranch headquarters came into view. Fitts brought them to a stop in front of the bunkhouse. He turned in the saddle and spoke to the deputy.

"Do you want to go in, or do you want me to?"

"Go ahead," said the deputy.

Fitts swung down and tied his horse at the hitching rail as he must have done many times. As he went into the bunkhouse, the deputy climbed down from the buckboard. Delaine dismounted and tied his horse next to the sorrel.

Fitts came out after a couple of minutes and said, "Ike's gone. All of his stuff is gone. The stove is cold."

The deputy said, "I imagine you already figured this out, but we came here to pick up some bodies."

"I didn't know," said Fitts. "I thought maybe you was goin' to arrest someone."

"We'll go over to the barn first." The deputy set out on foot as Baird shook the reins and put the wagon into motion. Delaine and Fitts followed, walking across the ranch yard under the grey sky.

They found Chamberlain where he had fallen. Baird let down the tailgate, and the other three men lifted the stiff body, carried it in staggering steps, and hefted it into the wagon. Delaine and Fitts climbed up and dragged the body to the center of the wagon bed. Baird had moved a couple of folded canvas sheets to one side.

Back on the ground, Delaine brushed his hands on his pants and said, "If we pull around to the back door of the house, we can get the others from there."

Fitts did not make a comment. He put on his gloves as he walked with Delaine, and then he took them off and put them in his coat pocket once again.

"In here," said Delaine. He opened the back door, which he did not remember closing. Chamberlain might well have come out that way. Delaine stepped aside when he came to Earl's body sprawled in the doorway.

"Oh," said Fitts.

The deputy, who had lingered to study the ground in back of the house, came in behind them. "Let's carry this one the same," he said.

They laid Earl on one side of Chamberlain and Cal on the other. The bodies made an unpleasant sight, with the patches of dried blood on their clothes and the frozen expressions on their colorless faces. Delaine was relieved to watch the deputy and Baird unfold a canvas and drape it over the three corpses.

Fitts rolled a cigarette, and Baird took a tailor-made out of a cigarette case. He lit a long match for both of them.

Fitts blew away a cloud of smoke and said, "Is that it?"

"Not yet," said the deputy. "While we're out here, I'd like to look for something else."

"I think Ike's gone. I didn't look to count horses, but I'd guess he lit out of here on a ranch horse."

"Something else," said the deputy. "Do you know

of a place where Chamberlain's men took horses that were of no use and shot them?"

"Culls? Oh, yeah. There's another little canyon back here. They took culls there and shot 'em."

"Did they bury them?"

"The culls? Nah. They just left 'em for the scavengers. Magpies, coyotes, buzzards. It wasn't all that many, just one every once in a while. I wasn't ever here for it. I just heard about it and saw the bones."

The deputy raised his head as he drew in a breath through his nose. "Well, I have been given to understand that there might be someone buried out there. A girl, maybe."

Fitts gave a look of caution as he held his cigarette to his lips. "Not the girl he had here. I think Cole had a girl, though everyone knew to keep their nose out of it."

"Not the girl who was her up until yesterday. She's alive and safe in town. What I mean is another girl, or woman, from before."

Fitts relaxed. "Don't know anything about that, but I can show you where to look."

"Let's do that. Can you find us a pick and a couple of shovels?"

Fitts blinked at his cigarette smoke. "Sure. I can do that."

Delaine followed Fitts on horseback, and the wagon fell in behind them. The trail led through the rock wall as Delaine had seen the evening before, and an area opened up into a smaller canyon, as Fitts had said. The distance was farther than it had appeared at first sight, maybe three-eighths of a mile, and the trail was rocky in places.

Fitts moved his horse to one side. "This is it."

The right side of the canyon floor had better grass than the left side, where rocks were scattered and dull bones were strewn.

"Let's take a look," said the deputy. He spoke to Baird. "How about you holding their horses, and the three of us will walk around." He spoke to Delaine and Fitts. "We'll keep an eye out for anything that looks like a mound of dirt or a mound of rocks, anything that's not the ground in its natural state. If they didn't bury the horses, then they didn't bury other things like dead calves. If there's something buried, I would guess it's something we want to look at."

The three of them spread out and walked through the rocky field. It must have been a dumping ground as well, as Delaine came across an old boot, a flattened bucket, and more than one whiskey bottle.

A call came out from the far left side of the area, where Deputy Erskine had stopped. He waved and called again. "Over here."

Delaine walked fast to catch up with Fitts, and the two of them arrived together.

"This looks like a mound of rocks to me," said the deputy. "No telling how long it's been here, at least a year with the bits of debris. I'd say there's something underneath."

Fitts nodded. "Shall we go for the tools?"

"I think so. I'll wait here. No need to bring the horses and wagon across all these rocks until we're sure we need 'em."

Fitts and Delaine walked across the field and told Baird what was up. He said, "We can tie these horses to the wagon, and I'll go with you." He let Fitts carry the two shovels and Delaine the pick, and the three of them walked across the rocky area to join the deputy.

Delaine saw soon enough that Baird did not intend to do any of the work but rather had come along to watch. Delaine loosened the rocks with the pick, and Fitts tossed them aside. The rocks were the size of melons and smaller, nothing too big for someone to have piled there.

"Could be that girl," said the hotel keeper. "The one that worked at the laundry." Delaine gathered that the deputy had told Baird something about their purpose. "Everyone knew she did it with men. This is just the kind of thing that could have happened to her."

The deputy said, "Do you remember what anyone said she was wearing when she disappeared?"

"Oh, yeah. It went around town. She was wearing a maroon-colored dress. Her sister knew all of her clothing, and that was the color of the dress that was missing."

"Keep an eye out for something maroon," said the deputy. "But if she was out here for a while, she could have changed into something else. Like the Ralston girl did."

Delaine and Fitts continued to loosen and toss rocks. Fitts stood up and straightened his back.

He said, "I wouldn't have ever thought to look for somethin' like this."

The deputy said, "It's something that people do."

"It is," said Baird. "No respect. Even if she *was* a crib girl."

Delaine kept from glaring at him. All the rocks on top had been cleared, and there remained a few embedded in the dirt. He pried them loose, and Fitts tossed them.

Delaine felt a fluttering in his stomach as he took a shovel in hand.

The deputy said, "Dig careful from the beginning. Sometimes they don't bury things very deep. Start in the middle. You don't know which way it's buried, and you don't want to hit the skull if you don't want to. Also, the middle is where the clothing is."

Delaine and Fitts worked one on each side, making shallow jabs and scoops. The dirt was hard and dry, but it was not packed as tight as the original earth, and they did not have to use the pick very much to loosen it.

When they were about two feet down, Fitts said, "Here's somethin'." He held his shovel almost flat as he lifted the broad end. The edge of the blade had a strip of pale maroon-colored cloth that was attached to something still in the ground.

"Careful now," said the deputy. "All around the edges, little by little."

It took another twenty minutes of slow work to reveal the upper layer of the body. The head was covered with a cloth bag like a flour sack, and the body down to the ankles had been clothed in a maroon dress that was frayed and separated in places.

The deputy spoke again. "We need to keep it all together as well as we can. Dig under, all around the edges, and we'll see if we can get it onto a canvas before we lift it out. Mr. Baird, if you can go for that other sheet of canvas, these men can keep excavating."

This was Nora, Delaine thought. She would ride back in the same wagon as the sons of bitches who put her here.

———

THEY RETURNED to town late that night. When they had the three bodies and the remains of the fourth safe in the back room of the barber shop, Deputy Erskine spoke to the others.

"We want to keep this as quiet as we can for a little while longer. It's too late tonight for me to interrogate Miss Ralston, but I want to talk to her again the first thing in the morning. Delaine, can you be there?"

"Yes, I can."

"Then let's meet again at eight."

15

———

Deputy Erskine conducted the meeting in Evelina's room, where Baird had furnished an additional chair before withdrawing in a proper way. Delaine wondered if he would listen at the door.

Evelina was wearing the same dress as the day before, and she did not appear as if a day of rest had relaxed her very much. Her face was still troubled, and she had a restlessness about her.

When the three of them were settled in their chairs, the deputy began. "Now, Miss Ralston, we're going to talk again to see if I can get the information I need to go further."

She did not give much expression.

"I have confirmed the deaths of the three men at the CC Ranch, though I didn't have much doubt. More to the point, now, is the fact that we found and dug up the body of another female who was buried in the canyon that you mentioned. So you helped us a great deal there."

She gave a small nod.

"We have a pretty good idea of who put her there —some if not all of the men we brought in on a wagon." He paused. "I have a pretty good idea of how she might have been taken there, just as I have a notion of how you were abducted and taken here. I think I know who the subject is, but before I try to arrest him, I would like to hear it from you."

The upper part of the light-blue dress rose and fell as she sat with her arms across her chest. She did not speak.

"I'm sure you remember what I told you yesterday. If I can arrest this party, he won't ever lay his hands on anyone."

Evelina did not avert her eyes, but she still did not say anything.

"We found a body of a young woman who disappeared a couple of years ago. As I am sure you have thought, something of the same nature could have happened to you. Now we need to think about who else it could happen to in the future if we don't do enough."

"I know."

"You know what I mean, or you know his name."

"Well, both."

"Then if you can tell me, you can do everyone a great deal of good."

She did not speak.

"Just his name."

She had her hand at her mouth, and she spoke in her low, mumbling way, but the word came out. "Mull."

"Mull?" said the deputy.

She nodded.

"Do you have a first name for him?"

"No. Just Mull. That's all I ever heard anyone call him."

———

Delaine and the deputy stopped at the registration area. Baird was wearing a tan corduroy jacket and a brown necktie, and he was clean-shaven.

"What can I do?" he asked.

The deputy kept his voice level and not loud. "Where can I find this man named Mull?"

Baird put his hands on the desk below the counter. "I don't know where he keeps himself. To save time, you could start with Ed Herbert at the land office."

"I know where that is."

"Mind if I go along?" said Delaine.

"No. Come on." The deputy settled his hat on his head, patted his coat where his revolver rode, and walked toward the door.

Snow was beginning to fall. The men turned left out of the hotel, crossed Center Street, cast a reflection on the windows of the bank, and kept going east. They covered the first block, passing the newsstand and the barbershop on the way. Delaine wondered if Marian had an idea that her sister's remains were wrapped in a canvas sheet next door.

They crossed the next street that went north, passed the mercery, millinery, and women's wear business where Evelina's dress would have come from, passed the bakery and its watchful proprietor, stepped down onto the ground in front of the shoe repair, and climbed up onto the wooden sidewalk under the awning of the Great Western Land Office.

The windows were dark, and the door was locked.

Still at a brisk pace, the deputy led the way back to the shoe repair. It was open, with a lamp shining in back.

The interior had the not-unpleasant odors of shoe oil and leather. The man whom Delaine had met when he and Gresham delivered the deer meat came to the counter, wearing a knit wool cap and a stained grey apron.

"Good morning," he said. "Something I can help you with?" His glance went to Delaine, and he nodded.

Deputy Erskine opened his coat to show his badge. "I'd like to know if you've seen Mr. Herbert yet today, and if not, whether you know where he lives."

"I haven't seen him, and I don't know where he lives."

"Thanks." The deputy turned around and led the way out. He turned, and when he came to the overhang in front of the bakery, he stopped. "Damned if I'm going to stop in every place in town."

The door opened, and the baker came out in his white shirt, pants, and apron. "Are you looking for something?" he asked.

"Mr. Herbert of the land office."

"He comes in almost every morning and buys pastry. He takes it to his office, where he makes coffee on a little kerosene stove he has."

"Have you seen him this morning?"

"Yes, but he didn't stop in. He seemed to be in a hurry. He walked past on the way to his office, and about ten minutes later, he walked back the other way. Looked like he had picked up a thing or two. He was carrying a small valise."

"Was he alone?"

"Yes."

"Thanks for your help."

"Always glad to help the law." The baker smiled with his mouth closed, and he went inside.

The deputy lingered under the shelter of the awning for a minute longer. "Let's try the stable."

The deputy set out again toward the middle of town, and Delaine kept up with him. They crossed the main thoroughfare on a diagonal. Snow was gathering in the street. They passed the train station and telegraph office and arrived at the stable.

Inside, Kent came forward to meet them. He was carrying a pitchfork, and he rested the tip of the handle on the floor as he stopped. "What do you need?"

"Do you know a man named Mull?"

"Of course I do. He keeps a horse here."

"Have you seen him this morning?"

"He left about an hour ago."

"What kind of horse was he riding?"

"He has a bay horse."

"Was he by himself?"

"No, he had his friend with him. Herbert. They each had a small bag. I thought they were fools to go out in this weather, but that's their business."

"What was Herbert riding?"

"I gave him the gentlest horse I have, a sorrel."

"Markings?"

"Narrow blaze, white feet in front."

The deputy heaved a breath. "I've got to go after them. Can you get my horse ready? I need to find someone to go with me."

"I'll go," said Delaine.

"I'd like at least two."

"You can have Hi again if he wants to go."

The deputy frowned. "Is he any good?"

Kent paused. He spit tobacco juice to one side and said, "Depends on what for. He can ride as good as you can, I'm sure of that. I don't know that he wants to take any bullets."

"I intend to put those two men under arrest, and I could use a couple of men to stand by me and to keep them from bolting away on the way back."

"I'll ask him. He's still asleep." Kent glanced at Delaine. "You can go get your horse yourself. That is, if you want to take him."

"I've used him two days in a row. I didn't work him hard, but it was a long way out and back each time."

"I'll get you a fresh horse. Let me wake up Hi first."

Delaine turned to Deputy Erskine. "I suppose I should have my rifle."

"Wouldn't hurt."

"It's in my room. I'll go for it and be right back."

———

KENT HAD a buckskin tied up for Delaine when he returned. Hiram Fitts looked as if he was clearing his head as he put his own saddle onto a slender grey horse. The deputy stood next to a large, dark-brown horse that was saddled and had a rifle attached.

Delaine brushed, combed, and saddled the buckskin, then strapped his scabbard to the near side. He checked the cinch and led the horse away. Outside, he felt the cinch again and tightened it a notch.

Deputy Erskine mounted up in a slow, deliberate motion. Fitts and Delaine swung aboard, and the party set out toward the main intersection. As the three rode abreast, the deputy said, "My guess is that they went north. If they had gone east, the baker would have seen them and told me. If they had gone west, Baird would have seen them out the hotel window. When the snow starts sticking like this, they'll make tracks. If we're not too far behind, it won't cover 'em up. The one thing in our favor is that Herbert isn't much of a rider, according to Kent. They won't go fast."

Fitts said, "You wonder why he'd go along to begin with, in weather like this."

"I don't think he had much choice," said the deputy. "He's a risk. He knows too much. He's been a risk all along, I'd say, but things are closing in."

"The long arm of the law," said Fitts.

The deputy gave him a sidelong glance and did not answer.

Fitts adjusted his reins. "I didn't bring a rifle or a pistol either one. Didn't think about it in all the hurry. So don't count on me to do no shootin'."

"I hope we don't have to," the deputy answered. "But you don't know what might happen."

At the edge of town, with the horses warmed up, the riders put them into a lope. After about a mile, the deputy slowed them to a fast walk. The horses were all breathing hard, but they seemed to have plenty of vim. As the land rose and the day progressed, more snow appeared on the trail. After ten or fifteen minutes at a walk, the riders loped for another distance, then alternated that way until they came to the fork.

The deputy dismounted to study the trail. "I think we're gaining on them," he said. "I can see tracks under the new snow."

On they rode to the northeast, following the same

route as the day before with the wagon, but covering the ground at a much better pace. By the time they reached the base of the pine ridge, two sets of hoof-prints were visible all along.

By nature, the horses wanted to run uphill, and the riders had to keep them from wearing themselves out. At last, the party reached the crest. After a few minutes for a breather, they moved on. When they emerged from the trees on the north side, the vast country to the north was a thick mist of snow. The horses took the slow descent at a walk.

"Rawhide Mountain should be straight ahead," said Delaine.

"It is," said Fitts. "This trail goes northeast, then east, like we went yesterday. But long before we come to the Lost Canyon turnoff, another trail goes north to the Rawhide Buttes."

The deputy spoke up. "I wonder if they would go there. In a way, it would make sense for them to go to the CC and hole up there."

Fitts cleared his throat with the sound that men who smoked made in the morning. "Rawhide's a long ways, more than twenty miles. But if he gets there, there's places to hide. They say there's a horsethief trail that goes through, with kind of a maze."

"He," said the deputy.

"Mull. He knows the way. You get out here, Herbert wouldn't know his ass from a banjo."

"We'll see where the tracks lead us."

They continued to follow the faint impressions left by two horses. When the trail leveled out, the deputy asked, "What's the country like between here and the Rawhide Buttes?"

"Like anythin' else," said Fitts. "Looks flat from a

distance, but it goes up and down. Breaks and bluffs here and there, cricks that're dry most of the year but might have a trickle in 'em now."

Delaine thought Fitts enjoyed being the knowledgeable one, and he did not blame him, as the deputy had not left his condescension in town.

To Delaine's sense of direction, it seemed as if they followed the trail northeast and east as Fitts said. Visibility was less than half a mile, so the hills and breaks along the pine ridge were clouded from view.

Delaine thought they had ridden for at least an hour since they crossed the ridge, all at a fast walk, when the deputy held up his hand and stopped.

"It looks like they've gone north. Two sets of tracks. Let me ride ahead and be sure, but I think this is where we make a turn." He rode the dark horse forward a hundred yards, turned around, and came back. "Nothing new up that way. I say we go north."

The country lay as Fitts had said and as Delaine would have expected, having seen it at a distance twice on clearer days. None of it was under snow yet, though the shortest grass was covered. Sagebrush stuck out. Leafless trees along draws showed their dark branches. Snow gathered in the pocks and ledges of the low bluffs.

After a distance of loping and then slowing to a walk, the deputy said, "They might know someone's following them by no. It looks like they moved faster here."

Delaine was thinking about how well the buckskin was working when, less than a mile later, the deputy spoke again.

"There's something up ahead."

He nudged his horse to a trot, and Delaine and Fitts followed.

The scene took shape as they approached. A horse stood by itself, saddled, with reins trailing. About a hundred yards to the west of it, in the direction in which the horse seemed to be looking, a human body was lying on the ground.

Deputy Erskine slowed. "Take it careful," he said. "That's a bay horse. Kent said Mull was riding a bay. But that doesn't look like him on the ground."

The supine body rose in the middle, the domed belly of a man wearing an overcoat. The man's hair was the color of old straw, and a hat with a small crown and a short brim lay nearby.

Little Hat, thought Delaine.

As they rode closer, the horse moved away, limping on its front left foot.

The riders drew rein and brought their horses to a stop. Snowflakes were beginning to gather on the body, and a dark red spot showed where the coat was open at the chest. The fleshy face was pale.

The deputy dismounted for a closer look. "Looks like Mull needed the other horse," he said. "I don't see a valise, so whatever they had, he took it all." He glanced around and gazed at the trail leading away. "Like Kent said, at least one of them was a fool to go out in this weather, but like I said, I imagine he didn't have much of a choice." The deputy climbed onto his horse in his deliberate way. "We'll come back to this. We need to go after the other one."

They set off at a lope, and after about a mile, they slowed and walked for a mile. Deputy Erskine said, "It looks to me like he's been running that horse since he took it away from his partner, and they were pushing before that. He's going to wear it out, I think."

The horses moved at a fast walk for a while longer, and at about the time Delaine expected to move into a lope, Fitts said, "That looks like him."

Less than a mile away, in an open area of grass and sage, a dark figure appeared against the whitening background. A man was leading a horse on foot.

"Let's go," said the deputy. "When we're within range of my voice, I'll tell him he's under arrest. If he shoots, we fire back. He knows he's at his last ditch, so that's what we can expect."

He led them off on a lope, slowed to a trot, and took them down to a fast walk. He put his gloved hands to the sides of his mouth and shouted across his horse's ears.

"Mull, this is Deputy Erskine. I'm an officer of the law, and you're under arrest. Give yourself up."

The man kept walking. The dull-black hat and grey coat were visible as separate tones, as was the sorrel horse.

The three riders moved ahead for another hundred yards, and the deputy called again. "Mull. This is the law. Give yourself up."

For answer, Mull stepped around and fired a shot from a pistol. The sound cracked, and a puff of snow jumped up in front of the group. Mull fired twice more, and the deputy's horse began to pitch. The fugitive fired again and again, and the bullets whoofed in the snow. Deputy Erskine leaned to one side, tried to regain his seat, but was thrown off. He landed in the snow, and his horse bolted, kicking up its hind legs.

Fitts spurred his horse and took after the runaway.

"Son of a bitch," said the deputy as he stood up,

holding his left hand against his hip. "My rifle is on my horse."

Mull fired again.

That's six, Delaine thought. He slid off the buckskin and pulled his rifle. As he knelt into position and levered in a shell, two more pistol shots cracked, and he felt the wave of air. The shots were going past him. Mull had not had time to reload, so he was using a second pistol, and it had a little more range.

The buckskin horse had pulled the reins from Delaine's hand when the last two shots passed, and it was gone.

Delaine held the rifle still and tried to find the right moment. He fired, and he did not see any impact or hear the thud of a hit coming back. He wished he had Gresham's shooting stick. He tightened into position again and tried to find Mull in his sights. The man was standing sideways, giving less of a target, with his arm straight out. The pistol cracked again, a bullet whistled near, and Delaine found the right moment a second time. He squeezed the trigger, and the tip of the rifle went up. When it came down, Mull was falling to the ground with his left arm outstretched above him.

Fitts came back with the deputy's horse and handed him the reins.

"Where's mine?" said Delaine, looking around.

"I'll get him." Fitts took off again.

The three of them rode their horses to the spot where Mull had fallen in the snow, and they dismounted. Mull's hat had fallen away, and he had rolled onto his left side so that his scar was not in view. His sallow complexion made a contrast with the white background.

Fitts said, "That's him, all right."

Deputy Erskine gazed at the dead man and said, "He caused a lot of misery for a lot of people, and this is what it comes to."

Delaine felt that the deputy did not miss the opportunity to deliver a moral message, but he did not disagree with it.

The deputy spoke again. "We're a long ways from town. This horse looks played out, and the other one is lame. I think we'll have to take turns riding double so we can transport the two bodies, but we can take it slow."

Fitts had rolled a cigarette, and he lit it. "We can do it."

Delaine let his glance fall on Mull. Here was another who would never see the world around him again. And as the deputy had told Evelina, he would not put his hands on anyone again, either.

———

DELAINE WALKED out of the Prairie Star Bakery with a sweet roll wrapped in brown paper. The trampled snow in the street was not melting, and he made a quick assessment of the route that had the most awnings and sidewalks.

A voice from the street interrupted his thought. "Delaine!"

At first he did not recognize the man on horseback, who wore a beaked winter cap and a dull-brown gabardine overcoat. As he focused on the face, he saw that the rider was George Mace.

Delaine stayed on the sidewalk as Mace guided the horse nearer. The cattleman's face and cap were framed by the grey sky. He was clean-shaven and clear-eyed, with a trace of displeasure showing in his features.

"I've talked to the deputy," he said. "And he tells me that you knew about Caswell rustling stock after all."

"When I talked to you, I didn't know anything for sure. Quite a while after that, his pal Hensley told me enough to make it more…definite. All I told the deputy was what Hensley told me. That's not the same as if Caswell told me or if I discovered it myself."

"I still think I deserved to know about it."

"It wasn't that long ago, and you know about it now."

"I don't suppose it matters much at this point. Just like it doesn't matter how much Herbert might have been caught up in it. Two-faced son of a bitch, but he's out of business with the rest of them."

Delaine understood him to mean Mull and Caswell and perhaps Hensley. From Mace's tone, which seemed relenting, Delaine thought he might offer him a job again, but he did not.

Mace said, "Mull was the worst. He was friends with Chamberlain. Who knows if he stole from him as well. But he's out of business, too. My thanks for your part in that."

Delaine nodded, and Mace rode away. Delaine took a seat on the bench outside the newsstand and unwrapped his pastry.

———

DELAINE WENT to the café that evening with the schoolteacher. The man who had waited on them before met them as they sat down.

"Good evening, Mr. Gresham." He nodded to Delaine with an expression of recognition and said, "And to you."

Gresham said, "Good evening, Phil. What's your dinner this evening?"

"Roast beef, mashed potatoes, and gravy. As good as always."

"That's what I'll have."

"So will I," said Delaine.

The waiter gave a semblance of a bow and moved away.

Gresham waved his hand at the illustrations on the wall. "Here we are at the deserted village and the country churchyard again."

"Peaceful scenes," said Delaine.

"Yes, though as I may have said before, melancholy and sentimental."

"Not doing anyone any harm."

"Not at all." Gresham folded his hands together on the table. "Has the girl gone back to Colorado?"

"Yes. Her father came for her today."

"I'm sure they'll have some adjustment to do, but at least they got her back."

"I'm glad she was able to get out of it. I'm also glad she came around and told us as much as she did. She held out at first. I haven't ever been afraid that way, or treated that way. It seemed as if, mixed up in it all, she had some kind of an attachment to Chamberlain. Sort of a mixture of fear and obedience and loyalty. As I told the deputy, I had heard of that in girls and women who had been taken by Indians. But the deepest thing she seemed to feel was a fear of Mull. I don't presume to understand it, like I say, but I sure don't blame her for anything she did or didn't do."

"Didn't?"

"Like run away."

"Oh."

"In her mind, it just wasn't possible."

Gresham said, "It wouldn't occur to me to blame her, but I know some people might. Say things like she should have just walked away. How would they know what it's like? I'm thankful she told you and Erskine where to look for Nora."

"Give him credit for asking. It seemed to me that he avoided her case, but when it came around, he didn't."

"At least Nora will have her elegy. It should give some peace to Marian."

"I hope so."

"So I thank you on her behalf. And on Nora's."

Delaine felt a tightness in his throat. "I did what I could. In some of the situations I was put in, I did what I had to. But I think the thing that moved me the most, at the beginning, at least, was my thought of her. She just deserved more." In his mind, Delaine also had Nora caught up with the pretty woman on the white mule, but he had no way of expressing it.

———

DELAINE WALKED along the quiet street with Rachel. The faint moonlight glowed on the snow all around, including on rooftops.

"It seems like a month since I've talked to you," he said. "What with the weather and everything that's happened."

"It's been five days."

"So it has."

"And have you decided what you're going to do next?"

"I'll look for work. Here. Hiram Fitts may go back to work at the CC, to look after stock and hold things together until the estate gets settled. I might go to work for Kent at the livery stable."

"That would be good."

"Better than nothing. I hoped you would approve."

"I did before, when you said you would look for work here, even if it was delivering coal."

"I hoped nothing had changed."

"Five days were not that long, at least when they were gone. You were busy doing what you had to do."

"I don't know what people have said of me."

"If anything, they see you as capable. At least as much as anyone else in town."

"Maybe it will help me get work in the future as well."

"And you won't have to leave. But let's worry about that tomorrow."

They stopped at the same time, and they met in a kiss, this time not on the cheek.

As they drew apart, she said, "I couldn't have done that if I thought you were going to leave."

A LOOK AT BOOK TWO
BROKEN HORN

In the wilds of Wyoming, a missing man's secrets are buried deep…and uncovering them may cost one cowboy his life.

When Jess Delaine agrees to look for Robert Sandoval in the remote town of Harrow, Wyoming, he expects an ordinary search. But he soon finds himself entangled in a deadly scheme involving Sandoval's late uncle, whose hidden secrets and dangerous business dealings lead to a trail of corruption and theft.

Teaming up with Rachel Valera, Delaine delves into Harrow's darkest corners, uncovering stolen documents, hidden alliances, and an unsolved kidnapping. As they inch closer to the truth, they come face-to-face with a ruthless rancher and his violent foreman—both determined to keep their secrets buried, no matter the cost.

With a deputy who remains indifferent in the face of ruthless men who kill without remorse, Delaine and Rachel must risk everything to bring justice to the innocent. But in a land where trust is a rare commodity, can they survive long enough to see it through?

AVAILABLE FEBRUARY 2025

ABOUT THE AUTHOR

John D. Nesbitt is the author of more than forty books, including traditional Westerns, crossover Western mysteries, contemporary Western fiction, retro/noir fiction, nonfiction, and poetry. He has won the Western Writers of America Spur Award four times—twice for paperback novel, once for short story, and once for poem. He has won the Western Fictioneers Peacemaker Award twice—once for novel and once for short story. He has been a finalist for the Spur Award twice, the Peacemaker seven times, and the Will Rogers Medallion Award eight times. He has also received two creative writing fellowships with the Wyoming Arts Council—once for fiction, once for nonfiction—and he has won the fiction award four times with the Wyoming State Historical Society.

www.johndnesbitt.com